Styled for Murder

Nancy J. Cohen

STYLED FOR MURDER
Copyright © 2021 by Nancy J. Cohen
Published by Orange Grove Press
Printed in the United States of America
Digital ISBN: 978-1-952886-21-8
Print ISBN: 978-1-952886-22-5

Edited by Deni Dietz at Stray Cat Productions
Cover Design by The Killion Group, Inc.
Digital Layout by Formatting4U.com
Cover Copy by BlurbWriter.com

ORANGE
GROVE
PRESS

Chapter One

"Ma, I can't just drop everything and drive over there. You're forty-five minutes away, and I have a bunch of errands to do this morning. What's so urgent that it can't wait until later?"

In the midst of doing chores at home, Marla adjusted her earpiece. She stood in her kitchen, gazing out the window at the brilliant Florida sky.

"There's a dead guy in our shower. You have to come right now." Her mother's voice rose in pitch.

"A dead guy? How is that possible?"

"Does it matter? Reed called the police, and they're questioning him like he's a suspect."

"Why? Is it someone you know?"

"It's Jack Laredo, the project manager for our bathroom remodel. Lenny Brooks, the tile guy, discovered him when he came to work this morning."

"That's horrible." Marla stared at a fallen coconut outside on the ground. Her mother had recently married Reed, a former literature professor, and they'd moved into a senior living community. This would throw a wrench into the happy life they had planned.

"Do you know how the man died?" she asked, needing more information.

"Not yet. I was out food shopping. When I got home, I found police cars in our driveway. I nearly had a heart attack thinking something had happened to Reed."

"That must have been scary. I'm glad you're both safe."

"Oy vey, I can't believe this is happening," Anita said.

Marla's heart wrenched at her mother's distress. "I'll be there as soon as I can. In the meantime, try to stay calm. Maybe the guy had medical issues and collapsed on the job. We can't make assumptions until we know more."

She hung up at the same time as a musical tone sounded in the faint distance. The dryer had finished. She crossed the kitchen in her ranch-style home and headed to the laundry room.

Almost by rote, she scooped the onesies, burp cloths and other baby items into a nearby basket. Her shoulders sagged as she carried the load into the master bedroom.

Since having her son, Ryder Harrington Vail, ten months ago in June, she'd been doing the laundry every day. Who knew an infant would require so many clothing changes? Marla had never expected to have a child in her late thirties and rejoiced in her blessings despite the repetitive routine. She sniffed the fresh laundry scent as she dumped the clean items on the bed.

As she folded clothes, she wondered how the job foreman might have ended up dead in her mother's shower. Was it an illness that had caused him to keel over? Or some sort of accident? When did the tile guy arrive to find the body? What was Reed doing while this was going on?

Marla wanted to leave immediately but had to follow her morning routine. At least this was Monday, her one weekday off from work. She'd thought of cutting back on her hours but knew her clients would protest. As owner of the Cut 'N Dye Salon and Day Spa, she still kept her own roster of customers.

She carried the clean clothes into the nursery to sort them into Ryder's dresser drawers. Dalton had already left for work and dropped the baby off at daycare. The image of her child's wide brown eyes, pert nose, and sweet little mouth brought her comfort. She missed his soft body and baby scent even now.

After she'd exchanged the soiled trash in his room for a fresh bag, Marla did her morning pumping.

A half hour later, she placed the bagged breast milk in the fridge and checked to make sure the dogs had enough food and water. Her head throbbed from lack of sleep. If one more thing piled onto her to-do list, she'd topple over like her son's set of stacking blocks.

"Spooks, stop rubbing against that chair," she told the cream-colored poodle, while Lucky, their golden retriever, nudged her leg. "You two behave while I'm gone."

Brianna, her teenage stepdaughter, had already taken the dogs out before leaving for school. Marla was the last one to exit the house. First, she texted Dalton to fill him in.

He responded with a volley of questions. A homicide detective, he was happiest when tracking down killers and bringing justice to their victims. Marla had experienced the same satisfaction with her sleuthing. Having given it up when Ryder was born, she missed the challenge. As a mother, though, she couldn't put herself at risk.

"Ma didn't say how the guy died," Marla wrote back. "I'll contact you when I know more."

She blinked to better focus her bleary eyes. While worry for her mother consumed her, a pang of resentment surfaced as she got into her SUV for the trip north.

Anita had moved away from Palm Haven right when Marla needed her the most. She'd always expected her mother to be present when she raised children of her own. But Anita had remarried and wanted a new life with her second husband. Although she deserved to enjoy her golden years, couldn't she have chosen a development closer to her only daughter?

Marla knew her attitude was selfish but couldn't help it. If Ma had bought a place less than a half hour away, it would be easier for them to get together for a quick lunch. Yet despite the distance, Ma made every effort to be there for her. She'd come over to stay for two weeks after Ryder was born. Marla shuddered at the memory of the sleepless nights, frequent feedings, and sense of helplessness at being responsible for a

3

baby's care. Dalton may have done it before, but she'd never faced such utter terror. At the very least, she could return the favor for her mother.

She glanced at the stately palms that flashed by the roadside and the fluffy white clouds in a bright April sky. The summer humidity would return next month, but for now moderate temperatures and drier air prevailed. Not that she could enjoy them. If only she could get one night of solid sleep, it might clear the fog from her brain.

Hopefully, she could calm her mother and be on her way. The remodeling job hadn't been without its hiccups, but she couldn't conceive how Jack Laredo might have died on the job unless it had been a natural death or an accident. She could think of all sorts of means for the latter, such as electrocution if he'd touched wiring that wasn't grounded or falling from a ladder and hitting his head.

Most likely, the project would be temporarily halted during the police investigation, but eventually it would resume. She hoped Anita and Reed didn't have too much disruption in the meantime.

Her self-assurance faltered once she arrived on their street and noticed the crime scene van parked there along with a bevy of patrol cars. A chill swept through her. Did the cops suspect foul play? Or did they investigate all unattended deaths in this county like they did in hers?

A surge of sympathy swept over her for the dead man's family. Had they been notified? How horrible to get a visit from the police with such tragic news. She wondered if he had a wife or children that would be left fatherless. Maybe she could send them a gift food basket or offer a donation toward their expenses.

Her heart rate accelerated as she emerged from her parked car. She approached the open front door of the sand-colored house with shaky knees, dreading what she might learn. The exterior white trim stared back at her with blank conformity, broken only by thorny plants with red flowers that lined the walkway. Somehow those seemed symbolic in the wake of a death.

Was blood involved? A horrifying vision of a man sprawled in the shower came to mind. If he'd bled out from an injury, the seepage would go down the drain. Her throat constricted at the mental images. Ma would never want to shower in there again.

She entered the foyer and firmly shut the door in her wake so the mosquitoes wouldn't get in. Voices sounded from the rear of the house. Instead of heading that way, Marla veered to the right toward the kitchen and family room at the opposite end from the bedroom wing.

"Ma, I'm here," she called, anxious to see how her mother was faring.

Inside the kitchen, maple cabinets faced her along with granite countertops, tiled floors, and stainless-steel appliances. Absent was the smell of chicken soup or brisket that Ma liked to make for her visits. The place seemed sadly empty. No one sat on the couch in the family room, either. They must all be down the hall.

She stuck her cell phone in a pants pocket and plopped her purse on the counter. Then she headed toward the voices at the other end of the house. Across from the foyer, she was about to pass Reed's office when a flash of white from inside caught her eye. Reed sat in his desk chair, a morose expression on his bearded face. Anita paced the room while wringing her hands.

Upon spotting Marla, she shrieked and opened her arms. "Marla, you made it! I didn't hear you come in." She rushed forward to embrace her daughter.

Marla hugged her back, feeling secure and comforted in her mother's arms and wanting to provide a sense of reassurance in return. After a moment, she stepped away to regard the pair. The scent of Reed's musk aftershave effused the air.

"Why are you two not sitting in the family room? It's more comfortable in there." Plus, they'd be less likely to hear the commotion coming from the master bedroom suite.

"The detective told us to wait in here for him," Reed replied in a somber tone. His face looked drawn with the corners of his mouth turned down. "He's already questioned us both. We can't give him much more information."

"I'm so sorry this is happening," Marla said, wondering what she could to do ease their anxiety.

Anita ran stiff fingers through her short, layered white hair. "It's still hard to believe. A man died in this house. It's horrifying."

"Did the detective confirm that it actually happened on these premises?" she asked. That might validate her earlier theory that it had been a natural or accidental death. Because if not, the man's body might have been moved inside the house. She shunted aside that notion, not wanting to consider this other possibility without further information.

"Detective Wanner hasn't said much," Reed responded, stroking his white beard.

"Ma, you said you'd been out food shopping. Did you unlock the bathroom door for the work crew like you've done every morning?" The master bath suite let out to a screened lanai at the rear of the house. Florida bathrooms were designed to open into pool areas so people didn't track water through the house from a dripping swimsuit.

Anita studied a spot on the wall. "Yes, I'd unlocked the door. Reed was busy working on his research paper. The same journal that published his last piece wants another article."

"That's great." Marla's attention swung to the retired literature professor who maintained his air of dignity despite the current disaster. A widower with two grown sons, he had an imposing presence that commanded respect. "So you were alone in the house until one of the workers discovered the body?" she asked him for clarification.

Reed nodded. "The guys usually enter on their own and go to work. I'll check on them periodically to see if they need anything, and then I leave them to the job. This time, I was watching the news on TV when I heard a howl from the rear of the house. I raced back there and found Lenny Brooks standing over Jack's body in the shower. Lenny is the tile installer."

"What else did you see?" Dear Lord, here she was jumping onto a case like in the past. But this was personal, so how could she resist? She'd just have to find a way to juggle baby care and work at the salon with snooping things out to help her mom and stepdad.

"Jack lay on his back on the shower floor," Reed stated in a flat voice. "It was pretty obvious he was dead, but I felt his wrist anyway. No pulse. That's when I called nine-one-one. Lenny stood there in shock and wasn't much help."

"Were there any signs of trauma or injury that you noted?"

Reed's complexion paled, and he glanced away. "One of my ties was wrapped around his neck."

"What?" Her eyes bulged at this revelation. "Good God, why didn't you mention this earlier? It changes everything."

"I know. Somebody else had to be inside the house. It wasn't me who put it there. Does that mean Jack was murdered?" His voice cracked, betraying his emotions.

"We won't know anything for sure until the autopsy is done. Let's wait to see how the man died before we jump to conclusions."

Nonetheless, she couldn't help the thoughts that somersaulted in her mind. Reed didn't have any enemies as far as she knew. He'd been respected by his colleagues. So why would someone wrap one of his ties around the victim's neck? Had Jack been strangled?

"What did Lenny say happened?" she asked, instead of voicing her fears aloud. Was the killer still around? Should she be worried for her mother's safety?

"He planned to finish tiling the shower seat," Reed

explained. "Lenny was here nearly all day on Friday. I could hear him arguing with someone on the phone from all the way down the hall."

"Maybe your tile guy had a beef with the foreman. Which one of them got here first this morning?"

Reed spread his hands. "I have no idea. We never know from day-to-day who will show up or when."

"Don't you get a message from the company beforehand on who to expect?"

"Unfortunately, no. Jack didn't communicate well with customers or his crew. He'd say someone was coming, and they'd show up three days later. We learned not to rely on his promises."

She noted the resentment in his tone but didn't comment on it. Hopefully, Reed hadn't complained about the foreman to the police detective, or that would make him even more suspect. "Did you notice anyone loitering outside?" she asked.

"Honestly, I didn't think to look around after... you know." Reed fell silent, his eyes sad. Regardless of how it happened, a man had died there. The heavy weight of a death put a pall on them all.

"Have you notified your sons? They might want to be here for you." Reed had one son still single and another who was married with two kids. They didn't live far and could help provide support.

"No, I didn't want to bother them at work. I'll tell them later. Besides, you and Dalton are more accustomed to this sort of thing."

"That's true. Listen, I'll go talk to the detective to see what I can learn. Wait for me in the family room." Her mother would be more comfortable on the sofa, even though Reed probably felt more in control in his home office.

As she moved down the hall toward the voices at the far end, her stomach pitted. This wasn't how she'd planned to spend her day off. But then again, the foreman hadn't anticipated a morning like this, either. What a horrible turn of events for everyone involved.

In the master bedroom, she halted to regard the melee of authority figures who had invaded her mother's privacy. Her gaze came to rest on a tall African American man with a trim moustache. He wore a slate gray suit and a commanding presence. He was pointing toward the bathroom while speaking to a white-haired fellow with a thin face and sallow complexion. They broke off their conversation upon noticing her arrival.

"Excuse me, gentlemen, but I'm looking for the lead investigator," she said, unable to control the tremor in her voice.

"That would be me," said the taller man. He had a deep voice like James Earl Jones. "I'm Detective Edgar Wanner. And you are?"

"Marla Vail. I'm homicide detective Dalton Vail's wife. He's with the Palm Haven police force. Anita Shorstein is my mother." Ma hadn't changed her name after she'd married Reed, saying it was easier that way at her age. "Can you tell me what happened?"

Wanner's tawny eyes narrowed. "It appears the supervisor of your parents' project ended up dead this morning. We're still trying to determine how he landed in the shower."

"Reed is my stepfather," Marla clarified. "Was the guy strangled? I know you can tell these things from petechia in the eyes and such."

"Then you also know our medical examiner will determine the cause of death."

Marla was dying to peek into the bathroom to get a glimpse of the body. Dalton would want to know the details.

"I've helped my husband solve crimes before. Maybe I can be useful." She'd noticed clues on previous cases that a trained investigator had overlooked. Her mind strayed to the time she had discovered a dead body in her neighbor Goat's house. The victim's pattern of highlights in his hair had led her to a former instructor from Marla's beauty school.

Detective Wanner snorted at her suggestion. "Thanks, but we have things under control. I'd appreciate it if you don't interview the witnesses until I've had a chance to get their formal statements."

Heat steamed through Marla's blood at his request. This was her family, not impersonal witnesses. "You mean my mother and stepfather? They're innocent bystanders."

"Bystanders who may have seen or heard something important."

Marla agreed but didn't say so aloud. "I understand the tile installer discovered the body. That means Jack Laredo, the foreman, got here first this morning. Are you sure he expired inside the house? Because if foul play was involved, his body might have been moved. I assume you'll check outside for footprints."

"Why would you mention foul play?" the inspector snapped. "What do you know about it?"

"My stepfather mentioned someone had wrapped one of his ties around the victim's neck."

Wanner's lips tightened. "Why don't you wait for me down the hall? We'll have a chat once I'm finished here."

Oh yeah? Don't expect me to rat on my mom or stepdad, not that they have anything to do with it.

She was displeased by his lack of concern for her family. At least Dalton took the time to express his sympathies and to make sure witnesses were safe while waiting for him.

"May I have your card, Detective Wanner? My husband will want to get in touch with you. I'm sure you understand we have a personal interest in this case. I'm worried for my mother's sake and want her life back to normal as soon as possible."

He pulled out his wallet and extracted a business card, handing it over to her. "That's exactly why you're unable to be objective. Please don't speculate or share information with anyone else other than your husband."

A young man with ebony hair leaned out of the bathroom and lifted a camera with a big lens. "Hey, Ed, I'm all done and so is Izzie with his sketches. We'll see you back at the station."

"All right, thanks. I'll catch you later." Wanner pulled out a notebook and pen. "Please spell your last name," he said to Marla.

She gave him her contact information without offering more than requested. Dalton had taught her not to volunteer anything on her own. She didn't appreciate this man's attitude. He might be competent at his job, but he could show more respect to her as a policeman's wife.

"May I ask how long it'll take to clear this area? My mother will want to get into the bedroom as soon as possible. As for the bathroom, it's been a loss ever since construction started. This job has had a number of delays and now things will be totally held up."

The detective zeroed in on her words with eagle-like sharpness. "Have there been issues with how the remodel is going so far?"

Marla cringed inwardly at her inadvertent slip. She would blame her ever-present fatigue, but she seemed to have perked up ever since she'd stepped into Ma's house. Why was that? Because there might be another crime to solve? What did that say about her, with a baby at home and a salon to run?

"You'll have to talk to my mother about their project," she told the detective. "Ma knows the details more than me."

He stepped closer and stared her down. She caught a whiff of garlic from his breakfast. "The people we're closest to are often the ones with the most to hide."

"What does that mean?" Marla asked in a sugary tone, refusing to react to his bait.

"Jack Laredo had not arrived yet when your mother unlocked the bathroom door this morning. From all indications, the man must have died between the time your mom left the house and when Lenny Brooks arrived. This means only one person was home alone with him, and that would be your stepfather."

Chapter Two

Marla met the detective's steely gaze. "Any number of people might have known Jack Laredo was coming here. If it turns out he was murdered, they could have set a trap for him. Or perhaps someone followed him here. I assume you'll interview his work crew and the design company staff?"

Wanner's brows drew together like thunderclouds. "I don't need a civilian's advice on how to pursue my case. I'll contact you if I require more information."

He turned his back on her and disappeared into the bathroom. She could see the sink area, but the shower and toilet were out of view.

It appeared Wanner no longer held any interest in interviewing her, thank goodness. No doubt she'd irritated him with her remarks.

She couldn't help it. Experience had shown her that when the cops fixated on a single suspect, they often missed clues. She recalled the incident again with her neighbor Goat, who had disappeared after discovering the dead body in his bedroom. The investigator had figured he'd done the deed and run, but he had been a scared witness. It was only through her persistence that the true killer had been found.

Then there was the time her friend Jill became a prime suspect in her sister's murder. The matron-of-honor had turned up dead under the cake table at Jill's wedding. Thankfully, Marla had uncovered the real culprit and saved her friend from going to jail.

It was merely good detective work to consider all the options.

With a grunt of annoyance, she headed back toward the family room on the other side of the house. She shared her observations with Anita and Reed.

Standing in front of their flat-screen TV, Reed stroked his jaw. "I'm still a person of interest if this turns out to be an unnatural death."

"Let's not make assumptions until the medical examiner's report comes in. Meanwhile, I'm sorry you have this *tsuris*. Do you want to stay at our house until things settle down?"

Marla had enough to do with Ryder, but this way she could keep an eye on her mother who might not want to stay in the house where a man had died. Plus, playing with her grandson would bring Ma comfort.

Anita swiped a hand over her face. Seated on the sofa, she looked weary. Lines creased the skin by her eyes and bracketed her mouth. "Thanks, *bubeleh*, but we're not going anywhere. We have three full bathrooms, and we've been managing without one of them. We'll sleep in the guest bedroom for now."

"Fine, but if you change your mind, you're always welcome at our place."

Anita gave her an appreciative glance. "I know. We could go to Michael's house, too. Your brother doesn't have a baby that needs his full attention."

"Oh yeah? I'll bet his kids are a handful when they're home from school. Can I get you a cup of tea, Ma? Your face looks like pastry dough. I don't want this to affect your health."

Anita patted her chest. "I'll be all right. I'm feeling a bit short of breath, that's all."

Alarm shot through her. "You're not having chest pain or pressure, are you?"

"No, it's just stress. Don't worry about me. I'm more concerned about Reed. I hope you'll ask Dalton to have a chat with Detective Wanner. It's comforting to have your husband on our side."

"I'm sure he'll step in to help. Wanner might be more willing to open up to him as a colleague." Not that Marla wanted to add to her husband's burdens. Dalton had been less talkative about work lately. She'd attributed it to lack of sleep, thanks to their son. But she feared he might be rethinking his choice of expanding their family this late in the game.

Marla had just hit forty and Dalton would turn forty-nine this year. He already had one child from his previous marriage. Brianna, a senior in high school, had been accepted at Boston University. Ever since her mother had died from cancer, she'd been aiming toward a research career in molecular biology. However, Dalton hoped that one winter in the historical city would be enough to drive her back to Florida. Time would tell. Marla had a feeling Brianna would love living in the city.

"Tell me what you know about this design company," she said, settling on the couch beside her mother and refocusing on their current dilemma.

"Amaze Design Center came highly recommended," Reed responded in his baritone voice. "We hadn't counted on the aggravation we've had since they started the project, though."

Anita jabbed a finger at him. "You're the one who insisted we hire this company. I would have chosen the one with the lowest bid instead."

Marla narrowed her gaze at Reed, wondering what had influenced him to make this decision. "Why *did* you choose Amaze Designs over the others?" she asked.

"I had my reasons. Although, I should have known better, considering…" Reed cut himself off and glowered at her, his Irish heritage evident in his graying red hair and his normally impish green eyes. Today they were a somber moss color and lacking luster.

Marla got the distinct feeling Reed had meant to finish that sentence. "Having problems with remodeling firms isn't news in South Florida," she said. "*Hurry up and wait* is the motto for most of them. Did you read reviews before making a decision?"

"All of the companies had complaints," Anita retorted. "In retrospect, we should have gone with the first estimate. At least their salesman warned me things could take longer than expected due to delays from suppliers."

"You'd told me two men came initially to do the demolition?" Marla asked, needing to learn who had access to the premises.

Anita smoothed her pants and nodded. "Yes, that's right. Pete and Juan were polite and cleaned up the site when done. Then several days after his visit was promised, the plumber showed up. I had to keep texting Jack, who lied and said the guy would be here on Monday, but he didn't come until Thursday. We stayed home every morning waiting for a no-show. I can't tell you how frustrating it's been."

Oh, great. If the cops obtained the cell phone records of the dead man, they'd see her mother's irate messages.

"Who else came besides the plumber and the two laborers?" Marla peered at the cherry wood bookshelves lining one wall. They held Reed's collection of classic literature. How many of those books had he actually read?

"The electrician did some rewiring. Then Pete and Juan returned to install the cabinets," Reed said with a sweeping gesture. "The drawers didn't have any knobs and they left huge gaps between the wood and the walls."

Anita bobbed her head. "The new cabinets were smaller than the old ones, leaving unfinished walls and missing tiles on the sides. I'd thought they would fill the same space. When I saw them, I panicked and sent Jack a text. He replied that the work wasn't done, and he was right. At Pete and Juan's next visit, they added fillers on the sides of the cabinets and installed the hardware. Now it looks much better."

"So let me be clear on this," Marla said, wagging her finger. "At every stage, one of you has sent angry text messages to Jack Laredo?" That would give the detective more fuel in his case against Reed. Annoyed customers would only take so much grief before they took stronger steps to gain satisfaction.

Marla recalled the angry client whose hair had become brittle after a bleach job because she hadn't told her stylist about a new medication she was on. Bleach was contraindicated in that case. Not only did the customer demand a refund along with a corrective treatment, but she'd insisted Marla fire the hapless stylist. In addition, she'd sent Marla a threatening letter from her lawyer. Fortunately, her insurance company dealt with the issue. But it showed how disagreements with customers could quickly escalate.

Anita plucked at the fabric of her pants. "Jack didn't tell us what to expect. He was lousy at customer service and should have been dismissed," she said, confirming Marla's thoughts on the subject.

"You don't have to worry about Jack's lack of skills any longer, Ma. The man is dead."

"I know, and it's terrible to speak ill of him under the circumstances, but that's the way it is. I'm sure we're not the only unhappy customers."

"Who else has been here to work on your bathroom?" Marla asked, making a mental list of potential suspects. She didn't have to wait for confirmation of a murder with the evidence of a necktie wrapped around the man's throat.

Reed paced the room, hands folded behind his back. He carried himself with a dignified air, although his steps dragged more than usual. "Lenny, the tile guy. At least he's good at his job. He does beautiful work and is a true craftsman."

Anita pointed a finger at Reed. "Don't forget the purple niche in the shower. It didn't match the beige tiles at all. I texted Jack that I hoped they didn't plan to leave it that way. He assured me the alcove would be tiled. I wouldn't have been upset if he'd told us these things up front."

Marla gave her a rueful smile. "They're knowledgeable

about the process, but they forget that most homeowners have no clue as to what's going on. What else still needs to be done?"

"The plumber has to install the fixtures on the sinks and shower. The electrician has to cover the outlets, install the vanity lighting, and connect the vent fan. Then the shower doors, towel racks and mirrors have to be installed. Did I tell you that when they took down the old mirror, the guys found tar there along with old wallpaper? It needed drywall repairs."

"You never know what you're going to find when you start a remodel," Marla said.

Anita shook her head. "We might have expected cracks in the floorboards or mold growing between the walls from an unforeseen leak, but not a dead person."

"Who else related to this project came to your house?" Marla swallowed, realizing her throat was dry. She could use another cup of coffee but didn't plan to stay that long.

"Nadia, the architect, came here for the initial consultation," Reed answered. "And the granite company sent a guy to measure the space. That's about it. These workers go from job to job instead of focusing on one project at a time. They would finish a lot quicker if they did one house entirely before moving on to the next. But I understand suppliers can take longer than expected, especially for items that have to be special ordered."

"Have you told Michael about any of this?" Marla asked her mother. Michael lived in Boca Raton with his family. Her brother was closer in distance and could have gotten there sooner.

"Michael and Charlene are both at work today," Anita replied. "I'll call them later and let them know what's been going on. By the way, have you spoken to your brother lately? Something is brewing there, but he won't tell me what's bothering him."

"Sorry, I haven't had time." Marla bristled at the implication that she'd been neglectful. She had too many responsibilities to keep up with everything.

Anita gave her a morose glance. "Maybe he'll confide in

you. I'm lucky if he answers the phone when I call. He doesn't respond to my texts, either. Sometimes, it's days before he gets back to me, if then."

"I'll get in touch with him when I have the chance," Marla promised. A daughter was often closer to her mother than a son. Besides, men were notoriously less communicative than women. Even Dalton had recognized how Marla's conversational skills helped him solve cases. She could connect to people in a way that he couldn't. Too bad she hadn't kept her cool with Detective Wanner, but the man lacked sympathy for her family.

A text message popped up on her screen, and her heart thudded. "It's Ryder's teacher. He has a low-grade fever, and I need to pick him up from daycare."

Anita's brows arched. "Oh, dear. I hope he'll be alright. Didn't he just get over a cold a couple of weeks ago?"

Marla collected her purse as her thoughts scattered. "Yes, but the pediatrician says these frequent infections will help him build his immune system. At least we've been resistant in catching things from him."

"Call me later and let me know how he is," Anita said, worry lines creasing her brow.

Marla could have texted Dalton and asked him to get their son, but she was ready to go anyway. She hugged her mother and departed, her heart heavy at leaving the older couple but wanting to be with her child.

Outside, a van had pulled up, and two men in white uniforms removed a gurney from the rear. Bile rose in her throat. What an awful end to such a beautiful day. If for no other reason, Marla wanted to identify the killer to serve justice. Then Jack Laredo could go to his final rest and her mother and stepdad could find peace.

It took her nearly an hour to get to the daycare center through heavy traffic. She signed in at the front desk and headed for Ryder's classroom.

Cribs lined the space that was brightly decorated with animal murals and scattered with toys. The room had two attendants for up to ten children who ranged in age from three months to two years. She'd made friends with some of the moms but most of them worked and had little time available for socializing.

After greeting the teachers, Marla washed her hands at the sink before proceeding to Ryder's assigned spot. Her child lay on his back, his wide brown eyes watching her approach. He whimpered his discomfort as she plucked him up and felt his brow. Definitely too warm.

"Has anyone else been sick?" she asked Tabitha, one of the teachers.

The pretty blonde nodded. "We sent Evan home the other day. He had a runny nose."

"Great. I'll be in touch." Kids had to be fever free for twenty-four hours before they were allowed back in school.

Outside, she secured Ryder in his car seat while wishing she could enjoy the sunny April day. She liked to take Ryder for walks when they had time. She hoped this sickness was fleeting and would go away without further symptoms.

After she got in the car, she sent Dalton a quick update. Maybe he could contact Detective Wanner before he came home.

Her muscles eased once she pulled into her driveway and got Ryder inside. He refused his bottle and wouldn't go down readily for a nap. Her son only calmed down when she held him in her arms and sat in the armchair in his room. She leaned her head against the cushion, her eyes half-closing as she stifled a yawn.

The rest of the day passed by in a blur. Fortunately, the fever turned out to be a short-term event, and Ryder went back to school on Wednesday. Marla had a busy day at the salon and looked forward to her free morning on Thursday.

That day arrived, and Marla groggily went about her

morning duties. She didn't have to go in to work on Thursdays until one o'clock. Brianna had left the house earlier, after taking care of the dogs.

The phone rang, and she saw on the caller ID it was her mother. They'd been keeping in touch via text messages and nothing alarming had arisen. At least, not until now.

"Detective Wanner called last night," Anita said in a tremulous tone. "He wants Reed to come down to the station to answer more questions. Wanner has officially labeled the case a homicide."

Chapter Three

Marla inserted her earpiece so she could pack the baby's meal for daycare while speaking to her mother. "Did Wanner say why he was interviewing Reed again?" she asked as she added Ryder's bagged and labeled snacks to his sack. Dalton was getting him dressed for the day. It took the two of them to manage one child, but they had the routine down pat by now.

"The detective was his usual tight-lipped self. Do we need a lawyer? What's the best approach for Reed to take? You're used to these things from helping Dalton, but we're not. My heart races whenever I hear the detective's voice."

"Calm down, Ma. You'll get through this. What does Reed say?"

"He shrugs it off, but I can tell he's concerned. It worries me why he was so insistent on hiring this company. I should have done more research on them."

Marla rolled her eyes. Ma would rather play mahjongg or meet her friends for lunch than spend time at the computer. She enjoyed going out, while Reed often stayed home with his books or the TV news channel. Lately, he'd been thinking about tutoring, which Marla thought was a great idea. He'd mentioned golfing lessons as well.

"Reed said he had his reasons," she responded. "I've hired people whose estimates were higher because I figured they'd do a better job. As for Detective Wanner, it's merely a matter of routine for him to question everyone involved, even if it seems repetitive. Tell Reed not to provide any additional information on his own."

"All right, thanks. He doesn't want me to go with him."

"I'm sure he appreciates your support, nonetheless. At any rate, I can't talk right now. We're getting Ryder ready for school."

"How is he feeling? I loved that photo you sent of him wearing sunglasses. He looked adorable."

"I know. He's such a cutie. He has his appetite back, thank goodness."

"We'll have to plan a family gathering after this awful business is resolved. Hey, you have some time free this morning. Why don't you stop over at Amaze Design Center? You can meet the staff there. It could prove useful."

So this is really why you called. You want me to put on my sleuthing hat. "Ma, I have a million chores to do this morning."

"The place isn't far from you. It's in Cooper City. Please, for my sake?"

Marla winced at her mother's pleading tone. How could she refuse? It would bring Anita peace of mind if she agreed.

"Okay, but then I'm booked solid for the rest of the week, and Sunday we're planning to take Ryder to the park. He loves the baby swings."

Anita offered a few parting words and signed off, leaving Marla feeling guilty that she wasn't doing more to help solve the case. She'd sworn off snooping when Ryder entered her life. If her mother weren't involved, she wouldn't step into those shoes again.

Her neck muscles taut, she relieved Dalton of duty in the baby's room so he could shave and get dressed. The shadows under his eyes proclaimed his lack of sleep. He'd gotten up at one o'clock when Ryder had started fussing. Was this one of the child's sleep regressive stages she'd read about, or were they already past that part? She couldn't remember it in her brain fog.

Marla proceeded to feed Ryder his breakfast. He played with his food more than he ate the pieces she'd cut up, but he drank most of his milk.

The sound of Dalton's footsteps alerted her that it was time to get ready for the day. As much as she loved being with Ryder, going into the salon each day helped her stay sane. It also made her more appreciative of the time they spent together.

By the time she dropped her son off at daycare, it was after nine. She looked online via her cell phone and noted the design center was already open. She could make a quick stop there to appease her mother before doing her other errands.

****

The warehouse district in Cooper City seemed out of place in a quiet residential neighborhood. As she pulled into a parking space, Marla contemplated how best to approach the staff. They might clam up if she admitted her mother's connection to the foreman. She could pretend to have an interest in their services. Her house in Royal Oaks might only be a few years old, but there were always improvements to make.

A few scraggly palms decorated the swale. The grass had been freshly cut, imbuing the air with a sun-kissed scent. The sweet floral fragrance of April blossoms drifted her way from a flowering tree that stood forlorn by itself. Its white blooms matched the color of cars in the parking lot. Next door to the design company was a framing studio on one side and an engraving business on the other. An auto body shop was two doors down, its bay doors closed.

Marla pushed open the door with the design company's logo and paused to survey the interior. Ahead stretched a vast expanse littered with decorating choices—sample showers, sinks, kitchen cabinets, bathroom vanities, lighting, drawer hardware and more. She paused inside the threshold, fascinated by the possibilities while sniffing the faint scent of sawdust.

Nobody occupied the reception area, but she heard raised voices coming from an office to her right. A man's angry tone was countered by a woman's snappish replies. Marla edged closer, figuring she should make her presence known.

"Hello? Is anyone there?" she called.

The voices stopped. A brunette scurried from the room, halting when she spotted Marla standing out front. The aggravated expression on the woman's face washed away, replaced by a falsely polite smile. It did little to disguise the irritation that still showed in her hazel eyes.

"I'm so sorry. I didn't realize you had come in. I'm Caroline Henderson, the company's administrative assistant." The woman spoke in a molasses-smooth voice with a slight Southern accent.

Marla scanned her flowery maxi-dress that perfectly fit her slim figure. With her wavy hair and flawless complexion, she could have stood in for a Belle of the South, minus the wide-brimmed hat.

"I'm Marla Vail. My husband and I are interested in redoing our bathroom." Marla handed over a business card, always ready to promote her salon.

"Awesome. You've come to the right place. Here's a questionnaire for you to fill out, and then I'll make you an appointment with our architectural designer." After handing Marla a clipboard, she nodded to a round table and chairs off to the side. "You can sit over there."

Marla put the clipboard down on the front counter, meaning to get the woman talking. "I just want to get a ballpark number on how much something like this will cost before I fill out any paperwork. We have a limited budget."

"That depends on what you want done. Is it a full renovation or a partial?" The woman's eyes narrowed as she assessed Marla's potential to become a valued customer.

"Probably a full makeover," she lied, thinking of their beautifully designed master bathroom. She and Dalton had paid extra for upgrades when they'd had the house built. She loved their spacious shower and modern cabinets.

"Filling out our form doesn't obligate you to anything. It gives us an idea of where to start," Caroline told her, a stubborn edge in her tone.

She must be hard-pressed to book new customers, Marla thought. Perhaps she got a commission from each person who signed a contract.

"I understand," she said, placing her hands on the counter and leaning forward. "When new clients walk into my salon, I have them fill out a questionnaire. It's important to know if they've had adverse effects from hair dye in the past or if they have medical conditions that could affect their hair. Our receptionist, Robyn, has them fill it out. How many people staff this place?"

Caroline smirked. "Three of us work here full-time. Nadia is our interior architect, although I call her a designer. She's the person who would work with you to meet your vision."

"What's the difference between a designer and an architect?"

"An interior architect designs building interiors, while an interior designer focuses on furnishing and decorating a place. Nadia has her own office as does Brad. That's where he works his magic with numbers."

"He's your accountant?"

Her expression faltered, and she glanced toward the suite of offices as a flush crept up her face. "Bradley Quinn is our president."

"Then what did you mean?"

"Nothing much. Brad keeps the company records, that's all." She winked at Marla. "My job is more important. I'm the person who hires the independent subcontractors and makes their assignments."

"It sounds as though you run the daily operations."

"Just so. Brad is very appreciative of my work."

In what way? Does the boss give you bonuses under the table, or is your relationship more than a professional one?

"You must be very knowledgeable about the business," Marla said since Caroline appeared to respond to flattery. What else did she do for the firm? They couldn't get many clients in here each day, so the receptionist job wouldn't take up much time. "Are you also in charge of social media and advertising? My receptionist does the marketing for our salon. I wouldn't have the time or the skill set."

Caroline lifted her chin. "That would be me. Now if you don't mind, I have work to do. You can give us a call if you have any further questions or look up our FAQ online."

No doubt they got people in there fairly often who made inquiries and never signed a contract. Marla wasn't deterred by the dismissal. Any tidbit of information helped her cause. The job foreman had died at her mother's house. Who were his associates? The office housed the administrative assistant, the in-house architect, and the company president. How about the guys who worked in the field?

The more she learned, the more suspects she could add to her list. She only hoped that Detective Wanner was being as thorough. Had he already been by here to question the staff?

"I have to go to work shortly, too," Marla said, fluttering her hand in the air. "But first, I need more details to tell my husband. Like, who could we expect on the job site? It's such a hassle having workers in the house. We'd have to stay home to let them in, for example."

Caroline's eyes narrowed. By now, she might be suspecting Marla had an ulterior motive for being there. "That's not a problem. You could hide a key outside or unlock the door for them if you have to leave the house. It's usually no more than two guys at a time. Our main contractors do the basic demolition and construction. Then you'd have various specialists come in to do their parts."

"Do the same crews work all the jobs?"

"We have several general contractors but only one project manager." Caroline's face puckered. "Unfortunately, Jack passed away recently. We haven't gotten a replacement yet."

"I'm so sorry. Had he been ill?"

"No, it was unexpected. We're still coming to grips with his death."

Marla clucked her tongue. "Poor man. His family must be devastated. Was he married?"

"Jack was divorced, and I doubt his ex-girlfriend will grieve for him."

"That's sad. At least his colleagues will miss him."

"Huh. Not with his track record. I mean, of course we'll be lost without him. Jack was skilled at his job."

Track record? As in, poor communication with customers? Caroline didn't sound very upset over his loss.

"What about the projects he was supervising?" she asked.

"We're working on it." Caroline gave her a pointed glare. "Would you like me to set a date for you to meet with Nadia?"

Marla took the questionnaire off the clipboard and lay the board on the counter. "Not yet. I'll take this home and fill it out with my husband."

"Here's our brochure. It lists our services and website." The woman handed one over and stood, clearly finished with their interview.

Marla exited, feeling satisfied by what she'd learned about the company's structure. It might allay her mother's worries if she knew Jack had other business associates that the detective could investigate.

Errands took up the rest of her morning and then it was time to head to the salon. Familiar scents and sounds impacted her senses as soon as she entered through the front door to an accompanying jingle of chimes.

Robyn Piper, the receptionist, greeted her from the front desk. She'd done a recent makeover, adding a magenta streak to her shoulder-length brown hair and switching from black-framed eyeglasses to contact lenses. She had even given up her corporate-style business suits for funkier clothes with flashy jewelry. But if she had hoped this change would improve her social life, she'd been disappointed. Nobody she'd dated recently had impressed her.

Robyn gestured for Marla to approach her desk. "I've put your schedule at your station. I hope it's okay that I plugged a color correction into your two-thirty slot. Some lady used an at-home kit and now has orange hair."

Marla grinned at the mental image. "It's fine. How was your date last night? Any luck with this one?"

"Nope. Wyatt was nice but bor-ing. All he talked about was how he sold HVAC units and the benefits of various smart thermostats."

"Will you be seeing him again?"

"I don't think so. Saturday night, I'm going out with Bruce. Remember, he's the dermatologist who wants to teach me how to play chess?" She stuck out her tongue at the thought. "I like him, though. He's funny and attractive."

"It isn't easy to find decent guys who are single when you're in your thirties. You can't be so picky. If he's into chess, you can always give it a try if you like him otherwise."

In Marla's view, Robyn was too skittish about commitment. She'd been burned before, having married young and divorced a short time afterward. But her biological clock was ticking, not that it seemed to matter to her.

"We'll see," Robyn said in a nonchalant tone. "If it's meant to be, it'll happen."

Not if you don't work at it, Marla thought.

"You'll never guess who called," Robyn continued. "We got an invite for our stylists to work at this year's garlic festival. They want us to do the hair for the contestants in their beauty pageant. The coordinator heard about us through one of the ladies on their committee."

Marla's jaw gaped. "Are you for real? That would be

awesome. Dalton and I were planning to go anyway. Did you respond?"

"Are you kidding? Of course I said yes. There's no pay, but we'd share in the publicity." Robyn clapped her hands. "It sounds like so much fun. I've always wanted to taste garlic ice cream, and they'll have all sorts of food booths."

"How many stylists would we need?" Marla asked, spinning the planning wheels in her head.

"There are twelve finalists. We'd have two hours total in the prep area."

"Hmm, if we bring three stylists, each of us could do four girls in that time. I'll see who else is interested. What kind of mention will we get?" While honored to have been asked, Marla couldn't help wondering how it might benefit the salon.

Robyn's eyes gleamed. "Besides a credit in the program book, we'd get free tickets and access to the V.I.P. tent. I'll include myself in the group, so that would make four of us." She paused. "Wait a minute. What will you do with Ryder?"

"Dalton can push him around in his stroller. Or maybe I'll ask my mother and Reed to meet us there, and they can watch him. With all that's going on, they could use a break. My mother is a nervous wreck. She asked me to stop by the design center to learn what I could about their operations. I went by there this morning." Marla had filled Robyn in on the case earlier.

Robyn gave her a questioning glance. "I thought you were going to let the police detective handle things."

"I was hoping to stay out of it, but I couldn't refuse Ma's request. Besides, I learned a few things that might be useful."

The front door chimes sounded, and their conversation ended. Marla's one o'clock appointment had arrived.

As she got busy with her customer, Marla nodded hello to the other stylists. Nicole at the next chair cast curious glances her way. Eager to confide in her mystery-loving friend about the morning's escapade, Marla managed to keep the latest news from her lips until they had a spare moment together.

Marla tossed the used foils from her last bleach job into the trash. Gosh, had it almost been a year since Nicole and Kevin had gotten married? She studied her friend's sleek figure, knowing she was trying to get pregnant. Nicole looked as slim as ever.

"What's up, Marla? You look like a snake that's just swallowed a meal." Nicole swiped a drop of cleaning agent off her warm brown skin. She was wiping down her counter before her next client arrived.

"I paid a visit this morning to the design center and met Caroline. She's an admin assistant who pretty much runs the place. The other full-time staffers are the company president and the interior architect."

Nicole's dark eyes sharpened. "Did you get to meet them, too?"

"No. Bradley Quinn, the company president, was there but busy in his private office. The architect wasn't present, either. She'd be the one to come to our house for an evaluation."

"Oh? Are you thinking of remodeling?"

Marla shook her head. "Not really, but I pretended we were in the market as an excuse to ask questions."

Nicole stuck a comb into the Barbicide jar on her counter. "Did you learn anything worth telling the detective?"

"The foreman had an ex-girlfriend. Wanner probably knows that already if he's been checking into Jack's background."

"Is the autopsy report back yet?"

"Not that we know. I'm not even sure Wanner will share the details with Dalton since he has a conflict of interest."

Nicole tucked a strand of hair behind her ear. She wore her raven hair pinned atop her head. "Is that detective still harassing Reed?"

"Yes. He wants Reed to come in for more questioning. Ma is concerned about why Reed picked this company when they had lower bids. I don't think that's unusual. We've done the same when we believed another place would do a better job."

"Have you looked at their reviews?"

Marla grimaced. "Do I have any free time these days? I can barely keep up with my email."

"You should ease up on your schedule, girlfriend."

"No, thanks. Work keeps me sane. Did Robyn tell you we were invited to do hair at the garlic festival for the beauty pageant contestants? It'll be great publicity. Dalton and I can bring Ryder. He loves being outdoors."

Nicole's eyebrows lifted. "I'd like to participate. Maybe Kevin could pick up some new sauces for his barbecue dishes."

"That would be great. I can't wait for your party on Memorial Day weekend."

"It'll be fun. Some of Kevin's friends from the fire department will be attending."

"Oh, yeah?" Kevin, a paramedic at the fire station, had helped to rescue Spooks when Marla's poodle got in trouble a while back. "Are there any single guys on your invite list? You could invite Robyn to meet them."

"That's an idea. I'll tell her to reserve the date," Nicole said with a grin.

Their next clients arrived, cutting off the discussion. Marla focused on doing hair for the next few hours.

Before she knew it, five o'clock had come and gone. This being her late night at the salon, she had her last client at seven.

She was grabbing a snack in the back storeroom when her cell phone rang.

"Dalton, what is it? Is Ryder okay?" Her husband would have picked him up from daycare earlier. It was almost time for the baby's bath.

"Yes, he's fine. I got a call from Detective Wanner. The M.E.'s report is back. The foreman didn't die from strangulation. His neck was broken."

Chapter Four

"That's a surprise. Did Wanner offer a theory as to why Reed's tie was wrapped around the victim's neck?" Marla asked her husband.

"No, and I didn't ask. I was happy Wanner was sharing information and didn't want him to clam up. He said Laredo's shoes had soil in the treads and grass blades stuck in his clothes, along with grains of dirt."

"You think he got killed out on the lawn and was dragged inside? If so, why?"

"To stage the body so Reed appeared guilty? Laredo could have encountered anyone in the backyard. He had to walk around the house to reach the bathroom door. However, the neighbors didn't notice any other strange cars outside."

"That doesn't mean anything. If someone meant him harm, they could have parked around the corner. Did the neighbors see anybody lurking by the house?"

"Not really. I imagine most people were getting ready for work and weren't peeking out their windows. Wanner would have canvassed the neighborhood as a matter of routine."

Marla grunted. "It's too bad this isn't your jurisdiction. I hope he's considering other suspects besides Reed, such as Jack's ex-girlfriend." She gave Dalton a summary of her visit to the design center.

"Hopefully, Wanner got a list of company employees, subcontractors and suppliers," Dalton said, his tone reflecting her own frustration. "Anyway, go back to work. I'll see you when you get home."

He didn't have much else to add that evening, and Marla was too weary by the end of the day to discuss the case in detail.

Dalton packed the baby's lunch on Friday morning while Marla fed and dressed him. It was her turn to drive Ryder to daycare.

She was in the car when she realized she'd forgotten to tell Dalton about the garlic festival. Oh well, it was nothing urgent. Hopefully, the weather would cooperate, and Ryder would have fun seeing the sights from his stroller when the time came.

Her schedule at the salon kept her fully occupied on Friday. She didn't give the murder case another thought until Saturday morning when her mother phoned.

"What's wrong? Are you okay?" Marla asked, her pulse accelerating.

"Reed had his interview with Detective Wanner. I'm afraid Wanner suspects him of being the killer. You have to do something to get that man off our backs."

"I'm doing my best, Ma. I went to the design center on Thursday as promised, and I met Caroline, the admin assistant. She said Nadia is their architect and Brad Quinn is the company president, but I didn't get to meet either one. I'm sure the detective has other suspects. He's just doing his job."

Marla glanced at the front door. She was waiting on her next customer, someone new to the salon. The whirr of hair dryers blended with the splash of water in the background. Scents of hair spray drifted her way as Nicole misted a client's hair at the next station.

"I hope you're right," Anita said in a forlorn tone. "Reed shuts up when I ask him questions. I'm afraid he's keeping things from me."

Maybe he's upset that you've lost faith in him. "Did you get any hint of a prior relationship between Reed and the victim when they were together?" Maybe they'd crossed paths in the past. It was an avenue that might be worth exploring.

After a moment, Anita replied in a squeaky voice. "Reed

did seem startled the first time they met. It was almost as though he'd recognized a ghost. But he denied any previous contact with Jack Laredo."

"Did he admit why he chose this firm if the price was better elsewhere?"

"He mentioned a celebrity endorsement. I'll ask him for the person's name. Then again, he's going out for a haircut later. He's so methodical that he must have kept notes on the estimates we got somewhere in his files."

"Don't snoop in his desk, Ma. That would invade his privacy. We'll find out the information another way. In the meantime, please trust your instincts. He's a good man."

Marla hoped her words rang true as she hung up. It was sad how the seeds of distrust had been planted. She hoped this blip in her mother's life didn't pan out to be anything more serious. Marla liked Reed and the way his eyes crinkled when he smiled. He treated her mother well and added an air of dignity to their family.

This brooked the question as to where else Reed might have encountered Jack. Their occupations were at opposite ends of the pole, and Dalton had vetted Reed's background before he married Anita. Maybe her mother had read things into their greeting that weren't there.

At any rate, her next client must have just walked in, because Robyn was waving at Marla from the front desk. The receptionist handed the lady a questionnaire to fill out. It was Jodi Fischer's first appointment for a cut and style.

After she'd completed their new customer form, Jodi walked over. Marla scanned the document then asked what kind of change the woman wanted.

"I'm tired of the same boring hair," said the young woman with wispy blond bangs and stick-straight hair. "Since I'm turning thirty this month, I don't want to look like I'm in college anymore, if you know what I mean. What do you suggest?"

Marla ruffled the woman's locks while studying her facial structure. "We could bring it up to chin length and add some layers. I think that would look great on you. Do you want to keep the bangs?"

"Yes, for now. I'm letting them grow out."

"Okay, we can work with that. Go on and get shampooed. Then come have a seat in my chair when you're done."

Usually when people wanted a change, they didn't mean for her to lop off all their hair. A new style could make a big difference same as a color change. Marla hoped Jodi would like what she had in mind.

A half hour later, she stood back to admire her work. Jodi smiled at her in the mirror.

"I love it," Jodi said after Marla gave her a final spritz of holding spray. "It feels so much softer and lighter than before."

"I'm glad you're happy. As a new customer, you'll get a ten percent discount on today's services. How did you hear about us, by the way?"

"A friend of mine told me about you. Caroline at the design center was impressed by your hair when you walked in to ask about their work."

Marla gave her a surprised glance. That wasn't what she'd expected to hear. "You're friends with Caroline?"

Jodi bobbed her head, her newly styled hair swaying with the movement. "We've known each other since we both went to FAU as business majors. I work in the office park over by Jacaranda."

"Oh, really?" This could be her opportunity to learn more about the administrative assistant. Then again, maybe Caroline had sent her friend to get the scoop on Marla.

"Caroline impressed me as being a savvy businesswoman," Marla said. "How did she end up working at the design center?"

"Caroline met Brad at a bar. I mean, Mr. Quinn, her boss. She's always been the type to snatch at an opportunity if one falls into her lap. He was looking for help at the office. It wasn't quite the job she'd wanted, but being out of work at the time, she took it. The salary isn't great, although she's found ways to supplement her income."

Jodi's tone hinted at disapproval and her eyes narrowed ever so slightly. Marla sensed old friction between them on that point.

"How so?" Marla asked in a sugary tone while Jodi stood and removed her cape.

"Brad put her in charge of hiring their subcontractors. She verifies their credentials." Jodi looked around and lowered her voice. "One time, she was tricked into signing with an unlicensed company. It might have cost Caroline her job if the boss found out, although she wasn't too worried about his reaction."

"I'm not sure I understand. Did their applicant provide false information? If so, Caroline couldn't be blamed."

Jodi winked. "She might not have verified things as well as she should have, especially when she expected to benefit from any subsequent assignments."

Do you mean she accepts kickbacks in exchange for her approval? Why are you telling me this?

"What happened when she realized her mistake?" Marla asked.

"Caroline removed the guys from her vendor list, but it was too late. The project manager had noticed their inferior work and called her out on it."

"You said Caroline wasn't worried about getting fired?"

Jodi's eyes gleamed as though she enjoyed spreading gossip. Marla still couldn't guess her purpose in being so talkative. "Caroline has herself covered in that regard. She was more concerned about any rumors Jack might have spread."

Marla couldn't decide which thread to follow first. Caroline knew she wouldn't be fired because she had a personal relationship with her boss? Then what threat did Jack pose?

"Who would Jack have told, if not Brad?" she asked.

Jodi waved a hand. "He had connections. It could have damaged the firm's reputation if anyone dug deeper."

Marla peered at her. "Are you afraid Caroline wanted Jack out of the way and took steps to make it happen?"

Was that why Jodi had come to her? So she could pass the tip along to her detective husband? Dalton wasn't involved in the investigation into Jack's murder. Nor had she told Caroline what Dalton did for a living.

Jodi stiffened. "Certainly not. Caroline might have been displeased with Jack, but she wouldn't hurt anyone. Tell me, do the police have any leads?"

Marla's suspicions intensified. Jodi would only ask that question if Caroline had put her up to it. That meant Caroline must have checked into Marla's background and knew all about her husband's job. "I have no idea," she replied. "Why would you think I'd know anything?"

"A little birdie told me you might be involved. I'm worried for my friend. If someone had it in for Jack, could she be in danger by virtue of association?"

"Tell Caroline to ask the detective in charge of Jack's case. I'm not privy to the details."

Jodi snatched her purse from the hook where she'd hung it and slung the strap over her shoulder. "I love my hair, Marla. Thanks for doing such a great job."

She hurried off to pay up front while Marla squinted at her retreating back. On the one hand, Jodi had implied that Caroline might have a motive to do away with Jack. But then she'd done an about-face and said she was worried for her friend's safety. She also knew Marla had a connection to the police investigator.

If Caroline had sent Jodi there on a fishing expedition, how much of what Jodi had said rang true? Either she did suspect Caroline in Jack's death and needed to unburden her fears, or Jodi had confided in Marla hoping to loosen her tongue.

Marla rubbed her temple, still confused at the purpose of their conversation. She'd let Dalton sort it out when she told him about it later.

That night at home, she gave him a brief summary. He tended to believe Jodi had been sent as a spy for Caroline, but he promised to follow up on her allegations regarding the subcontractor issue. Or at least, he'd pass the info along to Wanner when they spoke next.

Relieved of duty in watching the baby, Dalton plopped himself in front of the TV to watch a sports game. The dogs settled at his feet, content after being fed and petted.

Brianna waved a greeting on her way out the door to meet friends. By the time Marla put the baby to bed and did the dishes, she lacked the energy to think straight. She really should consider cutting back her hours, especially on Saturdays.

Sunday morning, Dalton took care of Ryder so she could sleep in. Once awake, she stretched her arms and started the day at a leisurely pace.

The morning had dawned bright and sunny, and she looked forward to their walk in the park. She dressed Ryder in a light jacket with a cap on his head and tickled him on the chin after placing him in his car seat. His big eyes stared at her as he babbled in response.

She loved his baby talk. Sometimes he woke up early and talked to himself in his crib. She'd even heard him laugh on occasion. How amazing it would be when he could communicate what was on his mind. Then again, that meant he'd learn how to talk back.

Spring blossoms scented the air at the park as they exited the car. Dalton transferred Ryder to his stroller and soon they meandered down the concrete path toward the playground. Brianna had decided to join them, surprising Marla that she hadn't wanted time alone at home. Going on nature walks on Sundays had been their family tradition, but Brianna had drifted apart as she neared graduation.

Dalton pushed the stroller. Marla enjoyed her freedom as she sniffed the perfumed air and savored the balmy temperature. Live oaks shaded the path, where woods lined the walkway on either side. Palm trees dotted the landscape in the distance while bird songs filled the air, broken only by an occasional raucous cry.

"I've too much to do today and a brisk walk will help clear my brain," Brianna said, her ponytail swishing as she strode beside Marla. She wore distressed blue jeans and a short-sleeved knit top in a jeweled pattern. Lately, she'd developed a fondness for Mardi Gras colors, purple and green. "We have debate team practice this afternoon. Then I need to finish the stupid homework that our statistics teacher gave us."

"You'll be finished soon, honey," Marla reassured her. "In the meantime, I'm sure you'll do great in the final debate. You're highly skilled at presenting an argument. Are you sure you don't want to change your college major from molecular biology to pre-law?"

"Nuh-uh. School is dragging on these last few weeks. It's torture to go to class."

"Don't worry. Before you know it, it'll be time for your graduation ceremony. Meanwhile, you have to get through prom. Has Jason made arrangements for transportation?"

"He and some friends have hired a limo. We've been invited to a party afterward. I hope you're not going to give me a curfew."

"No, but please send us a text as to when we can expect you home."

Jason and Brianna had been close since junior year. Dalton approved of the young man who seemed set on a career in finance. Personally, Marla didn't think their long-distance relationship would last once they each went their separate ways. Jason was headed to New York for his studies, aiming for a position on Wall Street. They were both math whizzes but had different goals in mind.

"The girls are excited about coming to your salon for our hair and nails," Brianna said, holding up her hand and wiggling her fingers. "It's generous of you to give them a discount."

"It's a benefit for Locks of Love," Marla reminded her. "We're happy to offer our services for a good cause. And it introduces our salon to their moms."

"I'll miss my friends but can't wait to start school in Boston."

"At least Glinda will be going there, too. It's great that you'll have someone you know for a roommate." It made Marla feel better knowing Brianna had a friend to rely on.

"How are Anita and Reed? I spoke to Grandma earlier and she asked about them."

Dalton's parents, Kate and John, lived in Delray Beach. Since this was Marla and Dalton's second marriage, Brianna wasn't related to Anita by blood.

"Ma is nervous about the police investigation," Marla admitted. "She's worried that Reed isn't telling her everything he knows about this design firm. Dalton, did you have a chance to call Detective Wanner about the things Jodi Fischer mentioned?"

"Not yet. I'll get to it during the week."

"Who's Jodi?" Brianna asked. She'd helped Marla with her sleuthing on more than one occasion. Despite Dalton's attempts to keep her away from the sordid aspects of life, Brianna had a curious nature that wouldn't be denied.

"Jodi is a new client at my salon. She's friends with Caroline from the design center."

"Is that how she got your name?"

"That's right. Jodi was overly talkative when she sat in my chair." Marla gave the teen a rundown of their conversation. "I'm not sure I believe her allegations about Caroline. Jodi might have been using this confession to lower my guard so I'd talk about the investigation."

"What are you planning to do next?"

Marla wrinkled her brow. "I'd like to revisit the design center to meet Brad and Nadia. I can use the excuse of thanking Caroline for the referral. Since we're apparently each trying to snoop the other out for information, maybe I can learn how Reed might have known Jack Laredo. Ma said he'd seemed startled when Jack came by for the first time."

"If there's something Reed doesn't want known, then it must be for a good reason," Dalton said, striding alongside them on the wide path. "That's a trust issue between him and your mom. If there's a secret he's hiding, he'll tell her when he's ready. It could be something completely unrelated. However, I can dig a little deeper if it'll put your mind at ease."

"I know Ma would be appreciative, although I'll feel like a snake if Reed finds out."

The baby whimpered, and they stopped so Marla could retrieve his bottle from their sack. Ryder grabbed it eagerly and suckled for a few minutes then pushed it out with his tongue.

"Don't you want more? You hardly drank anything." Marla nudged his cheek with the nipple, but he turned his face away. "I guess not." She capped the bottle after wiping dribble from his chin and replaced the item in her bag.

Brianna scooted ahead to watch an iguana scamper through the grass. She snapped a photo on her cell phone and then fiddled with the keypad, probably uploading it to social media.

Marla wished the murder case would go away as quickly. Unfortunately, the black stain would symbolically remain in her mother's bathroom until Jack Laredo's killer was found.

Chapter Five

Monday morning found Marla back at the design center, ostensibly to thank Caroline for the referral. In reality, she hoped to learn more about the firm and how Reed might have connected with their foreman in the past.

"Jodi looks so much better with her new hairstyle," she said, standing in front of the reception desk. "Thank you for sending her to my salon."

"I'm glad it worked out for her. I remembered you'd given me your card when she mentioned making a change." Caroline tucked a strand of wavy hair behind her ear. She looked very businesslike in a crimson blouse with a black pencil skirt. "Have you and your husband reached a decision about your renovations?"

"We've decided to use the money for garage shelving instead. Dalton has been wanting to improve the space since we moved into the house. We'll have to put off doing anything else for now."

Caroline's face remained expressionless. "You have our brochure and paperwork for when you're ready. Was there something else I could do for you today?"

"Jodi mentioned you'd been friends since high school," Marla said to keep their conversation rolling. "It was kind of you to refer her to us. Word of mouth is the best way to gain new customers. In fact, it was my mom who told me about your company. She's having a bathroom remodel done by your firm."

"Is that right?" The desk phone trilled. "Excuse me a moment. Hello, this is Amaze Design Center."

As Caroline listened, her brow furrowed and her lips pursed. "I'm sorry, ma'am. The delay can't be helped. We're waiting on your special order to come in. No, there's nothing I can do at this end to expedite the process. We're at the mercy of the supplier. Yes, I'll give them another call for an estimated delivery date. Thank you for your patience."

She hung up and glared at Marla. "The hardest part of my job is customer service. People can be rude and demanding when things don't go their way."

Marla's pulse quickened. This could be the opening she needed. "Tell me about it," she said with a sympathetic nod. "We get clients like that at our salon, too. They're not satisfied no matter what you do. But I understand how frustrating it can be from a customer's viewpoint, especially with renovation jobs. It disrupts your peace when you have to live with an unfinished bathroom or kitchen for several months."

"We always tell our clients to expect delays," Caroline said, her southern accent becoming more pronounced. "It happens with nearly every project."

"What is the actual process? You'd mentioned some of it in our last conversation, but I'm still trying to understand." Maybe Caroline would drop the names of their suppliers. Detective Wanner had probably obtained a list, but he wouldn't have reason to share it with Dalton.

Caroline clicked a ballpoint pen open and closed. The black and silver instrument had an expensive gleam. So did the pendant around Caroline's neck. Were those real diamonds with a ruby in the center? Her tennis bracelet looked genuine, too.

Marla wouldn't expect Caroline to make enough money at this place to cover living expenses plus high-end jewelry. Were they gifts from an admirer? Or perhaps part of an inheritance? For all she knew, Caroline could be independently wealthy.

"I'll assign our crew after the cabinetry comes in," Caroline explained in a somewhat haughty tone. Marla guessed that she liked to show off her superior knowledge along with the power she wielded in her role. "That alone can take several weeks depending on the supplier. Then we schedule the demolition. The same team installs the new cabinets. At that point, you'll have to wait for other items to come in. People get impatient and blame us for circumstances we can't control."

"Is that why your guys don't work on one project at a time until it's finished? Because they have to wait for special parts to be delivered?"

Caroline nodded. "Exactly. That applies to our craftsmen and their schedules, too. One person might be waiting for the plumber, while another one needs the electrician. Or things could be halted until a slab of granite is cut or the shower doors arrive. It's complicated. Things should be easier once we hire a new foreman. His job is to coordinate the various aspects of a project."

"Jack Laredo was in charge of my mother's renovation," Marla remarked, watching for Caroline's reaction. "She wasn't happy with how he communicated things."

The brackets deepened beside Caroline's mouth. "Jack wasn't the best at informing our customers about what was going on. When they couldn't reach him, they'd call the office. I had to smooth things over." Her mouth curved downward, revealing her displeasure.

"Still, his loss must be a blow to the company," Marla stated. "Are skilled project managers hard to find? I mean, how long had Jack been working here?"

"Why do you care? You're asking a lot of questions for someone who has postponed a project."

Marla was saved from a reply as the front door opened and a tall, lithe blonde breezed inside. A whiff of classic perfume accompanied her, similar to Ma's favorite Chanel No. 5.

"Good morning," the lady called in an accented voice. She

wore a conservative navy suit with a yellow gold chain around her neck and button earrings to match. Brushing past them, she dumped her portfolio case on the round table in the corner.

At Marla's curious glance, Caroline introduced them. "This is Nadia Romanoff, our architect. Nadia, meet Marla Vail. She's a hairstylist and a potential customer." She said the last with a touch of sarcasm, as though she knew that wasn't the real reason Marla was there.

In that event, why was she being so chatty? Was she hoping Marla would let something slip about the investigation?

Nadia's features brightened. "I'd love to hear what you have in mind. Come back here to my office."

Marla followed her to a suite of offices on the other side of the showroom. She caught a glimpse of the boss as they passed his open door.

Bradley Quinn had dark hair and eyeglasses and a harried expression on his face. He'd rolled up the sleeves on his white dress shirt and had a stack of papers piled on his desk. His square-jawed features reminded her of Clark Kent. Flashes of her brother's Superman comics entered her mind.

She'd remembered her promise to Anita to get in touch with Michael. She had called him and suggested they meet for lunch. To her surprise, her brother had agreed. They had a date for later this afternoon.

Nadia waved to her boss as they passed his office. Inside her own private enclave, she seated herself behind a modest oak desk. "What kind of project are you interested in, Mrs. Vail?"

Marla took a seat and crossed her legs. "Please, call me Marla. My husband Dalton and I are thinking of updating our bathroom. I'm just trying to gather information at this stage and gain an understanding of the process. I love your accent, by the way. Where are you from?"

"I emigrated from Russia as a child." Nadia fingered an amethyst ring on her right hand. She didn't wear a wedding band.

"Really? My ancestors are Russian. I would love to visit St. Petersburg one day," Marla said to put the woman at ease with a commonality.

Nadia smiled, the effect softening her face. "It's a beautiful city. We have a rich heritage."

"Yes, that's true. So what is it exactly that you do here?" Marla asked for clarification.

"When you're ready to move forward, we would discuss the improvements you'd like to make. Then I'll come to your house to take measurements. After you accept our initial proposal and send in your deposit, I'll draw the actual blueprints. I enjoy making customers happy. It makes me glad I took this job."

"Oh? Where did you work before?"

Nadia squared her shoulders. "I had a position at a high-end architectural firm in Miami. When I realized I couldn't go any further there, I left."

Marla noticed the framed certificates on the wall. "A lot of women hit a glass ceiling when it comes to professional opportunities."

"I see you understand. I'd like to open my own consulting firm one day, but meanwhile, this job provides for me and my son."

"You're a single mother? That must be incredibly difficult. I have a ten-month old child, and it takes two of us to manage him."

"Unfortunately, my ex-husband is not helpful in that regard." Something flickered behind her eyes, but then she plastered a smile on her face. "How did you hear about our company?"

"My mother is having her bathroom redone, but she's been having unexpected delays. Jack would tell her workers were coming, and nobody showed up until days later."

Nadia glanced at the door and lowered her voice. "That wasn't necessarily his fault, but things should improve when Brad hires someone new."

"I was sorry to hear of Jack's death," Marla mentioned, observing Nadia's response.

The woman folded her hands on the desk. "It was a shock, especially for him to die in such a manner. Poor man. He didn't get enough credit for the things he accomplished. Clients complained about him all the time over the silliest things. Sometimes all it takes is a patient explanation to satisfy them."

She stared Marla in the eye. "I don't mean to imply we'll be better off without Jack. Change can be a good thing, but not when it happens that way."

Isn't the former exactly what you meant? Marla thought. "Does this happen to you, too?" she asked. "Irate customers bother you with complaints?"

Nadia waved a hand. "We all get them. It comes with the territory of running a business."

"My mother's shower seat isn't finished. They can't use the bathroom until it's done. Is this normally the way things go?"

"Yes, it's nothing unusual. If we order granite for the seat top, there may not be enough left after the slab is cut. In that case, we'll cover it with tile instead."

"Lenny, the tile guy, came by to finish the job. He's the man who discovered Jack's body."

"So I heard. It must have been horrible. But how do you know this?" Nadia asked with a puzzled glance.

"Lenny found the body at my mom's place."

"Good heaven, I didn't realize the connection. Now I understand why you are here." Nadia's gaze chilled. "I hope you don't believe Lenny had anything to do with Jack's death. He's a good man and highly skilled at his job. Even if he and Jack didn't always get along, they respected each other's abilities."

Marla sat forward. "Did Lenny have any particular reason to resent Jack, aside from their problems in dealing with customers?"

"If so, I wasn't privy to it." Nadia tilted her head. "Although, there was that one time I heard their raised voices coming from the tile section. I was embarrassed because I was sitting up front with a customer. I had to go back and tell them to keep it down. I'd assumed they were arguing over a tile choice for some client. They should have come to me about it."

"Is Lenny the type to bear a grudge? Maybe they were talking about something totally different."

"It's not an issue anymore, is it? Besides, Lenny is a teddy bear. He wouldn't hurt anyone." Moisture glistened in Nadia's eyes. "Jack might have been a cog in our wheel more often than not, but we'll miss him. He always brought us our favorite coffee drinks when he came into the office. The man was good at noticing those personal details."

Not everyone appreciated him, Marla thought. Who had hated the man enough to break his neck? Moreover, who had the strength and knowledge to subdue him that way? Was it within a woman's scope to overpower a man and drag his body into the bathroom? Perhaps not, but that didn't mean she should eliminate Nadia or Caroline as suspects. Either one of them could have had a cohort in crime.

"Who else might have had a reason to resent Jack?" she asked, not ready to end their discussion.

"We've all had our petty disagreements," Nadia admitted, making Marla wonder if she'd had personal problems with Jack. "That isn't unusual when people work closely together."

Marla scanned the office looking for clues that would give Nadia a motive. The only item of a personal nature was a set of matryoshka dolls on a bookcase. Marla had collected the Russian nesting dolls herself after her sojourn to Sugar Crest Plantation Resort. That had been a wild Thanksgiving weekend when Aunt Polly had died and Marla met the ghosts at the haunted hotel. She'd also learned about her unusual ancestry there.

Her attention returned to Nadia, whose distant gaze indicated she was lost in thoughts of her own. "I'm trying to help my mother get things under control," Marla explained, hoping to loosen Nadia's tongue again. "Having a dead man in her house has been incredibly stressful. It would help to catch the person who killed Jack. If I'm asking questions, it's because I want this case solved as quickly as possible. Then everyone can move on."

Nadia responded with a sympathetic glance. "If your mother is patient, the police will find the person responsible, and her bathroom will get finished. We can only do what is possible under these circumstances."

"I realize that. It's just tough for me to be in the middle of things. Caroline seems to be keeping her cool. It must be helpful to work with someone who's so calm under stress."

Nadia snorted and picked up a paper clip to twirl in her fingers. "She would get riled at Jack, especially when he wouldn't reply to her messages. Maybe that's why she had words with him the other day. I could hear them shouting from down the hall. She's probably glad she doesn't have to deal with his lazy attitude anymore."

"Didn't Brad get involved? It's his company's reputation at stake."

Nadia's lips tightened. "He had his reasons for keeping Jack on."

Such as? And why had Caroline been arguing with Jack?

Marla tried another tact. "Caroline mentioned Brad likes to play with the numbers. Do you have any idea what she meant by that remark?"

"Sorry, I can't help you there." Nadia sorted through the folders on her desk and plopped one on top. "I've a client coming in for an appointment. I hope your mother is happy with her bathroom when it's done. Let us know when you're ready to proceed with your own project."

Marla rose and tucked her purse under her arm, feeling grateful the woman hadn't thrown her out earlier. "Here's my card. I own a hair salon and day spa. We give discounts to new customers if you're ever in the area and care to stop by."

"Thanks, I'll keep it in mind."

"Is it possible for me to meet Brad on my way out?"

"I'll see if he's available, but please don't repeat anything from our conversation."

Nadia introduced her to Brad as a potential customer and left her inside his office. The company president gestured for her to take a seat. Mounds of papers covered his desk in a disorganized fashion.

"I was sorry to hear about your project manager," Marla said, using the proper term for Jack's job. She took a seat as indicated. "Will that impact your operations?"

Brad's mouth thinned. "Caroline is managing the crew until we get a replacement."

"How terrible for his family. I imagine the police notified them. Will your staff be attending the funeral?" she asked, laying her bag in her lap. The faint scent of the fellow's citrusy aftershave reached her nose.

"That depends. His son lives out of town, so who knows what he'll decide to do?"

Marla's eyes widened. "I didn't realize Jack had a child. How sad for his father to die in such an awful manner. Did they have a close relationship?"

"Jack rarely mentioned him, but why do you care?" Brad drummed his fingers on the desktop as though impatient for her to leave. Had he been able to hear any part of her dialogue with Nadia through the walls?

"I like to know the people I'm working with when I have work done at my house. You can't be too careful these days, right? I thought I'd heard Jack had a girlfriend. Maybe she'll help his son make arrangements."

"I doubt it. Hannah and Jack broke up fairly recently." Brad's brown eyes bored into hers. "Are you here to discuss Jack or to talk about your project? Because we'll be filling his position with someone new. You won't have to deal with him."

Marla met his gaze. "As I understand it, that's a good thing."

Brad's fingers stilled as he regarded her with an icy expression. "Who referred you to our firm, Mrs. Vail?"

"That would be my mother, Anita Shorstein. She's married to Reed Westmore, my stepfather. It's their house where Jack's body was found."

The president's face reddened, and he pressed his hands to the desktop as though to rise. "Is that why you're here? To ask the same questions as the cops?"

"I want the case solved so my mother can find peace. I'll do what's necessary to expedite things in her favor."

Brad rose slowly to his feet, his steely gaze capturing hers. "If I were you, I'd be very careful about what you say and to whom. Otherwise, you might stir up more than dust in your wake."

Chapter Six

Once out the door, Marla phoned her mother. "I just left the design center, Ma. I've met Nadia and Brad. Along with Caroline, they're the only ones who staff the office. It seems everyone had a contentious relationship with Jack. I'd like to talk to the tile guy, Lenny Brooks. Do you know where I can find him?"

Detective Wanner should be done interviewing the top persons of interest by now, Marla decided, so she wouldn't be interfering if she had a chat with the man. He might be able to shed light on the office staff's relationships to the victim.

"I have his phone number since he's texted me a few times," Anita offered. "You're not going to do anything foolish such as inviting him to your house to look at your tile, are you? Because you have to be careful with these people. A man is dead, don't forget."

"I know." Marla adjusted her earpiece as she walked to her car. A lawn mower droned in the distance, an ever-present sound in South Florida. "It's possible Jack was killed for a reason that had nothing to do with his work," she reminded her mother. "Wanner must have spoken to his family and friends. Or at least, to his former girlfriend. It'll be interesting to see who turns up at his funeral."

"I'm texting you Lenny's number," Anita said.

"Thanks, I got it. Michael and I are meeting for lunch today. How is Reed doing?"

"He spends a lot of time in his home office. Something is eating at him. I can tell."

"Hang in there. Even if he had a reason to dislike Jack, he didn't kill the man."

"Do you know that for a certainty?" Her mother sighed. "I wish he'd open up to me. Same goes for your brother. I'm glad you're meeting him today. I hope Michael is more forthcoming about what's troubling him."

"We'll see. Anyway, I have to go. I'll talk to you later." She hung up, inwardly railing at men who didn't express their concerns.

Dalton could be that way, too, going silent when something bothered him. That reminded her that she'd meant to ask him about the police picnic on Memorial Day weekend. He hadn't said a word about it, and they usually attended. Wasn't that the same weekend as Nicole and Kevin's barbecue? Maybe she'd mixed up the dates.

She focused on driving as she headed north on Florida's turnpike toward Boca Raton. Michael was meeting her for lunch at Maggiano's, a favorite Italian restaurant by the mall. When the Glades Road exit came up, she took the ramp and headed east.

Her brother had already snagged a booth in the elegant dining room by the time she arrived. He stood to greet her with a quick embrace. He'd come from work and wore a dress shirt with belted trousers. His dark hair, now threaded with gray, was combed back from his forehead.

Marla slid into the leathery seat across from him, noting her water glass was already filled. The aroma of garlic and roasted tomato made her mouth water as a waiter strode past carrying a couple of platters.

She took the folded paper napkin from the red and white checkered tablecloth and spread it on her lap. "How are the kids?" she asked as a preamble to their chat.

"They're good. Here, I'll show you our latest photos."

Marla peered at his phone. It was incredible how fast they were growing. Rebecca, six years old, looked so cute with her pigtails and missing front teeth. Jacob, an active ten-year-old, was turning into a handsome young man. Marla couldn't imagine Ryder at his age. Would he be into rocks like her nephew? Jacob had enjoyed the crystal growing kit she'd given him at his last birthday.

"They're so cute," she told their proud father with a surge of affection.

"Jacob can't wait for summer science camp and Rebecca is excited about her dance recital." Michael rambled on about his children until the waiter took their orders. "Oh God, Marla. I don't know what to do," he said once they were left alone again.

Alarm made her pulse race. "What's wrong?"

"There's no beating around the bush. Charlene wants to move back north. I haven't told Ma yet because I know she'll be upset."

"Wait, Charlene wants to leave you?" Marla asked, her mouth dropping open.

"You know how she's always wanted to become a school principal? It's not happening for her in Florida. She cares more about fulfilling her goal than being with her family."

"So she plans to uproot herself and move out of state?"

He bowed his head. "That's right. I don't understand why this is happening. Is it some sort of midlife crisis? I've tried to make her happy, but no matter what I do, it's not working."

Marla reached across the table and squeezed his hand. "I'm sorry to hear this. Why can't she look for a position elsewhere in Florida? There must be something available."

Her brother shrugged. "I think it's just an excuse. She's become more distant lately, as though she's already detaching herself. I don't want to lose the children, sis."

"Is she considering a divorce?" Marla asked, aghast at the possibility.

He gazed at her, a lost expression in his eyes. "No, but she mentioned a trial separation. I can't understand why she is being so selfish. Whatever she does will hurt our kids."

Marla heard the pain in his voice, and her heart went out to him. Charlene had always been a sweet and caring wife, but she was also driven by her career. Normally, Marla would encourage a woman to follow her dreams, but not when it meant abandoning her loved ones.

"Does she mean to take the children with her?" she asked, unable to fathom a mother leaving her little ones behind.

"If so, she'll have a fight on her hands." Michael gripped his water glass so tight his knuckles went white.

"Maybe you should see a lawyer."

"Not yet. I'm hoping it won't come to that if I can convince her to stay."

Marla grimaced. "It's possible she needs to get this out of her system. Or is there more going on here than you're telling me? Have you two grown apart?"

Guilt assailed her as she contemplated her own neglect of her extended family. When was the last time she'd called her cousin, Cynthia? She could only do so much with the little spare time she had. Between the salon and her son, she had to stretch things to even help Ma with her problems.

Her brother shook his head, unwilling or unable to answer. This must be so difficult for him. He'd had his roadblocks in life, but he had overcome them. Marla had assumed he had the perfect life with a lucrative job in Boca Raton, an upscale house, and a beautiful family with two children. All they needed in her estimation was a pet.

Her lips twisted in a wry smile. *Nothing was ever as it seemed on the surface.*

What could she do to help? She didn't really want to call Charlene. Then she'd get caught in the middle... again. She didn't have the energy to take on another issue.

"I don't know what to tell you, bro. This is something you have to work out for yourself, but I'll support you no matter what happens."

"Thanks. It helps to talk about it." He sat back as the waiter delivered their meals. He'd ordered the Chicken Marsala while Marla got her favorite Eggplant Parmigiana.

She chewed and swallowed a piece of crusty bread and butter before digging into the steaming entrée. The combined flavors of tender eggplant and tangy tomato sauce mixed in her mouth. For a while, they ate in silence. Marla felt at a loss for words.

"What's going on with Ma's renovations?" Michael asked, his brows lifting.

Marla's mood rallied to the familiar topic. "It's come to a halt until the scene is cleared by the police. How much do you know?"

"They found the project manager dead in the shower and the cops suspect Reed."

"They're looking in the wrong direction. Reed wouldn't hurt anyone, although Ma thinks he might have had a past connection to Jack Laredo. But other suspects are more viable."

"Such as?" He stuck a forkful of spaghetti into his mouth while regarding her with mild curiosity.

"Caroline, the administrative assistant, approves the subcontractors and assigns them to each project. Nadia, their architect, does an initial assessment in people's homes and helps them with their choices in the showroom. Then there's Brad, the company president. I got the impression Caroline might be having an affair with him. It's possible she's also taking kickbacks from their contractors."

"What does this have to do with the dead guy?"

"Maybe he found out about Caroline's shenanigans. Here's something else. Caroline mentioned that Brad likes to play with the numbers. Could that mean he practices creative bookkeeping?"

"It's a possibility. Is Dalton looking into the company's finances?"

"It's not his case, but I'll mention it to him. Nadia isn't fully in the clear, either. Caroline heard her arguing with Jack, and vice versa. Clients complained about his poor communication skills.

The office staff would get angry calls from customers about unexpected delays. That couldn't have pleased any of them."

"How did this fellow keep his job if clients had complaints?"

"That's a good question. Nadia said Brad had his own reasons for keeping Jack on."

"Meaning what?"

"She didn't elaborate. It would help to learn more about Jack's background. All I know is he had a former girlfriend, and he has a son who lives out of state."

"Will there be a memorial service?"

Marla's brother knew she often attended funerals when sleuthing to see who would show up. "His body hasn't been released yet. It's been confirmed he died of a broken neck. The killer had wrapped one of Reed's neckties around his throat."

Michael winced. "Yeah, Ma told me about that. Did the killer want it to appear as though Jack had been strangled?"

Marla put down her fork. "That's what I thought at first. But now, it appears more likely the killer meant to cast blame on Reed."

"Who would do that and why?"

She shrugged. "I have no idea. Detective Wanner seems to believe Jack was killed out on the lawn and his body moved inside. Initially, it looked as though Jack had been murdered in the bathroom and Reed had used one of his ties to do the job. Why bother moving the body if not to implicate Reed?"

"What does Dalton say?"

"I've asked him to look more closely into Reed's background to see if he has a hidden agenda with this company. I hate going behind our stepfather's back, but Reed was the one who chose their firm even though they had lower bids."

"What's your next move? I know you won't let this go," Michael said, taking a sip of water.

"I'd like to talk to the tile guy. Lenny discovered the body. Ma gave me his phone number."

"You're not planning to meet him alone, I hope."

"No, I'll scope out where he works. I'll go there and say I need his advice on selecting the tile for my bathroom floor."

"Be careful, will you? I don't like the idea of you chasing after bad guys. You have Ryder to think about now." His face brightened. "How is my nephew, by the way? Is he doing anything new since I last saw him?"

Marla showed him some recent photos on her phone. She described Ryder's progress and her concerns about his sleep regressions. Speaking of sleep, her full stomach made her crave a nap. That was a luxury she couldn't afford, however. Too much to do and too little time.

She picked up the tab since she'd invited her brother to lunch, and they parted ways. Marla made him promise to keep her informed about Charlene. Her heart ached for him. She wished she could offer him better advice. Ma would be upset to learn about his concerns.

Marla gave her mother a quick call before she left the parking lot, saying her brother looked well and she'd share more details about their conversation later. She meant to go home and contact the tile man. Meanwhile, she had a list of errands to do along the way.

An hour and a half later, she walked through the garage entrance into the kitchen. She deactivated the alarm, plopped her purse on the counter, and greeted the dogs, who bounded at her for attention. She petted her furry friends and let them outside to the fenced backyard.

After putting away the groceries she'd bought, she settled at the computer. She'd thought about doing an online search for Lenny's name. That might be easier than giving him a cold call.

Sure enough, he was listed as an installer at Canyon Tile, a local business. Customers praised his work in their reviews.

Fantastic. Now she knew where to find him.

As long as she had the time, she did a search on review sites for the design company. People's comments were wildly mixed, some rife with complaints and others raving about the job done. Despite the problems along the way, most people seemed happy with the outcome. Their average rating was three-point-eight. It wasn't a company she would have chosen with so much competition in the area.

Her gaze flitted to the testimonial on their main page. Davinia Quincy, the daytime soap actress, highly praised the company. Marla admired her photos of a bright kitchen with modern lighting, a broad center island, industrial stainless-steel appliances, and wide granite countertops. She'd love to have a dream kitchen like that one, although she was happy enough with her own housing choices.

Was this woman's quote the celebrity endorsement that had influenced Reed to choose this company? How would he have heard about her? Surely, he didn't watch daytime TV.

According to a biography on the actress, she lived in West Palm Beach. It was possible they'd encountered each other at a local venue. Otherwise, why would her review have had such sway over him?

He had taught classic literature at the university. Maybe she'd performed at a Shakespeare festival or the like. There had to be a reason why he'd been impressed by her recommendation.

Further research showed that Davinia had gotten interested in acting as far back as high school, but it wasn't until she was crowned queen at the garlic festival that her career had taken off. A long list of TV and film credits followed.

Marla's brows lifted. That was interesting. Was this the same garlic festival she'd be attending?

Unfortunately, the woman's phone number was unlisted. Nor could she find any means to reach her despite calling the woman's casting agency and manager's office. They protected their client's privacy and railroaded Marla's inquiries.

Tabling that issue for now, she sent a text message to the tile man saying she'd been recommended to him as an independent installer. She wanted to redo her bathroom and was he available to work with her?

It took a couple of hours and several chores later before she received a response. "Have you selected your tile?" Lenny Brooks asked in his reply.

"Not yet. I was hoping for your guidance. I'm not sure what to get. It has to be non-slip for the bathroom. Could we meet at your showroom so you can show me the options?"

"I do installs for Canyon Tile," he wrote back. "They can help you choose the tile that's best for your needs. They'll even send someone out to measure. After your order comes in, that's when they schedule me for the installation."

"All right, I'll stop by their place. Thanks for your help." She signed off, weariness making her shoulders droop. In order to meet Lenny in person, she'd have to contact the tile place and ask when he was due in next.

She placed a call to Canyon Tile. When a female voice answered, Marla asked when Lenny Brooks might be in because she needed to consult him regarding a measurement. He'd forgotten to give her a business card when they'd met.

Fortune smiled upon her. The friendly receptionist said Lenny was scheduled to pick up a delivery order for an install on Wednesday. She'd text Marla his ETA later so she could stop by.

Excited by the prospect, she called Dalton and filled him in on her progress. She also told him the news about Michael.

"I'm sorry your brother is having to deal with this," he said, his deep voice comforting her. "Does your mom know?"

"I told her I'd call her back with the results of our conversation. I hate to worry her about it when she has so much on her mind."

"She already knows something is wrong since she asked you to intervene. I don't blame your brother for being distraught. His wife values becoming a school principal over their family. She should be willing to accept a compromise."

"I agree." Marla spoke hands-free through her earpiece while she put away the dishes from breakfast. "Charlene has never been thrilled about living in Florida. She hates the summers and the threat of hurricanes."

"That's no excuse. She's whacked out to leave her husband for a job she could find here if she really looked."

"You're right. There has to be some place in our state that needs a school principal and would meet her requirements. Maybe she *is* going through a midlife crisis as Michael suggested."

Voices sounded in the background, and Dalton responded to someone.

"I have to go," he said. "We've a homicide case on the east side of town. Looks like somebody knocked off a vagrant, and it's the second one this month. I'm hoping it's not a pattern."

"That would be terrible. At least you don't have to do the foot work." She was grateful he didn't have to risk himself anymore confronting the bad guys. He needed to stay safe for their son's sake and for her own peace of mind.

"The admin duties have gotten worse," he admitted. "Filling out forms isn't as fulfilling as being in the field. I'm beginning to miss those days of hands-on detective work."

"Are you sorry for the promotion?" He'd made lieutenant a while back.

"Not really. Things have changed in the department, though. City officials are breathing down our necks with their demands. We have to justify every single expenditure on the budget."

"Hasn't that always been the case?"

"Maybe, but it seems more onerous lately."

"Have you been able to look into any of the issues related to Jack's murder?" she asked, wondering if he was truly dissatisfied with his position or just feeling restless.

"Yes, I did, and here's the thing. Amaze Design Center has been in business for five years. I can't find any trace of Bradley Quinn before that time."

Chapter Seven

"That's weird," Marla said. "How could a person not have any history?"

"I can come up with a few reasons," Dalton told her. "Different identity, as in witness protection. Name change due to personal preference. You'd shortened your own surname from Shorstein to Shore for business reasons. Or the company could have been around but under another title."

"True, but you'd think something would show up on social media or elsewhere. Brad couldn't be a complete ghost."

"I'll dig deeper. In the meantime, be careful when you speak to Lenny Brooks."

"I haven't heard back from the receptionist at the tile place about his ETA. Maybe his plans have changed."

She wondered about it on Wednesday morning as she got busy with clients. An incoming text on her cell phone just after ten made her pulse quicken. It came from Canyon Tile.

"Lenny said he'd swing by around two o'clock to pick up his customer's order," the message read.

"Great, I'll be there," she wrote back. "Thanks for letting me know."

With a quick glance at her client getting shampooed, Marla figured she should finish the woman's haircut and style by one. Then she had some free time before her next appointment. The customer who would have taken the empty slot had cancelled a Brazilian blowout.

Her discussion with Lenny shouldn't take long. He'd be

impatient to make his delivery and get started on his installation. Anxious to meet him, she finished her current client and told Nicole to hold down the fort until she returned.

The other stylist gave her a wink. "Good luck, girlfriend. I hope you learn something new."

So do I, Marla thought during the drive to Canyon Tile located in Hollywood. She'd looked them up online. Their emporium appeared to be the biggest place in the area with referrals from designers, architects, and contractors. They even offered workshops, training, and certification programs for their vendor partners. Lenny would have had to meet their stringent requirements to do business with them.

The warehouse took up almost an entire city block, Marla noted as she pulled into a parking space. She should have come here to select the tile for their house when it was being built, but the developer had his own design center.

As she entered, several salespeople perked up. She halted, dazzled by the displays. Oh, my. If she didn't have a fairly new home, she'd be tempted to renovate from looking at these choices.

"Can I help you?" asked a guy in a rumpled charcoal suit. From the way he kept tugging at his collar, she surmised he preferred casual wear to starched shirts.

The receptionist's desk was empty. Perhaps the woman had gone for lunch? Marla had hoped to thank her for the phone message.

"I'm here to see Lenny Brooks, the tile installer," she said, glancing toward the rear. Would Lenny even come into the showroom, or would he merely stop by the loading dock?

"Does he know to meet you in here?" the salesman asked. His saggy face and large jowls reminded her of a canine.

"Not necessarily. I was told he'd be here to pick up a delivery order."

"I'll have to check at the bay outside, ma'am. Please wait here."

She scurried after the salesman, afraid that Lenny would deny knowing her. Worse, he might load his supply and leave. "Lenny might not remember me," she called. "He gave me an estimate on replacing the tile in my bathroom, but it's been a while."

She passed by galleries displaying different rooms in a house and a variety of tile options. The splash of water from a sink met her ears before the air-conditioning kicked in with a loud hum. Her heeled sandals clicked on the tile floor. She'd been through this selection process and was done with her house. Now baby toys and nursery supplies took priority.

The salesman exited to the loading dock and shouted to a tall African American man who was loading boxes into his van. "Hey Lenny, this lady is here to see you."

Lenny put down the carton in his arms and advanced toward them. "What can I do for you?" he asked Marla with a glint of curiosity in his brown eyes.

Her gaze swept from his close-cropped black hair beyond a wide forehead to his even features and thin moustache. "I need a few minutes of your time." She turned to the salesman who'd glanced at his watch in the interval. "I'll take it from here. Thanks for your help."

After he nodded and left, she addressed Lenny. "I'm Marla Vail, the lady who texted you earlier about using your services as an installer. Actually, you've been doing a job for my mother, Anita Shorstein."

His eyes bulged. "I know that name. I've told the cops everything I know, ma'am."

"It's Marla, and I have a few questions for you. I understand the experience must have been traumatic. My mom respects your work and says you're a skilled craftsman. It's sad that something like this had to happen."

"Sad for Jack. Maybe not so for others who knew him."

"Excuse me?"

"Please don't misunderstand," he said, raising his hand.

"Jack had the usual crop of complaints from customers. They'd blame him when anything went wrong."

Marla got the impression he was backpedaling from his remark. What *others* did he mean? "It's good you don't have to handle many customer complaints in your role. Had you worked with Jack for long?" Maybe if she got him talking about his work, he'd be more willing to open up about his colleagues.

Lenny moved a heavy carton closer to the van. "Nah, we'd done a few jobs together but not many."

"I imagine a highly skilled specialist such as yourself would be in demand. Where did you learn the business?"

He responded to her flattery with a grin. "My daddy taught me. He knew his way around a construction site. It's not what I'd planned to do, but when he died, I needed to support our family."

"You have siblings?"

"Two sisters." He took off his work gloves and tossed them on the pavement.

"Any kids?" She noticed he wore a wedding ring.

"Yep, but why do you care?"

"My mother is upset over Jack's death. I want to help her find peace. It must have been horrible when you found Jack on their shower floor."

He scrubbed a hand over his face. "It's hard to get that image out of my mind."

"My husband is a police detective. I know it affects me when he comes home and tells me about a bad case. He tries to keep things from me but sometimes he needs to talk it out."

"Yeah, I didn't want to tell my wife, but Bianca sensed I wasn't myself. I was scared the cops would think I'd done it. She said I should cooperate with the investigation. I've tried my best, but I get nervous around police officers."

She offered him a sympathetic smile. "Lots of people feel that way. However, the lead investigator seems more interested in my stepfather since it was his tie wrapped around Jack's neck. I want to help clear his name. Regarding Amaze Design Center, did Caroline assign you to a particular project or was it Jack?"

The whine of a siren in the distance mingled with the sound of traffic from the main road. A breeze stirred, bringing the scent of impending rain. From the corner of her eye, she noted dark gray clouds coalescing overhead. Hopefully, she could get back to the salon before it rained.

"Caroline would contact me to see if I were free to do a job. Then she told Jack, who coordinated the workers on a project. But I'm done with them," Lenny said with an emphatic shake of his head.

"I can understand your choice in light of what happened," she said, hoping to encourage him to keep talking.

"It's not Jack's death that influenced me, although that didn't help. The company still owes me for two previous installs, plus they're behind in payments to the tile company. This might be of interest to the detective looking into Jack's case, but you didn't hear it from me."

This was news. Were they behind in other bill payments as well?

"Have you had much contact with the company president?" Marla asked.

"Nope. Brad keeps mostly to himself, except for his assistant."

"Who is it that doles out the paychecks? Would that be Brad?"

"Uh-uh. Jack handed us the actual checks."

"Did you ask either one of them why you weren't getting paid? It's a serious issue if their company isn't meeting its obligations."

He grunted. "I barged into Brad's office one day and accused him of having cash flow problems. He denied any deficits."

Lenny donned his gloves and resumed loading his van. Marla knew that as soon as he finished, he'd drive off.

"My mother said Jack didn't communicate well," she said in a last-ditch attempt to gain information. "He'd promise someone like the plumber was coming but the guy would show up three days later."

Lenny's mouth curved downward, and his brow creased. "Everyone knew Jack was lousy at keeping in touch with people. When I complained, Brad told me to mind my own business."

"Can you think of anyone who might have held a grudge against the foreman?"

"No, ma'am." Lenny's arm muscles knotted as he hoisted another carton into the van. For a slim guy, he got in a daily workout handling those weighty boxes.

"Are you aware Jack wasn't strangled as it appeared?" Marla asked, meaning to startle him into providing more insights.

He paused from lifting another heavy carton and glanced at her. "How did he die?"

"I'm not at liberty to say. However, I'm disturbed by my stepfather's involvement. Were you aware of any friction between the two men?" She hated to ask but it had to be said.

Lenny put the box in his van then turned to face her. "I did overhear Mr. Westmore and Jack talking in loud voices one day. They were at the side of the yard, and I was working in the shower, so I couldn't make out what they said. Your stepdad was definitely riled about something."

Marla wasn't happy to hear this. Reed had neglected to mention a direct confrontation with Jack, just that he'd been unhappy with his customer service.

"I'd be angry if my valuable time was wasted waiting for workmen who never showed up. But killing Jack didn't solve those problems. Instead, it brought everything to a halt," she pointed out.

So what if Jack and Reed had a disagreement? She could understand Reed's annoyance with Jack's behavior, but it didn't follow that her stepdad would murder the guy for that reason. Then again, their discussion could have been about something else entirely.

Lenny kicked at a pebble. "If you're looking for other suspects, you might want to talk to George Eustice over at the granite yard. I'd met one of his friends on a job once and that man gave me an earful. George would have shot Jack on site if he showed up at his place."

Marla stared at him. "What did Jack do that made this man so upset?"

"You'll have to get the story from the horse's mouth, ma'am. And please don't tell him that I sent you there."

"Thanks for the tip, Lenny. I appreciate your time and the information. I'll feel better when my mother's life is back to normal."

Marla headed around the outside of the building toward the parking lot in front. She felt Lenny's eyes boring into her back as she walked away from him. He'd given her important clues in mentioning the paychecks owed to him and the tile emporium. But the best lead was the granite guy.

It seemed awfully convenient how Lenny had mentioned the man's name. Was he truly as innocent and cooperative as he seemed? Or was he deflecting suspicion away from himself as a person of interest?

Although he appeared to lack a motive, Lenny might still have had stronger feelings toward Jack than he'd let on. Had he suspected Jack of pocketing the money Brad issued for the payroll? If so, how far would Lenny go to replace their crooked foreman?

She also needed to follow up on his remark about Reed, although it would pain her to do so. Marla agreed with her mother that he was keeping things from them. Why wouldn't he tell his wife what plagued him? Was he afraid of losing her regard? He'd already lost Ma's trust.

Her cell phone pinged, and a message popped up. Oh, it

was a photo from Ryder's teacher. The baby was taking a nap, sleeping with his tush in the air. Her heart melted and a smile curved her lips at viewing his sweet little face, his eyes closed in slumber.

He's so adorable. I love him so much.

Her cares eased as she pocketed the phone and unlocked her car. Leave it to Ryder to put things into perspective. She needed to tend to her family above all else, and that extended to her family of clients and staff at the salon.

She showered attention on her next set of customers and then departed to pick up Ryder at daycare. The late afternoon evolved into a series of rote chores at home as she played with her son and prepared dinner. Brianna helped entertain the baby after she came home from school. She made funny faces at him during their meal and squeaked his toys.

Marla focused their conversation on Brianna's day. The teen groused about the statistics teacher who still insisted on homework even though the school year was nearly over.

"Don't you have to study for exams?" Marla asked, preferring to defer her conversation about the murder case until later.

Brianna shrugged, a frown marring her forehead. "They're not for a month yet, and I already know most of the material. These last few weeks are such a drag."

"It'll be over soon. In the meantime, enjoy being with your friends. You'll miss he closeness you have in high school once everyone goes to college."

Brianna got up to clear the dishes, then went to her room. Marla attempted to get Ryder to finish his milk, but he pushed it away. He gave her his sign language signal that he was done. Soon he'd be able to tell her verbally what he wanted. She couldn't believe how much he'd grown in the space of a few months.

She tickled his belly and her heart squeezed when he laughed. But then she got a whiff of his diaper and practicality took over. Dalton helped get his bath ready.

Ryder splashed water around in the tub and squiggled on the changing table as Marla tugged him into his sleepwear. She read him a story until he conked out, her own eyelids drooping.

Back in the kitchen, she placed the portable video monitor on the kitchen counter. He looked to be sound asleep and didn't move. With a sigh of relief, she washed the dishes that had accumulated. Most of them were Ryder's. As she cleaned the bottle gear, Dalton wiped down the kitchen table and refilled the dogs' water bowls. Marla still had a session of pumping to do before she could relax.

Nonetheless, she wanted to get the discussion off her chest that she'd waited for all afternoon.

"I need to tell you what I learned today," she began, admiring her husband's masculine form as he moved about the kitchen. "Lenny Brooks isn't happy with the design company. He said they still owe him for two jobs, and they haven't paid the tile place, either. He's done working for them."

"How did he feel about Jack?" Dalton came up behind her and massaged her neck. She sagged against him, her tired muscles demanding more. His practiced fingers felt so-o-o good.

"Lenny said Jack was the one who handed out the paychecks. When he went to Brad about the missing money, the president denied any problems with their cash flow. He told Lenny to mind his own business."

"That doesn't sound good."

"I agree. Is it possible for you to check into the company's finances?"

"Detective Wanner is likely already working that angle. I don't want to step on his toes."

"Maybe you can be unobtrusive in your inquiries? It would really help to know where the design center stands in terms of their financial obligations."

"It's not my case," he reminded her. "We have to trust Wanner to do his job."

"My mother's health is at stake. I can't just stand by and wait for him to share details with us. He's discounting the contribution we can make."

She dried her hands on a towel and turned to face him. "There must be public records you can access," she said in a coaxing tone. "Didn't you tell me how much you miss hands-on detective work? A bit of research on your part couldn't hurt."

He gave a resigned grunt. "All right, I'll see what I can do."

"Thanks, honey." She lifted on her toes and kissed him. "Lenny suggested I talk to George Eustice at the granite yard. This man had a reason to resent Jack. I thought I'd stop by there in the morning."

He tapped her nose. "Be careful, will you? I know you want to help Anita and Reed, but don't get yourself in trouble. You're a mother now. You need to stay safe."

Her heart twisted. She hadn't meant to get involved in sleuthing again. "I know, but I feel bad for my mom. She should be enjoying her new life instead of dealing with this situation. That reminds me, Lenny said Jack and Reed had words one day. Either Reed was annoyed by all the delays and was venting at the foreman, or there was something else going on between them. Ma fears Reed might be more deeply involved than he's telling her, and I'm tending to agree."

Dalton scowled. "If so, that won't help his case. He had means and opportunity, and he lacks an alibi. All Wanner needs is a motive and evidence to support the case against him."

Marla squared her shoulders. "How does he have the means? Do you believe Reed could break someone's neck that way? Would you know how to do it without police training, because I sure wouldn't have a clue."

"That's a good point."

Ryder whimpered, diverting their attention to the baby monitor. Oh, no. His eyes were wide open. *Go back to sleep,*

Marla urged him in a silent plea. She and Dalton watched in mute suspense until his whimpers ceased and his eyelids drifted closed.

"Whew. I'd better shower while I can," Dalton said with a tired grin.

"Go ahead. I still have my pumping to do." All thoughts about her mother's problems evaporated from her mind as she trudged after him into the bedroom, the baby's monitor in hand.

Ryder awoke again at one a.m. and this time he didn't go back to sleep so quickly. Dalton got up to sit with him while Marla rolled over and drifted back to oblivion.

It was her turn when the baby woke up for good at five-thirty. Her mind groggy, she held him in the comfy armchair in his bedroom, but his cries wouldn't cease. She'd better get his bottle ready and then prepare for the day.

Her blood thrummed as the early hours sped past and she performed her usual tasks. She looked forward to the challenge of talking to the granite dealer. Maybe she should get someone to go with her in case the fellow had a temper.

She dropped Ryder off at daycare and lingered in the parking lot. She'd try her best friend, Tally. They needed to catch up with each other's news anyway.

"Hey, what's up? I'm wondering if you're free this morning to join me on an adventure," Marla said after their preliminary greetings.

"What did you have in mind?" Tally responded in her bubbly voice.

Marla, who'd already filled her in on the case, mentioned the granite yard.

"Holy smokes, that sounds like fun. I'm afraid I have to stick around this morning, though. We've new inventory coming in today. Any chance you can stop by the dress shop later?"

"I'll see what time I'm done. We need to make a real date to get together. How is Luke?"

"He's so active. It exhausts me running after him," Tally replied, launching into a series of anecdotes about her son. "Anyway, I have to go. Text me when you're available and we'll make plans."

Marla rang off, picturing the toddler's dancing blue eyes and blond hair. Tally's son shared the same exuberance as his mom, whom she'd known since high school.

They'd parted ways during college and met again later in South Florida. Marla had been married to Stan, a domineering attorney, when she was maid of honor at Tally's wedding. Unhappy in her marriage, Marla had divorced Stan at Tally's urging and attended cosmetology school.

Tally had reinvented her life after her husband died in a tragic car accident and relocated closer to Luke's daycare center. She owned Dressed to Kill, a dress boutique where she sold social occasion wear for special events. The store's new bistro tempted shoppers to linger over coffee or light bites while trying on evening gowns. Marla admired her friend's strength as a working single mother and regarded her as a role model.

Wishing she could meet Tally for lunch as often as in the past, Marla got into her car, turned on the engine, and phoned her mother.

"Hi, Ma. I'm checking in. How are you holding up?"

"I'm fine, thanks. I was wondering when you were going to call. What's going on with the murder case?"

Oh, you don't care to ask how I'm doing or how is your grandson? Resentment flared but she tamped it down. Ma was in a nervous state these days. Her security was at risk and so was her marriage.

"I spoke to Lenny Brooks at the tile store." She related their conversation and the main points she'd gained.

"We need to get this wrapped up," Anita said. "Reed is becoming more withdrawn every day."

"Has the detective been badgering him?" Marla hadn't

mentioned the argument Lenny said he'd overheard between Reed and Jack.

"No, but he did get a call from an old colleague at the university who said Wanner had been there to question people."

"That can't be good. Why doesn't the detective investigate Jack's other associates? The job foreman didn't have a reliable reputation."

"That's why we need your help, *bubeleh*," Anita responded. "Wanner is stuck on Reed as his prime suspect."

"I'm heading over to the granite yard now. I'll let you know if I learn anything new."

It took her half an hour to reach the place. It was wedged between an auto collision plant and a glass repair shop in a seedier part of town east of the railroad tracks.

A fountain in front of the entrance spit water into the air, rendering a fresh scent like a bubbling brook. It softened the impact of row after row of granite slabs on display. She peered around the open space for a salesperson and jumped in fright when a gravelly male voice sounded from behind.

"Hello, ma'am, can I help you?"

She spun to face a middle-aged man with a droopy mustache that matched his gray-streaked hair. He wore a Cuban shirt hanging out over baggy pants. His nose appeared irregular with a crinkled look as though he spent too much time in the sun. His tanned complexion lent credence to that theory.

"I'm looking for George Eustice," she replied, realizing the towering slabs of granite must have hidden his approach.

He pointed to his chest. "That would be me."

"I'm a potential customer at Amaze Design Center. I wanted to talk to you about Jack Laredo."

"That sonovabitch? I got nothin' nice to say about him. If that's why you've come, you can leave now. I heard he's dead, and I'm glad of it. The man got what he had coming."

Chapter Eight

"I understand Jack riled lots of people," Marla told the granite guy. "I'm not sure I want to do business with his company." George glowered at her. "What does it matter now that Jack is dead?"

"His death has shut things down, meaning projects will be delayed more than usual. If you don't mind my asking, did your problems with Jack relate to his job?"

George lifted a hand to shade his face from the sun. "Their firm hadn't paid me for the last two orders. I refused to extend them anymore credit. Jack burst in here one day and chewed me out in public. Apparently, a customer had blamed him for the delay in installing their granite countertops. This client wrote a nasty note to the company president."

"How did Brad respond?"

The granite dealer snorted. "Jack didn't say, but I knew Brad wouldn't care. He could never fire Jack. They knew too much about each other."

"Is that right? Like what?"

"Things from the past," George said, hunching his shoulders.

His stance indicated an unwillingness to elaborate, so Marla tried a more sympathetic approach. "It must have been upsetting when Jack came here and railed into you. He shouldn't have blamed you for his troubles. It's understandable that you wouldn't fill another order until the company's debts were paid."

"You said it. I could have punched him in the face for

yelling at me in front of customers." George curled his fists for emphasis.

Marla noted his stocky figure and muscular arms. He'd have to be strong to move those pieces of granite around. Did he also do the precision cutting to meet client's needs? A closed door led inside. Maybe the interior housed a machine shop in addition to an office. Or perhaps that partition at the far end led to his workbench. Regardless of his role, he looked powerful enough to kill someone with his bare hands.

"Did you contact Brad directly about your missing payments?" she asked, resisting the urge to take a step back.

"Brad wouldn't take my calls. He was always too busy. Or so Caroline said when she answered the phone. He's in her pocket, after all."

Don't you mean, she's in his pants? "I noticed they were close," Marla commented.

He made a distasteful face. "You got that right. Caroline has her hooks into him well and good."

Marla rubbed the back of her neck. The sun beat down on her exposed skin with relentless intensity. Should she suggest they go inside to an air-conditioned space? Then again, she'd prefer not to be alone with this fellow who may have a murderous temper. At least outdoors, passersby could see them.

"Lenny Brooks, the tile specialist, mentioned he hadn't been paid recently, either. How can their company stay in business when they don't clear their debts?"

"Heck, I'm not surprised by anything they do," George said with a snarl.

A teenaged girl emerged outside, her eyes squinting against the sun. She had straight black hair that flowed down her back and wore shorts along with a shirt tied at her midriff. Her exotic looks reminded Marla of a Hawaiian dancer. Even her movements were graceful.

"Papa, you have a phone call in the office," she said, pressing her pink lips together.

"I'm busy, Amelia. Take the person's name and number. I'll call them back."

The girl pointed to Marla. "Is this lady a customer? If so, I can fill her in on the different grades of granite." Her eagerness was evident in her voice.

"I know you can, *mi cielito*." He introduced her as his daughter then gave a furtive glance at the parking lot. "Go inside. I warned you not to show yourself."

"That man is gone, papa. He can't bother me anymore. Now I can help you at work."

George growled. "Most of our customers aren't as nice as this lady. Do as you're told and stay out of sight." He turned back to Marla with a false smile. "Today is a teacher workday so she has the day off from school. My wife works, and I don't want Amelia home alone."

Marla couldn't let those remarks pass. "Is someone harassing her? If so, I can understand why you'd want to keep your daughter close." Adjusting her sunglasses, Marla moved into a shady patch where the temperature was more tolerable.

"It was Jack Laredo," the granite yard owner said, nearly spitting his name. "He'd noticed *mi hija* working here during winter break and showed up with excuses, but I saw the way he looked at her."

"Oh, no. What did you do about it?" Marla kept an interested expression on her face, but her heart leapt with excitement. This guy might be a viable suspect in Jack's murder for personal reasons that had nothing to do with Amaze Designs.

George's eyes narrowed. "I did nothing at first. I'd hoped he would lose interest. But somehow, the devil learned that Amelia had entered the garlic queen competition at the spring festival. The prize is a college scholarship."

"No kidding? I'm attending the festival this year. I'm a salon owner, and my stylists have been hired to do the girls' hair. How awesome that your daughter is one of the contestants." Marla handed over her business card.

"It's a small world, yes?" George took the card and pocketed it.

"That's true. We got the name of Amaze Design Center from my mother, Anita Shorstein. It's her house where Jack's body was found. Have the cops been by to talk to you about his death?"

He jabbed a finger at her. "Not yet, and I'd like to keep it that way. I don't want my name associated with that snake."

"You're aware he was murdered?"

"*Si*, so I heard."

"My stepfather's tie was wrapped around his neck, and we're trying to understand what that means. Reed Westmore is my mother's husband. Would you know anything about Reed's relationship to Jack?"

"Never heard of him."

His response appeared to be genuine. "You said Jack had learned your daughter entered the garlic festival pageant?"

George's complexion darkened. "Jack waited one day until I was in my office and then he drew Amelia aside. He offered to sway the judge's vote in her favor if she let him touch her. She ran away and told me what happened. I wanted to smash Jack's face right then and there, but he'd already left the premises."

"Did you go after him?" She could understand his rage. If a pervert ever approached Brianna, she'd want to take drastic action against him.

"No. I figured things would work out on their own," George admitted with a sardonic smile. "He and Brad were a team. I knew Brad's history. It was only a matter of time before he shut down the company and moved on. Jack would have gone with him, and then he'd be out of our hair for good."

Marla shifted feet, yearning to get out of the heat. "I'm not sure I follow you."

George's hulking presence blocked the sun as he stepped forward. "I don't suppose you're aware that the garlic festival judge whom Jack mentioned was Brad's sister? Davinia Quincy is a former winner. She's made quite a name for herself as an actress since her early days."

Lord save me. Davinia is a judge in the pageant? And she's Brad's sister? Wheels spun in Marla's mind. Davinia was the celebrity who'd given Brad's company her endorsement. Once again, Marla wondered about the connection between Reed and this woman. Despite his claims, he couldn't have been swayed by one testimonial, no matter how famous the client.

"What does Brad's sister have to do with him moving on?" she asked, confused by George's statements.

The granite dealer spread his hands. "It's his pattern. Davinia knows it, too. She's been smart in disassociating herself from her liar of a brother."

Marla meant to ask him to explain further but a truck drove up in a cloud of dust and a couple of husky workmen lumbered out. They waved to George.

"We're done talking, *señora*. And don't think I'm not onto you. You came here to pick my brain. I hope you got what you wanted and will leave us alone."

She had no choice except to go, but there had been one good thing to come out of this conversation. She'd be seeing Amelia again at the garlic festival and possibly her dad, too. George Eustice, as an enraged father, made a valid suspect in Jack's murder. He could easily have lied about not taking direct action against Jack.

Once in her car, she drove off to work, eager to share her news. Before heading into the salon, she remained in the vehicle with its engine on and updated both her mother and Dalton with the results of her visit.

Nicole asked about the case after Marla had applied color to her first client's roots and set the timer. Dressed in a flattering maxi-dress, Nicole put down the comb in her hand.

"You have that look on your face," she told Marla from

the next station. "You've learned something new about Jack's death, haven't you?"

"I believe so." She filled Nicole in on the most recent events.

Nicole nodded, her glossy black ponytail swinging. "Let me see if I've got this straight. Lenny Brooks, the tile guy, claimed he hadn't been paid for the last two pay periods and the tile place was owed for a couple of orders as well. Ditto for the granite dealer."

"That's correct."

"How does this give Lenny a motive to kill the foreman?"

"Jack handed out the paychecks. Maybe he pocketed the money himself and Lenny suspected as much."

"So how would killing him solve things? George seems a more viable suspect. He had personal reasons to do away with Jack."

"I agree. But something is still fishy at the design center. Caroline had mentioned Brad playing with numbers."

Nicole's eyes rounded. "As in, using a bookie to place bets on the horse races or falsifying their business accounts?"

"I would assume it's the latter. George called Brad a liar and seemed to believe he'd close the firm and move on. I don't get that part, but he also mentioned Davinia's name. The actress is Brad's sister. She's a judge in the upcoming garlic queen festival."

"No way? This case gets stranger and stranger."

"It does, especially since George's teenage daughter is a contender in the pageant. Jack offered to sway the judge in her favor if the girl let him touch her."

"Eww. That's reason enough to give George a motive for murder," Nicole said with a grimace. "Hey, wait. Aren't we doing the hair of these beauty queen contestants?"

"Yes, and that may give me a chance to talk to the girl away from her father. George claimed he did nothing to lift a finger against Jack after his lewd offer, but that seems unlikely. He's still angry, even though Jack is dead."

Nicole waved to her next client who'd walked through the door. She put their conversation on hold and strode over to greet the woman.

After her client headed to the shampoo chair, Nicole returned to her station. "What does Detective Wanner say about all this?" she asked Marla.

Marla straightened the supplies on her roundabout. "He hasn't spoken to George. I hope he's interviewing everyone associated with Jack and just hasn't gotten to the granite guy yet."

"Is there anyone else who might have had a reason to harm Jack?"

Marla consulted her mental list. "Caroline and Nadia work at the design center, but they wouldn't have the strength to snap a man's neck."

Nicole put a hand on her hip. "How do you know? With the proper training, anyone could do it. Women can be warriors, too."

"Or maybe they got a male friend to do the deed," Marla suggested. A whiff of holding spray entered her nose. Zoey was spritzing her customer across the aisle.

"Do either of them have a possible motive?"

"Nothing that seems strong enough. Nadia isn't satisfied with her position, but she's getting paid and has benefits. She'd like to open her own architectural firm someday. This job will add to her credentials, but not if the company goes under. George seems to believe that's where they are headed. I don't understand why he'd think so."

"What about Caroline?"

"She and Brad are tight together. I don't see why either one of them would knock off Jack."

"What about those missing paychecks? Could they have suspected Jack of taking the money?"

Marla spread her hands. "If so, why kill him? They could have demanded restitution or fired him."

"Not if Jack had some hold over Brad. Your granite guy mentioned he and Brad were a team. They must have known each other's secrets."

"True. Or maybe Jack was about to rat on Brad? The company president could be the one embezzling funds and Jack suspected him. He got tired of being blamed for the deficits by everyone and threatened to expose his boss. Brad got rid of Jack as a liability."

Marla's timer dinged and she sent her client to get shampooed. They only had a few more minutes to schmooze.

"Can Dalton look into the company finances?" Nicole asked, glancing at the sinks where her customer was nearly done.

"I've already asked him to check on it."

"It sounds as though you're on top of things then. How's the baby? I don't see how you have time for sleuthing when you've so much else to do."

Marla's face split into a grin. "He's teething and is drooling all over the place. I think that's why he's been fussy at night, although yesterday he slept well."

"Your dark circles are showing, girlfriend. You need to use more concealer."

"Who cares? I can barely get dressed in the morning. Each day is exhausting."

"That's motherhood for you," Nicole said with a wry twist of her mouth.

What did that mean? Marla knew her friend had been trying to get pregnant ever since she and Kevin had gotten married. Was she wishing she had the same problems?

"Do you still want me to bring my wild rice and barley dish to your anniversary barbecue?" she asked, remembering the event.

"Yes, please. Memorial Day weekend is coming up too fast." Nicole draped a clean cape around her client, who'd sat in her chair.

"I've been meaning to ask Dalton about the police picnic. It's the same weekend. I'd make two batches of my side dish and bring one there as well. I'll mention it to him tonight."

As Marla got busy working on her client, she wondered if Dalton was merely being forgetful with so much on his mind. Or was he not planning to attend the picnic this year? He missed his field work, but that shouldn't have anything to do with it. He'd see his friends there.

Troubled for no particular reason, she determined to broach the subject that evening.

Chapter Nine

Marla remembered to ask Dalton about the police picnic after dinner as she washed the baby's bottles. Ryder was asleep, his eyes closing as soon as Dalton had laid him down in his crib. She prayed he'd stay sleeping so she could get some rest. Her neck ached from the long day at work. She hadn't gotten home until eight-thirty.

"I spoke to Nicole about her anniversary party today," she began, scrubbing the nipples and propping them to dry on the mat she'd bought for that purpose.

"Oh, yeah?" Dalton said as he wiped down the kitchen table.

Marla had waited to mention the event until after her husband filled his stomach. *Wait until a man has his dinner before bringing up a touchy subject*, her mother had advised. *A meal always mellows a man.*

"I'm taking my wild rice dish to Nicole's event. I could make a double batch if we're attending the station picnic that weekend."

"Good idea," he said, his head bent over his task. "Do we have a gift for Nicole and Kevin?"

"The first anniversary is paper. I thought I'd order a set of personalized stationery. You know, memo pads, sticky notes and such."

"That's boring. How about a picture frame or one of those online albums that you put together from digital photos?"

She gave him a shrewd glance, aware he'd changed the subject. "I'll do more research on it. Have you bought tickets yet for the picnic or notified Betsy we'll be coming?" It was a potluck meal held at the park under a roofed pavilion. Betsy, one of the officer's wives, coordinated the gathering.

"Not yet. I wasn't sure if you wanted to go or if we should spend a quiet day with Ryder."

"Are you kidding? He'd love the park, and you could show him off to your friends." They were always looking for ways to entertain their son and use up his energy during the day. Why would Dalton think she'd want to do otherwise?

Dalton scraped a hand through his hair. "All right. I'll let Betsy know we're coming." He almost sounded reluctant, which struck her as odd. Usually he enjoyed the department's social functions.

Marla dried her hands on a towel. "Is there something you're not telling me?"

"Nuh-uh. This just slipped my mind, that's all. I'm glad you reminded me."

She narrowed her eyes at him. He still wouldn't meet her gaze. "We also need to talk about Brianna's graduation party. I haven't done a thing to plan it. Do you know how many friends she wants to invite?"

"Are you talking about me?" the teen said, wandering into the kitchen and opening the refrigerator door. Dressed in her pajamas and without any makeup, she looked ten years younger. A pang struck Marla's heart at the thought of her leaving for college.

"Yes, we were discussing your graduation. Where do you want to have the celebration and when? There will probably be a lot of parties that weekend."

Brianna closed the fridge door, a container of yogurt in her hand. "It's more your party than mine, with both sets of grandparents and your stylists coming."

"Maybe so, but we're proud of you, honey. We want to celebrate your accomplishments with our family and friends. You can invite whoever you want to come."

Dalton waved at them. "I'm going to take a shower while I have the chance." He tossed his cleaning sponge on the counter and bolted from the room, leaving them to their social planning.

Brianna was unfazed by his departure. "Let's hold the party at a restaurant," she told Marla. "That would be easier. Would it work for Ryder?"

"We'll have to schedule it before his nap, unless we get a sitter."

"No way. He's part of the family and the grannies would want to see him. We can do a brunch. Then I can go to other parties that day."

"Okay. Do you have a place in mind?"

Brianna shrugged. "Not really. We'd need a restaurant with a private room. I'll do the research if you're busy with other stuff."

"That would be a big help, thanks."

"Will Dad be inviting anyone from work?" the teen asked, lifting her brows.

"I wouldn't know. He rarely talks about things there anymore. I think the desk job is getting to him." Marla tilted her head, wondering if Brianna had made the same observation.

"He's good in a leadership role. I feel better about him being in an office instead of out on the street." Brianna got a spoon from a drawer, popped the lid on her container, and dug into her strawberry-flavored yogurt.

"I agree." Marla leaned against the counter and folded her arms across her chest. She appreciated these talks with her stepdaughter and hoped they wouldn't lose their closeness once Brianna left home.

"By the way, how's your mom's case going?" Brianna asked with a sparkle in her eyes.

"I've met the people at the design center as well as the tile guy and the granite dealer. But I'm too tired to talk about it."

"You look exhausted. You'd better go to bed before Ryder wakes us all up."

Marla gave her a tired smile. "I'll bet you can't wait until you're out of here. You'll be able to sleep through the night again without interruption. But we're going to miss you terribly."

"You'll get over it. See you in the morning." Brianna tromped off, her long hair swinging at her back. Marla gazed after her with fondness.

She got ready for the night but couldn't go to sleep right away with so many things on her mind. Cradling her laptop, she sat up in bed and checked her email. Dalton lay beside her, snoring with his eyes closed. She tapped lightly on the keyboard, not wishing to wake him.

After looking up anniversary gifts for Nicole, she brought up the schedule for the garlic festival. She'd have to figure out the logistics for her stylists at the pageant unless Robyn had already taken care of that task.

Uh-oh. A warning at the festival site popped up saying the restrooms were under construction due to renovations. Portable potties would be available. That would be inconvenient when they had to change Ryder.

Dalton would have to watch the baby while she was busy backstage. She hoped he didn't get called away by a case that weekend, although it happened less often now that he was engaged in administrative duties.

Her eyelids drooped and she shut down the computer. Now if only she could succumb to slumber as easily as her husband.

****

Marla awoke when light seeped into the room from the window blinds. Her cell phone read six-thirty. She stretched with a groan. Either Ryder had slept through the night, or she hadn't heard Dalton get up to tend to him. His space was rumpled and empty. He must be doing the morning feeding.

Nancy J. Cohen

She crawled out of bed, did her morning ablutions, and trundled into the kitchen still in her pajamas. Dalton sat feeding their son, a tender expression on his face. He glanced up at her entrance.

"Morning, sweetcakes. Did you sleep well?"

"Yes, thanks. I was so conked out that I didn't hear Ryder at all."

"He woke up a short time ago. I have an early meeting this morning. Would you mind taking over so I can get dressed?"

"Sure. Go ahead."

Ryder seemed to take forever to eat, throwing half his food on the floor and laughing at her response. After he'd finished his breakfast, she put him down on his play mat in the family room. Dalton came inside, looking handsome in a charcoal suit. He'd brushed his hair back from his forehead, its silver highlights adding to his distinguished air.

"Listen, I have something to tell you," Dalton said, his glance raking her over. Still in her pajamas, she flushed under his perusal. "It's about Reed. I meant to mention it last night but got distracted."

She stiffened. "What about him?"

"Jack's son was enrolled at the university when Reed was teaching there. The kid dropped out for unknown reasons. He'd been a student of Reed's in his literature class."

"That's not so unusual." She gazed at him warily. From the glint in his eyes, there was more to tell.

"Remember how Reed mentioned problems with kids who cheated on exams or plagiarized their school papers? What if he caused the boy to get kicked out?"

"You said the kid dropped out from school, not that he'd been expelled. Even if Reed were to blame for his departure, it would give Jack a reason to resent him and not the other way around," Marla pointed out.

"What if Jack had retaliated in some way? Reed would want to avoid any further contact with him. It doesn't make

88

sense that he'd have chosen the design firm under those circumstances."

"It's likely Reed had no idea who would be assigned to his project or even that Jack worked there," Marla said. "That could be why Reed seemed startled the first time they met on the job."

"You may be right. I'm still curious as to why Reed picked this place. He must have had some connection to Davinia that drew him to her endorsement."

"Could they have known each other back in Reed's teaching days? That would have been when Reed was married to his first wife."

"Who knows? Maybe you can ask the actress at the garlic festival since she'll be there as a pageant judge."

"That's assuming we get a chance to meet. There's so much going on that day. Various bands are booked for the main stage. Competitions and cooking demos will draw crowds, not to mention the exhibitors and food vendors. I can't wait to try the garlic conch fritters, crab cakes and jerk chicken."

Dalton's face brightened. "I'm more interested in the Argentine barbecue, gator bites and garlic ice cream. Hey, don't look so surprised. I looked up the menu, too."

"Of course, you'd be interested in the food." She should have known that would appeal to him. "I'm hoping we can watch one of the guest chefs."

"You'll be busy with your stylists, and I'll be with Ryder. We'll have our hands full."

"I suppose so. What should we do in the meantime to help my mother and Reed? Did you have a chance to look into the design company's finances?"

"Not yet." Dalton snatched his keys from a set of wall hooks. "I'm still trying to learn more about their inception. I can't get anything earlier on the firm's president. It's damned odd."

"Davinia might have the answers. She could shed light on her brother's past."

"Maybe she'll come to the funeral. I got word from Detective Wanner that Jack's body is being released. His son will be holding a local graveside service."

Marla perked up at this news. "One of us should go to see who shows up."

"Let's talk about it later. You'd better get dressed. I have to leave for work."

****

Hours later during a break at the salon, Marla headed into the back storeroom to grab a cup of coffee and to do more research on the case. She'd decided to reach out to the company's customers via social media. For this purpose, she signed into her neighborhood app. A quick search found someone who had asked for recommendations on bathroom remodels.

This request had garnered a number of responses including several mentions of Amaze Design Center. She sent off a series of private messages to the commentators of those posts.

By the end of the workday on Friday, she had a load of replies. People were descriptive in their tales of woe.

"The company cuts corners by sending unlicensed workers to do their electrical work. I almost had a fire in my kitchen due to improper wiring behind our oven."

"This company doesn't provide the products they promise. I'd ordered sliding glass doors for my shower. The installers came and put on a fixed door instead. When I said it was wrong, the foreman tried to convince me this type of door was the popular choice. I insisted they change it to the ones specified in the blueprints."

"The mirror guys were awful. They didn't remove the label. We have a smear now because we had to scrub it off."

"I suspect the foreman and the permit inspector are colluding together. There's no way the latter would pass their sloppy work. I noticed an exchange between the two of them in our backyard. I didn't see any money switch hands, but I wouldn't be surprised."

Marla reread that last one. Was this customer implying the inspector accepted bribes to approve inferior work? Had their foreman been Jack Laredo?

She shot back a query asking for the job supervisor's name. She also asked for the name of the permit inspector, which might be listed on their paperwork.

What if the permit guy truly was accepting bribes? Jack might have threatened to expose him. Had this person killed the foreman to protect his reputation?

Chapter Ten

Saturday morning at the salon, Robyn greeted her from the front desk. "We have the schedule for the garlic festival. They want us there at ten-thirty. We'll have to do makeup as well as hair. Is that okay?"

"Sure, that will work. I'll have to drive separately from Dalton. Then he can leave with Ryder if the baby starts fussing."

"Any new leads on the murder case?" Robyn asked, thrusting a strand of hair back from her face. She wore garnet lipstick, a new look for her. It gave her a gothic vibe with her nails painted the same color and heavier than usual makeup. Did she have a date after work?

"Jack's memorial service is tomorrow," Marla said, not wishing to pry into Robyn's personal life at the moment. "Dalton and I plan to attend. He called his parents to ask if they'd babysit. Kate and John haven't seen Ryder in a couple of weeks, so they were happy to agree."

"You're lucky to have both grandmothers nearby." Robyn gave a rueful chuckle. "You and Dalton probably go to more funerals than anyone I know. It'll be interesting to see who shows up at this one."

"Tell me about it. I'm hoping we can learn more about the people who knew Jack."

Marla went to work as her first appointment arrived. She didn't get a chance to discuss the case again until later. Feeling an urge to touch base with Tally, she called her friend during an interval between clients. She sat outside on the salon's front bench for privacy and a breath of fresh air. Her hair stirred in the light breeze.

"How is Luke?" Marla asked to start the conversation. "I can't believe he'll be three years old in August. That's your milestone birthday, too."

"Don't remind me. How does it feel to be forty, old lady?"

Marla grinned at Tally's teasing tone. She was six months older than her friend and never heard the end of it. "Thankfully, it feels no different. However, being a mother has aged me ten years."

"No, it hasn't. You're a great mom. And Luke is doing well, thanks. At least, he doesn't have a cold this week." They laughed, both of them having experienced their child's frequent infections. "What's new with the murder case? Has the detective arrested anyone yet?"

"Not to my knowledge." Marla gave her a quick update.

Tally gasped on the other end of the line. "Davinia Quincy is related to the design company president? She comes into my shop to buy gowns for award ceremonies."

"For real? I thought actresses wore famous designer dresses and borrowed expensive jewelry."

"That's for the big awards, like the Emmys or Golden Globes. These are smaller events."

"How much do you know about her? Does she come in alone?"

"Hah, are you kidding? She's always accompanied by that manager of hers, Oscar Fielding. I can't stand the twerp. He has this creepy way of looking at a person and is rather rude."

"Does she ever mention her brother?"

"Not that I recall. Besides, we usually discuss what event she's attending and what style dress she wants. Money doesn't appear to be an issue. She's purchased gowns for several thousand dollars in my store."

"It's surprising that she lives in Florida and not California."

"We have a film industry, although it's not as well known."

"That's true. Anyway, you and I still have to set a date to get together. Any chance you're going to the garlic festival? We could meet up there."

"I'm afraid I have other plans that weekend. Can you do lunch a week from Monday? That's the only opening on my calendar. It's been crazy busy here."

"Sure, that would be great." They talked a few more minutes about work and children before ringing off. Marla fell into her routine at the salon and didn't finish until five.

She let Dalton sleep in the next morning and got Ryder up and fed. Her husband was more than willing to do his share, but he deserved a day of rest. Or at least, a few hours' worth.

Kate and John would be arriving at nine o'clock. Marla had a mountain of chores to get done first, including getting ready for the funeral.

By the time the doorbell rang, she'd done her morning pumping, thrown a load of baby laundry into the washing machine, prepared a meal for brunch, and dressed Ryder in a preppy shirt and pull-on pants.

Spooks and Lucky bounded to the front door as Marla ushered her in-laws inside. She shooed the poodle and golden retriever aside so the older couple could enter. John held a shopping bag that he handed to her.

"Something for the baby," he said, his gray eyes twinkling behind his wire-framed eyeglasses. His eyes matched the color of his hair.

Kate went straight for Ryder, held in Marla's arms. "There's my grandson. Hello, sweetie pie. You're my little doll."

Marla let her hold him while she drew out the box inside the bag. "He'll love this," she said, viewing the colorful xylophone instrument. She put it on the activity table Dalton had set up.

He couldn't help buying things for their son, showing a playful side that she adored. She'd frowned at the finger-paints he'd brought home last time, but they didn't create as big a mess as she had feared. Ryder had a good time smearing the paint around, grinning with pride as they praised his efforts. Now they had several examples of his artwork taped to the fridge.

Brianna wandered in, still sleepy-eyed and in her pajamas. She greeted her grandparents and then went to get dressed. The men watched Ryder play with his toys while Kate helped Marla put food on the table.

"Dalton said Anita and Reed are going through a hard time," Kate said, slicing a tomato on the cutting board. Her auburn hair gleamed in the sunlight streaming in through the window.

"Yes, it's been tough on them. The sooner this case is solved, the better. Ma feels guilty about not going to the memorial service today, but she'd be too stressed out. I told her to stay home and relax."

"That was good advice."

Marla fell silent, hoping they'd learn something useful at the funeral to make their time worthwhile. Once this issue was behind them, Ma's life could get back to normal. But would any of them truly be able to return to the way things were after the killer was behind bars?

The aroma of her zucchini and egg casserole permeated the kitchen. She plated the bagels and cream cheese Dalton had bought yesterday while Kate set the table. Since they were eating together, Marla had made more of a production than normal. She stuck a quick-fix peach cobbler into the oven for dessert.

"Does John have any art shows coming up?" Marla asked, changing the subject. Her father-in-law, a retired attorney, had gotten interested in stained glass art and now displayed his work at various craft shows.

Kate rolled her eyes. "He has an event on the west coast.

It's the same weekend as my bridge tournament, so he's going with a buddy of his from the studio."

"It's good he's keeping busy." Marla remembered how Kate had difficulty adjusting to her husband's retirement. His presence at home all day had upset her routine and then thrown her into a flummox when he'd announced his intention of entering art shows. She'd learned to compromise and became more adept at being flexible.

"Tomorrow is National Garlic Day," Kate said. "You're going to the festival in two weeks, aren't you?"

"Yes, we'll be attending the final day. Do you want to join us?"

Kate's brow creased. "I'd love to, but we signed up for a trip to Vizcaya that day. It sounds like fun, though."

"Ryder will enjoy being outside. Did I tell you my stylists will be doing the hair for the garlic queen contestants?"

"No, but that sounds wonderful. I'll be eager to hear all about it."

Brianna and the men joined them for the meal. Brianna strapped Ryder into his highchair and entertained him while Marla retrieved the food she'd cut up earlier for his late breakfast. As they ate, she told his grandparents how much he loved daycare. He played with different toys there than the ones at home and learned important socialization skills.

Kate praised his progress, making Marla swell with pride. It was too bad they had to leave this happy environment to attend a funeral.

****

Marla's mood sobered as she and Dalton arrived at the cemetery close to two o'clock. He followed directions to the gravesite where the service would take place. Already a number of vehicles were parked under the shady oak trees bordering the lanes.

The scent of freshly turned earth reached her nose as she and Dalton exited his sedan and padded across the dry grass to the designated area. She'd worn a black blazer with a cream shell and a black skirt along with sensible closed-toe shoes. She wouldn't want to tempt fire ants by wearing sandals, although she expected the funeral home kept their lawns sprayed.

The seats under the awning were taken. She didn't recognize any of those people, but she did give a nod of acknowledgment to the staff from Amaze Design Center. Brad, Caroline and Nadia stood in the wings. They cast startled looks her way upon noticing her presence.

A number of strangers made up the rest of the guests. It wasn't a large crowd but enough for a decent showing. Her gaze flitted from person to person as she tried to identify the people who'd known Jack Laredo.

She bent her head as a minister began the service, which was brief and devoid of any personal eulogies. A young man who must have been Jack's son scattered the first symbolic handful of dirt onto the coffin after it had been lowered. Then they went through the sad ritual of taking turns shoveling piles of dirt into the hole.

Marla stood back, blinking away moisture from her eyes, the scene reviving memories of her father's death. Dalton, too, had a haunted look on his face, doubtless remembering his first wife's funeral.

She gripped his arm, and they gave each other watery smiles. They had each other to lean on now. The feel of his solid arm through his sport coat brought her comfort.

Marla continued to hold onto him when the ceremony concluded and people split up. A number of people she didn't know huddled in clusters to speak in low voices. Caroline conferred with Brad off to the side. Their heads almost touched as they spoke quietly. Then Caroline made a vamp-like wiggle that left no doubt about her intentions.

As Marla surveyed the scene, she noted a stocky fellow in

dark sunglasses who stood observing the crowd. He wore a bowtie with a tailored suit and vest that must have been uncomfortable in the heat. When he caught Marla's glance, he smirked at her. The hairs on her nape rose and she looked away.

"We should introduce ourselves to Jack's son and offer our condolences," Dalton said, pointing in the man's direction. "Maybe we'll get a hint about their relationship."

"It didn't sound as though they were close. Did Jack have a will? It might be enlightening to see who inherits his estate."

Dalton gave a rueful chuckle. "More likely, they inherited his debts. I doubt Laredo had much to leave anyone, but that's a good question. I'll see if he filed a will as a public record."

"How will you introduce us?" Marla asked out of curiosity. "As a police detective and his wife, whose mother's house was the site of Jack's murder? That might not go over too well."

"I'll just say we were acquaintances. Speaking of detectives, Wanner is standing over by that leafy tree. He must have arrived during the ceremony."

"Has he spotted us? I'll bet he won't be happy about our presence."

Before they could gracefully slink away from his line of vision, Nadia sidled up to them. "Mrs. Vail, is this handsome man your husband? It's kind of you to attend poor Jack's funeral."

Marla introduced them. "I'd heard Jack's son planned to hold a service. I felt it was only right to pay our respects since Jack was, um, in charge of my mother's remodel. Ma wanted to come, but I felt it would be too stressful for her and advised her to stay home."

"I understand. Are you two really considering renovations? If so, you might want to attend the Home Expo next weekend at the convention center. Our company has reserved a booth in the exhibition hall. We're giving away a generous prize on Sunday."

Marla's interest perked at the mention of a free giveaway. "Like what? If it's a thirty-thousand-dollar kitchen makeover, I might show up to enter."

Nadia chuckled. "Now where would we get those funds? I'm afraid it's not that generous an offer. You could win a free double vanity for your bathroom, however. That is, if a remodel is truly on your agenda."

Marla didn't respond and Dalton remained on silent mode, letting her take the lead. She released her hold on him and stepped to the side, waggling her brows in his direction. Nadia might be more forthcoming if they spoke privately.

"This situation has been rough on my mom," Marla admitted once Dalton had wandered off. "I want to see Jack receive justice so we can put him to rest. I know I may have asked this question before, and forgive me if I sound insensitive, but who do you think might have done him in?"

Nadia glanced around. Marla followed her gaze, noting Brad who stood off to the side, glaring at them like an evil ogre. Standing under a shady tree, Caroline gave them the stink eye. Detective Wanner was chatting up the son, while others stood around in small groups.

"Jack didn't have many friends," Nadia replied, "but it's hard to single out any one person who would have done such a horrible deed." A strand of blond hair loosened from her twist and she tucked it behind an ear. Her jerky movements betrayed her state of nerves.

"George and Lenny weren't happy with him," Marla remarked, aware that they hadn't attended the service. "George said he hadn't been paid for his last two orders, and Lenny was missing a couple of paychecks. I'm wondering why your company is having problems meeting its payroll. I hope this shortcoming won't affect my mother's remodel. She only needs a few things done for the job to be completed."

"You've been talking to our contractors?"

"I've been asking around."

Nadia's mouth pinched and her eyes took on a worried cast. "You might want to be more careful. People could be watching."

What people? You just indicated you had no idea who might have wanted to harm Jack. Were you lying?

Before Marla could follow up on those remarks, Brad strode up to them and grasped Nadia's arm. He leaned in and spoke close to her ear. Whatever he said made the architect lurch away, mumble a hasty goodbye to Marla, and hasten toward her car. Was Brad angry she'd been speaking to Marla? What was he afraid Nadia would say?

Instead of accosting her next, Brad spun on his heel and stalked away. Relieved he hadn't stayed to berate her, she searched for her husband. Her glance caught him speaking to the homicide investigator, so she meandered toward a young woman who stood dabbing her eyes with a tissue. Could this be Jack's ex-girlfriend?

"Hello, I'm sorry for your loss," Marla said. "Were you a friend of Jack's?"

The willowy brunette gave a sad smile. "We used to be together. We'd broken up, but I couldn't let him go without saying a final goodbye."

"I'm Marla Vail. And you are?"

"Hannah Brody."

"Did you come alone, Hannah?" It didn't appear as though anyone waited for her by the line of vehicles, at least no one who was visible.

"Heck, yes. My brother would be furious if he knew I'd come."

"Oh? Why is that? It's reasonable for you to want to pay your respects."

The younger woman rubbed her belly. "Stuart wasn't very fond of Jack."

"I'm sorry to hear that," Marla responded, noting her gesture and mentally filing it away. How long ago was their breakup? "It was thoughtful of Jack's son to hold a service for him here. I understand he lives out of town. From what I've gathered, he and Jack didn't have a close relationship."

"To be honest, I'm surprised Kit held any kind of memorial for him."

"Maybe Jack had left his son a generous legacy."

Hannah gave a snorting laugh that turned into a hiccupping cough. "Please excuse me," she said, swiping at a tear trickling down her cheek. "The idea of Jack being generous to anyone except himself is a hoot."

"I never knew him that well," Marla admitted. "It's sad that now I won't get the chance. What kinds of things did he do for fun? Did he tinker with work tools in his garage?" she asked with a loopy grin meant to encourage confidences.

Hannah waved a hand. "He rented an apartment, so he didn't have a garage. He loved the old Jackie Chan movies and took martial arts classes. Jack had quite a few trophies from tournaments."

"Really? He must have been quite good then." This also implied that either his killer got the drop on him or the murderer was someone even more formidable than they'd thought. A shiver danced down her spine at the notion.

"How did you say you knew Jack?" Hannah asked, a suspicious gleam springing into her eyes.

"We were acquainted through his work." Marla fumbled for a way to keep their conversation going. She was learning about Jack's personal life and didn't want it to end.

Hannah glanced at her wristwatch with an exclamation of dismay. "It's getting late. My brother will wonder where I've gone. I told him I was visiting a friend, but he might check up on me. It's getting too hot out here anyway."

"Here's my business card," Marla offered. "I'm a hairstylist if you're ever looking to change your style. Also, my husband is a detective. This isn't his case, but he does keep in touch with Detective Wanner." She mentioned it in hopes the woman would get the hint that she could pass along any relevant information through Marla.

"Thanks, I'll keep it in mind. Bye for now." Carefully stepping between the graves, Hannah headed to the road.

Flummoxed as to who to speak to next, Marla wasn't aware someone was sneaking up on her until she felt a tap on her shoulder. She whirled around to face Bradley Quinn, whose face was twisted in a snarl.

"Mrs. Vail. I see you are interfering again where it doesn't concern you. First you attack Nadia and now you're speaking to Jack's former girlfriend."

"I didn't *attack* Nadia. We were having a friendly chat."

"You've also visited our business partners. I won't let you spread rumors and damage our firm's reputation."

"It's already damaged. Your contractors aren't being paid. Customers are angry over unexpected delays. For the most part, they've blamed Jack for these problems. Why did you keep him on with all the complaints against him?"

Brad's complexion darkened. "He knew the business and was good at his job. It wasn't his fault if a supplier promised a shipment that didn't come through. Or if the plumber, for example, was due on site but got called away by an emergency."

"True, but shouldn't he have informed his clients? They'd wait at home and nobody would show up. I'd be annoyed if my time were wasted that way."

"Nonetheless, people loved the results. We're the best remodeling company in the area."

"So what's the problem with paying your partners, as you call them?"

If steam could have emitted from his ears, she'd see it now. "We'll get it fixed. We're due some deposits that haven't come in, not that it's any of your business."

She had to admit that did sound logical. "Nadia seems to be a very talented member of your team. I hope you weren't angry with her on my account."

He squared his shoulders. "Nadia is a skilled architect, but she wants more. She needs to think about her son. In our company, she has a steady job with good pay and benefits. It doesn't behoove her to risk her position."

Marla bristled. "Talking to me was risking her position?"

"Talking to anyone about our company affairs is against our policy and will not be tolerated."

"You and Caroline seem to get along," she said, unable to help her snide tone.

"She's the rock in our organization. We all work together as a well-oiled machine. I'd advise you to drop your inquiries, or I'll have to take steps to shut you down."

Chapter Eleven

During the drive home, Marla shared her findings with Dalton. Her husband glowered at the mention of Brad's threat. She couldn't decide if the company president meant he would take legal action against her or if his words implied something more sinister.

"Regardless of his intent, you'd better steer clear of that man," Dalton advised. "I suspect he's up to no good. I'll keep checking into his background and the company's financial status. Unfortunately, I don't have access to their books and neither does Wanner without a warrant."

"I have faith in you. You'll find out what we need to know. How was your chat with the detective?" They had missed the opportunity to meet Jack's son after the service. By the time they were both free, he'd already left.

"Wanner believes Jack was killed in your mom's backyard and his body moved into the shower," Dalton replied, his hands on the steering wheel. "That indicates either the killer meant to implicate Reed, or he intended to leave a message of some kind."

"What, like a warning? Could the murderer also have a grudge against Reed?"

A frisson of alarm shot up her spine. Was her stepdad in danger, and by association, her mother as well?

"I can't help feeling there's a link we're missing," Dalton said, focused on driving. "Wanner hasn't eliminated Reed as a person of interest. It's possible he staged things this way on purpose, so the investigators would assume it was a setup. I'm not sure what to believe except we might not know the professor as well as we'd thought."

"I should talk to his former colleagues," Marla suggested. "They might be more willing to open up to me than to Wanner."

He shot her a concerned glance. "That could be helpful, but if you go down that road, watch your back. As Nadia said, somebody could be watching."

****

Marla got a break in the case on Monday morning. She received a text message from the customer who'd commented online about the permit inspector. He gave her the man's name.

She'd already dropped Ryder off at daycare and was heading to the supermarket. Instead, she changed lanes and veered toward city hall. That was the most likely place where she'd find the fellow. She meant to investigate the customer's allegations that Tobias Banyan had accepted bribes and confirm that the other man seen in the yard with him had been Jack.

She pulled up to the white-columned building amid stately queen palms and flowering hibiscus bushes. She'd had few occasions to come here, having signed up online for water service when she and Dalton moved into their house three years ago.

Night-blooming jasmine perfumed the air as she climbed the steps to the entrance. Inside, she faced a reception desk staffed by a middle-aged woman.

"Hi, I'm looking for Tobias Banyan, the permit inspector."

"Is Toby expecting you?" the lady asked, while Marla admired her hairstyle. Her auburn hair had been smartly cut in a flattering bob. The color complemented her warm green eyes.

"I don't have an appointment," she replied, "but I've an urgent matter to discuss with him. It won't take long."

"All right. Please sign our visitor log and I'll give you a badge."

Marla complied then stuck the adhesive label onto the

amethyst top she wore over black pants. The receptionist gestured to a hallway on the right.

"Go down that corridor. His office is a few doors down."

Marla thanked the lady and headed down the hallowed halls, impressed by the hard-working city staff she saw busy in their offices. Glass panels on the doors let her see inside. On her way out, she should pick up one of the brochures she'd seen detailing the city's seasonal activities. Maybe they had mommy and me classes she could do with Ryder.

She stopped at the door with the designated name plaque and rapped on the wood.

"Come in," a man's voice called from inside.

She twisted the brass knob and entered. A quick survey revealed overstuffed bookcases, a wilted potted plant on a battered file cabinet, a collection of glass paperweights, and several framed family photos. The room smelled of old paper and dust.

Marla closed the door so they wouldn't be overheard. She introduced herself and took a seat opposite the man's desk. He had tousled wheat brown hair and tired eyes. Her gaze surveyed his stocky frame and ill-fitting jacket and tie.

In a brief flash of memory, she saw the shadowy figure at Jack's memorial service who'd stood by observing the crowd. It wasn't this guy, though. That man had favored a bowtie and vest even outside in the heat. The suit had fitted his bulky figure like a second skin.

"How can I help you?" Mr. Banyan asked in a gruff voice. A mound of folders covered his desktop in a disorganized heap. The quiet hum of an air-conditioner droned in the background.

"I've been looking into Amaze Design Center," Marla said, debating how to ease into her questions. "My mother is having work done by their company, and I understand you're the inspector who signs off on their jobs."

He snickered. "I sign off on most of the jobs for this city. They only have the budget for one other guy."

She pointed to a framed picture of a couple and two children. "Is that your family? It's a beautiful photo. I hope you don't have to work weekends so you can spend time with them."

"Fortunately, this is a weekday job, although some days I work late."

"You're lucky. I'm a hairstylist, and I work every Saturday. It's tough on my husband. He has to stay home and care for our son when I'm at the salon." She figured sharing family stories might encourage Tobias to open up to her.

"I get it," he said, nodding. "Our daughter has health issues, and it's hard on my wife when I don't come home until after dinner. She has to manage the two kids by herself."

"Is she a stay-at-home mom?"

"No. Olivia runs a cleaning service. Her company is licensed and bonded. Are you in need of a housekeeper?"

"Not really, but I could refer her to my friends if you have a business card."

They exchanged cards, and Tobias included one of his own.

"You didn't come here for a friendly chat, Mrs. Vail," he said after scanning her data. "My time is valuable. What can I do for you?"

She crossed her legs to get more comfortable. The chair could have been better cushioned. "As I said, my mother is having renovations done by Amaze Design Center. I grew concerned when I read reviews from former customers."

His brow furrowed. "What do you mean? They do good work."

"It appears many of their clients weren't happy with the foreman, Jack Laredo. I'm sure you're aware he was found dead in a homeowner's shower. That would have been my mother's house. Naturally, she's extremely upset. I'm trying to gain information that might help solve the case so she can move on."

"All right, but why come to me?" he asked, spreading his hands.

"Have you ever cited this company for faulty construction?" Marla ventured.

His left eye twitched. "If I did, any problems would have to be remedied before a re-inspection."

"How about materials? For example, have their contractors installed things like cabinetry with wood that seemed mismatched?" She remembered that had been one guy's complaint.

"I deal with safety issues, not aesthetics." Tobias's gaze swung to the window with its view of the parking lot.

"According to some reviews, you've given this company's projects a passing grade more often than not." Marla was guessing, but maybe he'd slip up during their conversation.

His lip curled in a snarl. "What are you implying? Customers complain all the time. It's not my fault if the kitchen wiring looks sound, but then an appliance goes bad. Or if a client whines about his cabinets because he doesn't like the amount of space inside. People are picky about every detail."

Wouldn't you care if it were your dollars spent? You should be just as critical with your inspections. You're on the side of the consumer, not the installer.

"At least this design company files for permits," Marla said with a sympathetic smile. "I realize people often get work done on the sly and don't bother with legalities. This happened to us with a former neighbor. He tried to erect a fence between our properties without getting a survey. We had to file a code violation for him to correct his mistake. Otherwise, his fence would have encroached upon our land."

Unfortunately, this neighbor—the homeowners' association president—had ended up dead shortly thereafter. Dalton, who'd been seen arguing with the fellow, had been removed from the homicide case due to a conflict of interest.

Tobias's mouth curved downward. "There are also

unscrupulous companies that tell their clients a permit isn't required because they want to skip the proper steps. Most laypersons don't know the difference."

"I'd want to go through proper channels," Marla said. "Tell me more about Jack's relationships. Considering the negative reviews, is his company better off without him?"

Are you? she wanted to ask but didn't. If Jack had been paying him off, Tobias might have considered eliminating him as a liability.

What would be the permit guy's motive in accepting bribes in the first place? Tobias couldn't make much salary as a civil servant. Did he need money to pay for his daughter's medical care? That would be motivation enough to loosen one's scruples. And if he'd taken bribes from Jack, had he murdered the foreman to keep his lips permanently sealed?

Tobias shifted in his chair. "Jack may not have had many friends, but he knew his job."

"Do you have any theories as to who might have been responsible for his death?"

He snorted. "Ask Caroline at their office. She runs the place and knows everyone involved."

Marla's attention returned to the design center. What if Jack had been siphoning money that Brad issued for the payroll? He might have used the funds to pay off Tobias. But why feel the need to bribe him about the inspections? As Tobias said, if there were construction errors, the company merely had to fix them.

But if Jack or Brad were making money by ordering inferior materials or by sending in unlicensed subcontractors, that could be a reason to pay off the permit inspector. She should talk to Pete and Juan, her mother's work crew.

"My husband and I attended Jack's funeral to pay our respects," she said, wishing she could learn more about the foreman's personal life. "I didn't see you there."

"We weren't that well acquainted."

"Had you ever met his girlfriend? Hannah came to say goodbye even though she and Jack had broken off their relationship."

"As I said, I wasn't on personal terms with Jack. We rarely discussed family." His gaze skittered toward the exit.

"Hannah said her brother didn't like Jack," Marla persisted. "I'm wondering why."

"Jack had a temper. Make your own guesses." Tobias's face reddened. "Now if you don't mind, I have to sort through this paperwork."

Marla gripped her purse and rose. She'd learned a few things but didn't get any hints that Tobias had a strong reason to get rid of Jack.

"When do you think Brad will get a new foreman?" she asked in a final attempt to gain information.

Tobias stood and strode to the door, opening it in a clear message of dismissal. "I wouldn't know. Hiring someone is Brad's duty. Good day, Ms. Vail."

Marla left, pondering their conversation. Tobias hadn't admitted to skirting the rules, but the customer might have been right about him. If he did accept bribes, had he done away with Jack to ensure his silence? Yet Tobias had given her no overt cause to suspect him.

Something still didn't sit well with her about this interview, though.

If Jack was slipping money to Tobias, where did he get the cash? Was he stealing the funds from the payroll money Brad had made available?

But how often were inspections required? It couldn't be that frequently. So this begged the question, what if Jack was paying off Tobias for another reason?

Her temples throbbed as this notion didn't wash. Then Jack would have killed Tobias and not the other way around.

As she reached the lobby, she tore off her visitor badge and tossed it in a trash can. Outside, bright sunlight gleamed off the cars in the parking lot. The glare hurt her eyes. Standing at the top landing, she dug inside her purse for a pair of sunglasses.

She should contact Pete, one of her mother's contractors. Ma had given her the man's phone number. It could be Pete and Juan who took the shortcuts that jeopardized safety. If Jack had called them out on it, they might have acted to silence him.

Or was she grasping at straws? George Eustice, the granite dealer, still had the most likely motive. Jack had stalked his daughter. Any devoted father would be enraged under those circumstances.

After running a few errands, she went home to call her mother with a report on her visit to the permit inspector. The dogs nipped at her heels until she threw them each a couple of treats. She sank into a chair at the kitchen table and sipped from a mug of coffee as she placed the call. Her eyelids drooped. She needed the fix of caffeine to stay awake.

"Hi, Ma. How is everything?" she said when her mother answered.

"I'm glad you called. You'll be happy to know I have a mahjongg game this week. It'll be good to get out."

"That should cheer you up. Has Reed been any better at telling you what's on his mind?"

"Not really. He stays shut in his office most of the day."

She detected her mother's frustration in her voice. "Have you ever asked Pete or Juan, the contractors working at your house, about Reed's past connection to Jack?"

"Pete said he'd been unaware the two had met before. His main complaint was not getting paid for their last two jobs. Plus, he didn't like how Jack failed to keep customers informed about schedule changes. People would get angry when the workmen didn't show up as expected."

"So Pete resented Jack for his poor supervisory skills and possibly for stealing his paycheck."

"I suppose."

Marla updated her mother on the interview with Tobias Banyan. "I wonder if Detective Wanner has been to see him. Has the detective shared anything with you?"

"Are you kidding?" Ma said. "I was going to ask you the same question."

"Wanner believes Jack must have been killed in your backyard and dragged into the shower. But that doesn't explain how Reed's tie ended up around the man's neck."

"You said Reed knew Jack's son from his teaching days," Anita reminded her.

"I know. But surely, Kit wouldn't have murdered his father and tried to cast the blame on Reed. I'd had that thought, but it's too far off to be plausible. Kit lives out of town. He'd have to have made a trip here earlier."

"If only Reed would trust me," Anita said with a sigh. "There's more to their relationship than he wants us to know."

"We have to learn what really happened between them. How about if you and Reed join us at a home expo on Sunday? Maybe we can get Reed to loosen up if we act supportive as a family."

Anita clapped her hands in the background. "That's a great idea, and I'd love to see Ryder. How is my sweetie?"

Marla latched onto this happy topic. "He's feeding himself better, but he likes to throw his food on the floor and laugh at our reaction. It makes a mess but he's so cute."

She rambled on about Ryder's antics until another call came through. "Oops, I have to go. Dalton is calling. I'll talk to you later." She switched to the other line. "Hi, hon. What's up?"

"I have news," he said in a curt tone. "You know the granite guy you went to see? Apparently, George had been a former partner of a man named Brad Quincy. They had a disagreement and split up after dissolving their company named Jazz Kitchen Designs."

"What? Are you saying Brad Quincy and Bradley Quinn might be the same person?"

"It seems obvious. They folded their business and took down the website."

"That's interesting. George did call Brad a liar when I spoke to him. He claimed to know Brad's history and said it was only a matter of time before he moved on. Maybe he was talking about the business. Do you think Brad's done this switchover more than once?"

"It's a possibility. I'll have a talk with Wanner. He's moving too slow on this case. I agree with you that he seems fixated on Reed as his prime suspect. George Eustice has a more valid reason to want Jack dead, from what you've told me about his daughter."

She nodded, glad he agreed with her viewpoint. "I spoke to the permit inspector this morning. Sorry I didn't text you earlier, but I got caught up in errands and then I called Ma when I got home. I invited her and Reed to join us this weekend at the home improvement show. Maybe we can get Reed to open up about his relationship to Jack's son. Plus, it'll cheer my mother to see Ryder."

"I saw the screenshot his teacher sent. He looked so cute sitting in that toy car." Dalton's voice softened when he spoke about their son.

"I know. He looks so small compared to the other kids in his class, but at least he's not playing by himself anymore."

Marla and her brother hadn't gone to school until they were three, and the two of them had turned out fine despite the lack of early socialization. That reminded her to call Michael to see how he was doing. She'd forgotten all about his problems with so much else on her mind.

Bad Marla. But how could she keep up with everything? Add one more item, and her life would topple over. She could barely manage as it was to get all her tasks done.

"The permit guy is married and has a child with medical issues," she told Dalton. "His wife runs a housekeeping service. According to his story, he and Jack weren't acquainted that well."

"How about the customer's insinuations that he was on the take? Maybe he needs to pay for his kid's doctors."

"I couldn't come out and accuse him directly."

"Oh, no? That hasn't stopped you before."

She heard the wry amusement in his tone and could imagine his wide grin. Her heart somersaulted at the image.

She put her earpiece in so she could move around the kitchen. "I did ask Tobias about the quality of building materials and workmanship at Amaze Designs," she said, rising to take her empty mug to the sink. She grimaced at the mound of dirty bottles that needed cleaning. "He said the company's clientele were usually satisfied and complaints went along with the job."

"Not when so many of the complaints were directed against Jack," Dalton pointed out. "It makes me wonder why Brad didn't fire him."

"He got the jobs done, didn't he? Maybe that's all that counts in the long run," Marla said.

"Not if there's any truth to the rumors about inferior products or unsafe craftsmanship. It's possible the foreman had some kind of leverage over Brad for job security. Brad got rid of him in the only way he could."

"Or perhaps Caroline is the guilty party," Marla suggested. "If she's having an affair with the company president, she might do anything to preserve the status quo. Jack brought unwanted attention their way by garnering customer complaints. She could have killed him—or gotten someone else to do the deed—to protect Brad."

"Then again, we shouldn't discard Nadia, a single parent who needs her job. She seemed innocent to you but that could be an act," Dalton said.

"I don't really think she'd care that much. With her skills, Nadia could get a job elsewhere even if it didn't meet her standards." Marla rubbed her eyes. Despite the boost of caffeine, she wasn't feeling any more energetic.

"We can debate this later. You sound tired. Go take a nap."

"You're right. I can barely keep my eyes open. We'll talk more about it after dinner."

Yet Marla couldn't sleep. She worried about the toll this situation was taking on her mother and on what it might do to Ma's marriage. It didn't bode well when you couldn't trust the man you married. Why was Reed being so damn stubborn?

Was he wary of incriminating himself, or could it be that he was nervous about a killer being out there? What did he know that he wasn't telling them?

Maybe Reed wasn't afraid of being accused of murder. It could be he'd realized that unless he kept silent, he might become the next target.

Chapter Twelve

Marla called her mother back and warned her to be careful, just in case she and Reed were in any danger. She didn't relate it to Reed's reticence to talk but explained her warning based on logic.

"I'm just nervous thinking about a murderer being on your property. Don't let your guard down. Somebody might hold a grudge against Reed, and that could be why he wrapped that tie around the dead man's neck."

"Oh, my. Should we put our alarm on during the day?" Anita squealed into the phone.

"Not if you're home. Just be vigilant, that's all. Listen, I'm planning to call Michael to see what's new with him."

If she'd hoped to sooth Ma's fears by discussing her brother, it didn't work. Their conversation only brought up his marital issues.

"Don't worry. I'll talk to him," Marla promised before ringing off. She'd failed to reduce Anita's worries and instead had only added to them.

Not in the mood to get involved in anybody else's affairs and busy with chores, she didn't get around to making the call to Michael until the following afternoon.

She had a free moment on Tuesday during her lunch break at the salon. After grabbing her turkey sandwich from the fridge, Marla sat on a stool and dialed Michael's number.

"How is Charlene doing? Any change in her plans?" she asked, unwrapping her sandwich and taking a bite.

"She's still intent on leaving," Michael said in a morose tone.

116

"I've consulted a lawyer as you suggested to see what my options might be regarding the kids. I'm not certain, but Florida law might not allow Charlene to take them if she leaves the state."

"I'm sorry you have to go through this. How much do Jacob and Rebecca understand about what's going on?" At ages ten and six, respectively, they could tell something was wrong.

"Jacob realizes his mommy isn't happy. I've reassured him that it's about his mother's job and has nothing to do with him. She still loves him even if she's annoyed with me."

Marla hoped they didn't argue in front of the children or talk loud enough that little ears could hear. "Have you talked to Ma about it?"

"I don't want to bother her. She has her own problems. What's new with the murder case?"

Marla updated him on their progress.

"Who's your strongest suspect?" Michael asked, while voices sounded in the background. She'd caught him at work at his investment firm. They didn't have much time before his next client appointment.

She took a gulp from her water bottle. "The granite dealer has the best motive as a parent protecting his child. My other bet is on the home office. Brad, the company president, clearly has something to hide. His assistant may know what it is, but she won't talk. We have a few other possibilities as well." She mentioned the celebrity actress and her manager, the girlfriend's brother, the tile installer, the permit inspector, and Jack's son. Their motives might be fuzzy, but they weren't out of the picture.

"Be careful, sis. You don't know which rock you turn over that will hide a snake."

"You're right. I've told Ma to watch her back. I'm wondering if Reed is keeping silent to protect her. He might be afraid to reveal what he knows because then the killer will go after him next. And by association, his wife as well."

"That's a scary thought. What other reason would he have for being uncooperative? I don't like that he's not confiding in Ma."

"I agree. We've invited them to join us at a home expo this coming weekend. Maybe we can coax Reed into revealing what he knows."

"Good luck. I hope it works out."

"Keep me posted on your situation, too. I'm here to support you, whatever happens with Charlene."

Marla rang off, depressed by their conversation. She'd hate it for Michael to get into a custody battle over the kids. Things were bad enough with their mother's issues.

As she polished off her sandwich and the bottle of water, she mused over her findings in the murder case. It irked her that the lead investigator hadn't made an arrest yet. Why was Wanner dragging his heels? He must not have enough evidence to convict anyone. But did he still suspect Reed of masterminding the foreman's death?

If so, why would her stepdad wrap his own tie around Jack's neck?

That tie could be the clue to determining why Jack was killed and how Reed fit into the scheme. Surely Wanner had spoken to Reed's former colleagues by now. What had he learned about Reed's relationship to Jack?

There had to be some factor she and Dalton were missing.

As she headed back into the salon, Marla decided to review the case with Nicole. The other stylist was sharp at coming up with new angles.

But this time, Nicole didn't have anything to add. She put a hand on her belly as she regarded Marla. "I hope you get this case solved fast. I'm excited about our Memorial Day barbecue and want you to enjoy it. Kevin got me a new apron to wear. Wait until you see what it says." Her eyes sparkled and her lips quirked in a half-smile.

Marla's gaze dropped to her friend's hand and where it was positioned. Hmm, was something brewing that Nicole and Kevin meant to share?

It made her think of Jack's girlfriend who'd made the

exact same gesture outside at the gravesite. Could this possibility also apply to Hannah?

Her next customer arrived, and Marla's thoughts evaporated. She didn't consider the case again until later that evening when Dalton raised the topic.

"I spoke to Wanner this afternoon," he said, sitting in bed wearing only a pair of pajama bottoms. He'd picked up a book, the biography of an explorer, and rested it on his lap.

"Oh? What did he say?" Standing by the dresser, Marla let her gaze roam from his manly chest to his angular face. Her interest stirred, but she tamped it down. After caring for Ryder and dealing with her other chores, she lacked the energy for lovemaking.

"He shared the suspects' alibis. Nadia was at her kid's school function that morning. Caroline and Brad alibied each other. They met at the office to confer on a new project that had come in."

"That's convenient. How about the tile guy? He's the one who found the body."

"Lenny Brooks claims he'd left his house around eight-thirty. It's normally a half hour drive but traffic held him up. He didn't get to your mom's house until nine-fifteen or so."

"What's the estimated time of death?"

"Between seven and nine. Your mother left to go grocery shopping around eight. There were no other cars out front. She was home by nine. Lenny's truck wasn't there yet."

"He could have arrived earlier and parked elsewhere. How about the others involved?"

"Pete had another job, although he didn't get there until ten. He can't account for his earlier hours. Juan had a leak in his tire and was waiting for it to get fixed at the auto place. Wanner verified his statement."

"So Pete's movements were unaccounted for during that time, and Lenny may have arrived sooner than he said. Anybody else?"

"That's all Wanner gave me."

She moved to her nightstand to check the portable video monitor. Ryder was sound asleep in his crib. He looked so adorable that she had to resist the urge to go in there and kiss him.

Dalton followed the direction of her glance. "He's lost his pacifier. Should we put another one near him?"

"No, we might wake him up. He's conked out, thank goodness."

Marla and Dalton had sworn they wouldn't use the device, but one day, Ryder had been howling and nothing had soothed him. They'd stuck a pacifier in his mouth and were awed by the instant silence. Now he was addicted, but the doctor said it was better than his thumb.

"Is there anyone else who didn't have an alibi that you know about?" Marla moved to the bedside and plumped her pillows, appreciating the freshly laundered scent. She'd finally been able to do their sheets and towels in between the baby's loads.

"An employee at the granite place said George Eustice had gotten to work late that morning. He's still a prime candidate in my mind. But Wanner agrees there's something fishy about the design company. We'll see those folks again at the home expo. It'll be a good chance to ask around about them."

"That's a long way off yet. I've too much to get done before the weekend."

Weariness dragged at her. With a groan of fatigue, she lay back on the bed and closed her eyes. She murmured an affectionate goodnight and turned off the light.

Soon blissful sleep pulled her into its embrace.

The girlfriend's image wafted into her mind from a dream. She mentioned it to Dalton as they went through their morning routine the next day.

"Did Wanner ever interview Hannah as a person of interest?" she asked as she sat at the kitchen table feeding Ryder his breakfast.

"We didn't discuss her. They'd already broken up, so what

reason would she have to get rid of him?" Dalton, in a rush to get to a work meeting, collected his wallet, keys and other pocket items from where he'd tossed them on a counter the night before. She sniffed his favorite spice aftershave in his wake.

"Hannah was afraid her brother would find out she'd gone to Jack's funeral. When I asked the permit inspector about her, Tobias said he'd never met the girl. However, he did admit Jack had a temper. Do you think Jack might have been abusive toward Hannah, and the brother took steps to end their relationship on a permanent basis?"

Dalton's brows lifted. "I can suggest to Wanner that he talk to the woman and ask about the brother. You could be far off base, but it's an idea worth checking out."

Another idea jolted her. "Here's a different possibility. Maybe Jack and Hannah split up because he lost interest in her. That could have happened when Jack got fixated on George's daughter."

"I'll mention these theories to Wanner. You never know what'll pan out in a case."

Ryder babbled from his seat at the kitchen table, drawing her attention. He pushed the bottle away when she offered him another drink and made a grimace that she recognized.

"Uh-oh. He's pooping. I'll have to change his diaper again before we leave."

"Can you manage by yourself? I've got to go." Dalton put a hand on her shoulder, his eyes shining with love and concern.

"Yes, of course. Have a good day."

Her morning off to a good start, she hummed on her way to the salon, after dropping Ryder off at daycare. But her happy mood evaporated when Robyn handed her an envelope at work with her name typed on it.

She turned it over in her hand, puzzled by the lack of a return address. "Where did you get this?" she asked the receptionist.

"It was on the front bench. I brought it inside, figuring one of our customers must have left you a note."

Marla waited until she'd reached her station and put away

her purse before opening it. What she saw made her blood run cold. She stared at the message typed on the paper.

STOP ASKING QUESTIONS. YOU DON'T WANT YOUR FAMILY TO BE HURT.

Her breath came short. She stood frozen, her hands shaking. When reason returned, she dropped the paper on the countertop, aware she shouldn't put her fingerprints all over it.

"What's wrong?" Nicole asked from the next chair over. The other stylist had been reviewing her schedule. She put it down and stepped closer. "Did that note upset you?" Her eyes narrowed as she scanned the contents. "Omigosh, Marla, do you know who sent it?"

"How would I? It could be from anyone." Her pitch rose as she fought hysteria. Any potential threat to Ryder had to be taken seriously.

"You have to tell Dalton."

"I know." She steeled herself to face this problem rationally. After taking a cell phone photo of the message, she donned a pair of gloves, carefully refolded the paper, and put it back into the envelope. She put this inside a paper bag from the storeroom and hid the nasty item in a drawer.

"You realize what this means, don't you? You're getting close to the killer," Nicole said, hovering nearby. "Who have you spoken to most recently? Something must have triggered this warning."

Marla waved a hand in the air, her body still trembling. "I talked to guests at Jack's funeral, then I had a chat with the permit inspector. Actually, we mentioned our families."

"This note was delivered to your business address. It's possible the sender doesn't know where you live. That's a good thing," Nicole pointed out.

"You could be right. I have given my business card to everyone I've encountered."

"Do you think the threat refers to Ryder or to Anita and Reed?"

She stared at Nicole. "I've no idea. It could be either or both. I'll send Dalton a photo along with my text."

He called her back almost immediately. "You're done investigating this case, Marla. You can't jeopardize yourself or our family when we have Ryder to consider. Have you noticed any unusual cars cruising the parking lot there? It's likely the person who left the message stuck around to make sure you got it."

Her gaze flew toward the front window as she squinted for a better view. "If true, it's too late for me to spot anyone now. I stuck the envelope in a bag in case you want to check it for prints, although Robyn and I have both touched it."

"I'll come over and pick it up."

"Will you tell Detective Wanner about this?" she asked, realizing the fellow might confiscate the item if he thought it related to his case.

"I'd rather send the note to my lab," Dalton replied. "Meanwhile, I'm going to call Ryder's school and tell them to notify us if anyone comes around asking about him. Their security is tight, but we can't be too careful. That goes for you, too."

"I know." As her first client walked in, Marla cut their conversation short. "My nine-thirty appointment just arrived. I'll see you soon."

Busy working on her customer's hair, Marla paused when Dalton walked through the door twenty minutes later. He hadn't wasted any time in coming over.

She gave him a peck on the mouth in greeting. With her client waiting for her to finish a cut and blowout, she couldn't stop to discuss the case. She handed Dalton the bagged envelope and nodded her farewell.

All through the day, she startled easily and kept glancing toward the entrance. Obviously, she'd riled someone enough to warn her off. The most logical person was Tobias Banyan since she had spoken to him last.

The permit inspector had dodged her questions about sketchy actions by the design company and his own possible complicity. Yet he could be much more culpable than he'd appeared. She moved him a few notches higher on her suspect list even though he lacked a strong motive. Would Jack have really ratted him out for taking bribes? If so, Jack would be admitting his own involvement in offering the payments.

Then again, the annoyed customer in the review had only mentioned an exchange between the permit inspector and a workman. He hadn't said who had paid whom, assuming money was the item passed along. What if Tobias had been the one paying off Jack for some reason?

That idea deserved consideration, but she didn't have time. Work occupied her attention throughout the rest of the day.

Finally on her way home, she peered into her rearview mirror to make sure she wasn't being followed. Fortunately, it had been Dalton's turn to pick up Ryder at daycare.

"I'm worried for you," Dalton said as they got ready for bed. They'd spent hours playing with Ryder, feeding him and performing their myriad other evening duties.

"I'll be careful. I'm not going to stop what I'm doing. This proves we're on the right track," Marla said, laying out her clothes for the next day. "Thursday morning, I can go to the college campus and talk to any of Reed's colleagues who are left there."

"I spoke to several of them," her husband said, picking up his book and sitting on the bed. "Reed is highly respected and no one had a bad word to say against him."

Marla shrugged. "I'll see what I can find out. There has to be someone who remembers what occurred between Reed and Jack's son, Kit. I can approach it from a different angle. As Reed's stepdaughter, I want to help prove his innocence."

She didn't voice her fears aloud. Who knew what might surface once she found somebody willing to gossip?

Chapter Thirteen

The campus at Nova Southeastern University had expanded from the last time she'd been there. Now comprised of more than three hundred acres, it boasted concrete buildings with beige or sunyellow façades, brick-paved walkways, decorative sculptures, and a variety of palm trees among other tropical plants.

Fortunately, Marla had called ahead as to where to park or she'd be hopelessly lost. She followed signs to the designated lot, feeling secure that she hadn't been followed. She'd taken a circuitous route to get there and hadn't noticed a tail in her rearview mirror.

She emerged from her car to enter a maze of tree-lined paths weaving between stately structures and manicured lawns. The smell of freshly cut grass mingled with a floral scent as she crossed an intersection near the library. Groups of kids charged past, intent on getting to their next class or meeting their friends at the student center.

In the distance, the drone of a lawn mower competed with airplanes coming in for a landing at Fort Lauderdale-Hollywood International Airport.

Nostalgia for her college days invaded her mind. She'd only spent two years at the university where she'd aimed to become a teacher. A tragedy had cut short her incipient career. However, if not for that horrible event, she'd never have realized her potential as a hairstylist. She was proud of her accomplishments as owner of a successful salon and day spa. Besides, now she used her teaching skills in continuing education classes for her staff.

125

A balmy April breeze ruffled her hair as she located the College of Arts and Sciences. Her palms sweated as she entered the hallowed halls and headed to the main office. Perhaps she should have made an appointment. What had caused her to believe one of the professors would have time for her?

Nonetheless, this was her best chance to discover what had happened between Reed and Kit. If Reed had somehow caused Kit to drop out of school, then Jack might have held a grudge against Reed ever since.

But that notion didn't equate. Then Jack would have gone after Reed instead of the other way around. Reed was the one under suspicion of murder. There had to be something else she was missing.

"Hi, my name is Marla Vail," she told the administrative aide inside the office. "I'm looking to speak to faculty who might have known my stepfather when he taught here."

The middle-aged woman, whose golden blond hair swirled above her head like threads spun by Rumpelstiltskin, regarded her with curiosity. "What was his name, dear?"

"We call him Reed, but he was known as Professor Renfield Westmore."

"May I ask your purpose in making this request?" said the woman, whose desk plate identified her name as Bonnie.

Marla had conceived an excuse during the drive there. "Our family is planning a surprise party for Reed and my mother to celebrate their one-year anniversary. It's a second marriage for both of them," she explained with a gushy grin. "At that age, it's rare to find love again, and our family is so happy they've found each other. We want to make the event special, but Reed is reticent to talk about himself. We'd like to invite some of his former friends in his honor."

Bonnie arched her penciled brows. "Do you know what years he taught here? I'm a new transfer from the engineering college, so his name isn't familiar to me."

Marla bit her lower lip. How long ago had Reed retired?

"He's seventy-two. If he retired at sixty-five, that would be seven years ago." Reed had already left his position when Ma met him. She'd introduced him to the family at their New Year's Day party, right after Val Weston had died in her day spa and just before Tally and her husband went missing. That had been a memorable holiday season and not in a good way.

A few minutes passed while Bonnie did the research. "I see him in our records, but Dean Palmer wasn't in office then. A couple of Professor Westmore's colleagues have since retired, so you can't talk to them right now. Wait, Stanford was present during that time. He teaches British lit. Or you could try Donnelly, our drama and poetry instructor."

"What was Reed's specialty?" Marla asked out of curiosity. If he'd told her, she had forgotten.

"Professor Westmore specialized in Irish lit, but he also taught classes in world literature as well as the history and structure of the English language."

Marla grimaced inwardly as visions of early grammar classes came to mind. "Would either of those two instructors you'd mentioned be willing to talk to me?"

"I'll text them to see if either one is available."

While Bonnie contacted the men, Marla considered making her excuse into reality. It might be a nice thing to do for her mother and stepfather, especially with all the grief they'd been having. She'd suggest it to Reed's sons and see if they wanted to weigh in. They'd have plenty of time until September to plan an anniversary party.

Bonnie glanced up and beamed at Marla. "Professor Donnelly can see you. He's in between classes and is working in his office. Go down the hall, take a right, and look for his name on a door along the corridor. But first, please sign in here so I can give you a visitor badge. You're not allowed in the hallways without one."

Marla complied, thanked the administrative assistant, and

hurried off, aware of the clock ticking. She'd have to leave soon for the salon.

The professor ushered her into his office with a kindly smile. He had disheveled wheat hair streaked with gray, an off-kilter nose and a bristly jaw.

His eyes twinkled as he bid her to take a seat. "Bonnie says you're thinking of holding a surprise party for Reed. I didn't even know he'd remarried. His wife is your mom?"

"Yes, that's correct. It'll be a year this September since their wedding."

He grinned, deepening the crease lines around his eyes. "I'm glad for the old sod. We'd lost touch in the last year or so. I'd love to come to your event and catch up."

Marla poised her cell phone to take notes and wrote down the contact info he gave her. "Can you suggest anyone else we should invite? Or not?" she said with a small laugh.

Donnelly mentioned a few names that Marla jotted down.

"I do hope their bathroom renovations are finished by then if we hold the event at their house," she mentioned. "Have you ever done any remodeling? It's such a nightmare."

"I know." The professor chuckled. "We had a mess when we did our kitchen. My wife couldn't wait until it was finished."

"I can't even imagine the upheaval. You were lucky to get a reliable company."

"Yes, they were good, but we were careful about who we chose."

Marla leaned forward and lowered her voice. "It came as a shock to my stepdad when the job foreman for their renovation company turned out to be the father of that kid who'd caused Reed problems back in the day."

Donnelly's gaze shuttered. "I have no idea what you mean. Professor Westmore was an outstanding instructor. He weaved myth and legends into his lectures in a way that made kids eager to do their assignments. That man had true talent as a teacher. I thought he'd hire out as a private tutor once he retired, but I guess I was wrong."

"He seems to have given up that life entirely," she said with a sad nod.

The educator fell into silence. He rolled a pen back and forth while Marla's gaze roamed from his polished wood desk to the piles of papers stacked everywhere to the souvenir shot glasses displayed on a bookshelf. A collection of framed certificates and commendations decorated the walls.

She inhaled a faint musty odor, no doubt from those old books on his shelves. An unexpected wave of nostalgia hit her once again. Majoring in education may have been the wrong choice for her, but she'd enjoyed campus life.

"You have to be so careful nowadays," Donnelly mused, startling her. "One careless gesture and disciplinary action ensues. It's almost not worth the effort. Throw in interdepartmental politics and things can get chaotic."

Was he speaking about sexual harassment or political correctness? Either one would apply to his statement. "Every workplace has the same concerns," she said in response. "It must be difficult to constantly have to be on guard against saying something or making a friendly overture that can be wrongly construed."

"You're right. We can't be too cautious in this climate, can we?" The professor let go of his pen and straightened his spine. "Anyway, I'll look forward to your invite."

Marla got the hint and rose. Why had he brought up this topic? It struck her as odd coming out of the blue, unless it related to Reed. Was Donnelly trying to clue her in with his oblique remark?

Outside in the corridor, she peered up and down the hallway at the array of closed doors. The exit sign had an arrow to the left. A grizzled man in a tan uniform was mopping the floor at the opposite end.

Should she see if he knew anything? It would be a long shot, but with his white beard, he looked old enough to have been employed here back in the day. Maybe he'd heard mention of Reed's name. Janitorial staff often overheard gossip since people rarely paid them any attention.

"Hello there," she said, aware of the noise her pumps made tapping on the tile floor. She stayed away from the wet section he'd just finished, wrinkling her nose at the vinegary smell from his cleaning solution.

The man gave her an appraising glance. "Can I help you, miss?" he said in a New York accent that reminded Marla of her friend Arnie Hartman, owner of Bagel Busters two doors down from her salon.

"I was wondering if you were around when my stepdad taught at the college. Do you remember Professor Westmore? We're holding a surprise anniversary party for him and my mom, and I'd like to invite some of his old friends. I've spoken to a couple of people here about his connections, but you might have more insights to share."

The man's eyes narrowed to slits. "I don't discuss what I hear in these halls."

She thought of offering him money in exchange for information but had a feeling that would backfire. "All right, thanks. Sorry to have bothered you. Have a good day."

Her footsteps echoed as she proceeded toward the exit. A uniformed security guard stood by the door, reading announcements written with a dry erase marker on an easel board. He wore accessories similar to what Dalton had put on during his patrol days. This guy appeared to be in his fifties or so, judging from his lined face and balding head. A retired police officer or former military?

Schools were no longer the secure havens of knowledge they'd once been. Now campuses had video surveillance, armed guards and hidden security devices. It was a sad world for kids who had to do shooter drills in class and watch for predators on their way to school. Marla worried about Ryder growing up in this environment.

"Excuse me, I need some information," she said, approaching the guard.

"Sure, lady. Where do you need to go?"

"Oh, I'm not lost. I'm here on a research mission. Have you been working at the university for long?" she asked, offering him a sweet smile.

He raked her over, his gaze impassive. "I've been on the security team for years, ma'am."

"I'm wondering if you'd known my stepdad, Professor Renfield Westmore, when he worked here. Reed retired about seven years ago." She'd have to verify the date with Ma for future reference. "He and my mom got married in September. I'd like to invite some of his old friends to an anniversary party."

The security guard's expression softened. His name badge read Sam Friar. "Sure, I knew the man. He always greeted me with a kind word. How's he doing?"

"He's great, but an incident from his past has surfaced that's upset him."

The guard scrunched his brows. "There ain't no truth in those tales." He grabbed her elbow and steered her to a corner away from the entrance. The foyer was quiet, but students would pour out of the classrooms once the period ended. "What are you really doing here? Some detective came by to talk to people in the office about him."

Bonnie hadn't mentioned this. How recent was her transfer? And was that why Donnelly had been reluctant to talk openly to her?

"My mother is anxious to learn the truth about what happened. I understand Kit Laredo had been a student of Reed's... Professor Westmore. Something happened between them and the boy dropped out of college. He blamed my stepfather."

Sam's lip curled. "It wasn't his fault. The kid cheated on an exam."

"Oh, really? Wouldn't Kit have gone before a disciplinary committee?"

"Yes, and they suspended him, but then he lost his scholarship. That made him drop out. The professor's evidence was only the catalyst."

"It's sad that Kit felt he had to cheat to pass a test. Didn't his parents encourage him to study?" she asked, hoping to get a hint about his home life.

The security officer peered at her like she had a few screws loose in the attic. "Are you one of those folks who don't allow a kid to take responsibility for his own actions?"

"Well, no, I'm just wondering—"

"I don't care about his freaking upbringing. I could see where the kid got his nasty manner, though. His father burst in here one day ranting against Professor Westmore."

Now we're getting somewhere. "An angry parent can be difficult," she remarked.

"I'll say." Sam glanced over his shoulder and then jabbed a finger at her. "That might have been the end of it, but then the kid retaliated."

"How so?" Marla asked in a mild tone. She shifted her feet, anxious to hear the whole story.

Sam's eyes glittered. "I was here the day it happened. A female student requested help with an assignment. The professor was always kind that way, tutoring kids past hours to work with them. Kit Laredo took advantage of his generosity."

"In what way?" Marla's senses heightened. Maybe now she'd find the answers she sought.

"The girl was alone in his office with him and claimed he'd made an inappropriate advance toward her. She had recorded part of their conversation and must have led him into it. He'd been talking about literature, but the snatch of dialogue had obvious innuendos. I got called in when she raised a stink, and later I assisted in the internal investigation."

Marla's heart twisted. Poor Reed. This would have been

an affront to his dignity and honor. "Was there any truth to the girl's accusations?" she forced herself to ask.

"Heck, no. It smelled of a setup from the get-go. Westmore denied the allegations and was deeply distressed by the incident. You could tell it hurt him."

No wonder he's so devastated by this murder case. It has to be déjà vu for him in terms of being implicated in a crime he didn't commit. But why doesn't he tell Ma about it? Is he too embarrassed? Or is he afraid she'll begin to doubt him?

Too late for the latter. Doubts had already taken root.

"Did the girl confess that she'd lied?" Marla wanted to know. "And how was Kit Laredo involved?"

"Kit put her up to it. Professor Westmore was exonerated due to the witness's lack of credibility, and the matter was expunged from his record. He was careful afterwards not to be alone with any of his female students, and he cancelled his private tutoring. He'd lost his mojo, even though the girl finally admitted Kit had paid her to make a scene."

"Could it have been Kit's father who'd instigated things? He must have been disappointed when his son lost the scholarship."

Sam's gaze darkened. "Nah, it fits the kid's M.O. He was a rotten egg from the start."

Like father, like son, she thought, although Kit had done a decent burial for his dad. Maybe he'd turned his life around once he moved away.

Or not. Perhaps he'd shifted blame for his problems to Jack and finally got his revenge.

"I appreciate the info," she told the guard. "It'll put my mom's heart at ease to learn the truth."

"Give the professor my regards, will you? Tell him we miss his jokes. And if you really do plan a party, I'd love to be invited."

Marla walked away shaking her head. Reed had told jokes? He always seemed so staid and distinguished. Yet her mother had mentioned that he made her laugh, and he did lighten up at family events.

Anyway, why would this incident disturb him now? The student who'd made the accusation against him had confessed it was a lie.

She recalled Ma's words that Reed had been startled upon meeting Jack on the job. What if Jack, upon realizing Reed's identity, had threatened to tell his new wife about his disreputable past? All of Reed's shame might have come back to haunt him.

Jack might even have demanded money to keep silent. That could also be why Reed didn't cancel his contract once he learned Jack worked for the design center. Jack might have insisted the project go forward with Reed making extra payments to him on the side.

Would this have given Reed a strong enough motive for murder? Perhaps not in her view, but it could be the reasoning behind Detective Wanner's suspicions.

Chapter Fourteen

The day of the home expo arrived. Marla planned to confront Reed with her newfound knowledge, but it would also provide another opportunity for her to question the design center staff at their exhibit booth. First, she had to complete her morning routine before Anita and Reed arrived.

She had just finished feeding the baby when the doorbell rang. Dalton unstrapped Ryder from his highchair and took him to get dressed for the day.

Marla flung open the door and greeted her mom and stepdad. "Hi, come on in. Can I get you a cup of coffee?"

"No, thanks," Anita said, breezing inside. They exchanged hugs. "What can I do to help?"

"You can say hello to Brianna while I pack our gear. She has plans for today and won't be joining us. Dalton is busy changing Ryder's diaper."

As Marla went through her checklist of things to bring, she wondered how her life had gotten so complicated. B.C., or Before Children, she used to fly out of the house with only a purse strap strung over her shoulder. Now she brought along several sacks full of baby items.

"Can I offer assistance?" Reed asked, standing awkwardly by the kitchen entrance. He wore a button-down blue shirt with navy trousers. His trim reddish-gray beard added to his dignified air, reinforced by the flat tweed cap on his head.

Marla swallowed the questions that sprang into her mind, saving them for later. Now that she'd learned about the incidents with his students, he appeared more vulnerable to her. She would have to be careful how to approach the sensitive topic.

"Thanks, but I have everything under control." Marla placed her bulging bags and other necessities near the garage door where Dalton could grab them. "Lucky, stop bothering our visitor," she told the golden retriever who nudged Reed's leg.

The dog bounded to her side, nipping at her ankles until she produced a treat. Spooks, who'd been chasing one of Ryder's toy balls, must have sniffed the tantalizing aroma because the poodle came looking for his handout. Marla tossed him a biscuit then refilled their food and water dishes.

Finally, the group headed out. Anita and Reed squeezed into the rear of the SUV next to Ryder's car seat. Dalton stuffed the stroller and bags into the trunk area.

During the drive, Marla kept the conversation light, bragging about Ryder's latest accomplishments. She looked forward to the home expo and getting some new ideas for their house. They could only stay a few hours, needing to get back before Ryder's afternoon nap.

Despite Marla's attempt to avoid the topic of the murder until later, Anita inevitably brought it up. "It's miserable not having our bathroom finished. I don't know if I'll ever want to take a shower in that room after what's happened, but at least we'd be done with workmen in our space."

"Technically, Laredo wasn't killed there," Dalton pointed out.

"Does it matter where he died?" Reed snapped. "We'll have to live with that memory. It will help when the culprit is behind bars, but Detective Wanner still believes I'm guilty."

"Because you had a reason," Marla said, exasperated by the secrets between them. She'd meant to speak to Reed in private, but it was time for her mother to learn the truth. She had shared her information with Dalton the night before.

"I'm sorry to air this in public, but Reed, did you ever tell Ma about the episode with Jack's son?"

Reed coughed. "Excuse me?"

She twisted her back to regard him from the front seat. "You don't need to hide this from us any longer. We're aware Kit Laredo was your student. You caught him cheating at exams. A disciplinary committee suspended him, but then he lost his scholarship as a result and dropped out of school."

Anita spread her hands. "Reed has already told me about this boy, so what's the big deal?"

"Do we have to discuss this now?" Reed demanded.

"Yes, we do," Marla bristled at his imperious tone. "Did you also tell Ma how Kit tried to get even because he blamed you for his problems? He paid a female student to get you alone in your office and set you up for a case of sexual harassment." Marla related the story to her mother.

Anita gave Reed a frosty glare. "You should have told me the rest. I'd have known it wasn't your fault."

His face reddened. "I didn't want you to think less of me. It was an embarrassing event in my life. I had to watch my every step at work thereafter."

Anita's gaze softened, and she stroked his cheek. "You should have more faith in my love for you. I couldn't be prouder to be your wife. Nothing will ever erase that from us."

"It must have been hurtful to you," Marla said, her voice oozing sympathy. She wanted him to know that he hadn't lost her regard, either.

"I'm sorry I didn't confide things sooner, but I didn't want to turn the kettle black," Reed admitted. "Things were bad enough with Wanner breathing down my neck."

"I imagine it was a surprise when you met Jack on the remodel project. Once he recognized you, did he ask for payment in return for his silence?" Marla needed confirmation that her theory was correct.

Reed hung his head. "He did, but I refused. Instead, I agreed to honor the contract with his company rather than cancelling it."

"Now we know why Detective Wanner is so focused on you. He must have gotten wind of your prior relationship to Jack," Anita said quietly at his side.

"Who else would know our history and use it against me?" Reed asked with a hint of desperation. "Somebody wrapped my tie around the victim's neck for a reason."

"Jack's son?" Marla guessed. "Maybe Kit never forgave you for his lost opportunities. He came into town early, killed his father, and set the scene to cast suspicion on you. It's a similar M.O. to what he'd done before."

"That may be so, but why would Kit murder his own father?" Dalton cut in. "I can ask Wanner to check into his flights. He should be able to verify when the kid arrived in town, but this idea makes no sense to me."

Marla put a finger to her mouth. "Or, maybe Kit was the one who set the detective on Reed's tail. Jack could have told his son that he was project manager for Reed's job. When Jack was killed, Kit figured Reed had done it. He informed Wanner about their past connection."

"I'll have another chat with the good detective," Dalton promised.

"Hey, can we talk about something else?" Anita said in a high-pitched voice. "This is supposed to be a pleasant day."

"It will be, now that we've aired the dirty laundry," Marla said with a sense of relief. "No more secrets among us, okay?"

As the others murmured their consent, Ryder squirmed in his car seat. Their tension must be transferring to him. "Neh-neh," he called, his agitation rising.

"Oh, his passie fell out," Marla told her mother, realizing what he wanted. Neh-neh was his name for a pacifier. "There's another one in the bag below if you can reach it."

"Maybe you'll find some new ideas for your vegetable garden at the expo," Reed told Dalton in a conciliatory tone, while Anita played with the baby.

"I'd like to add eggplants, cucumbers, and squash," Dalton

replied, his gaze focused on the road. "We're more likely to find plants at the garlic festival since it's being held at a nursery. This home expo might help me plan for an outdoor kitchen, though." He rambled on as though he knew Reed needed to be put at ease.

They'd bought a house with enough land for an elevated garden in the backyard. Marla hadn't wanted a pool after the tragedy in her past. Images still haunted her of little Tammy's body. The toddler had drowned while under her care as a babysitter, and it had taken years for her to come to terms with it and move on. No way would she tempt fate with a swimming pool on their property. Instead, Dalton hoped to hire a landscaping firm to create his dream vegetable garden.

The arrival of their son had put a halt to those plans. Between the baby, their two dogs, and a teenager in the house, they had enough to handle for the moment.

As they approached the parking garage at the Broward County Convention Center, Marla considered her goals for the day. Caroline was sure to be present at the design company booth, since she ran their office. Would Brad or Nadia accompany her? Either way, Marla hoped to learn more about their operations.

She put off these thoughts as Dalton found an empty space. He retrieved the stroller from the trunk while Marla grabbed their baby supplies. Ryder was happy to get out of the car and into the fresh air.

April flowers provided splashes of color amid regal palms and manicured lawns on the path leading to the convention center. Sunlight gleamed off the rippling current from the waterway in back. From her vantage point, Marla glimpsed a cruise ship docked at Port Everglades. She remembered her own voyage to the Caribbean with a pang of nostalgia. It would be a long time before they'd be able to travel in luxury again.

A citrus scent infused the air as they entered the convention center lobby. She paused to admire the towering glass windows and the turquoise and coral carpet. Its seashell design, along with a series of potted palms, added to the bright and airy tropical ambiance.

They followed the crowd toward the exhibit hall. She'd bought tickets online, so they got right in. The attendant handed them each a canvas tote filled with promotional items. Marla stuffed the goody bag into the back of the stroller.

She unfurled the hood so the glare from overhead lighting wouldn't hurt Ryder's eyes. People crowded the exhibits and cruised the aisles, chatting in small groups or watching demos.

"Where should we go first?" Marla scanned the banners decorating the spaces where black-clothed tables held brochures, pens, wrapped candies and other tempting giveaways.

"Look at those spa tubs," Anita exclaimed, pointing. "That's what I need for my arthritis."

They walked past booths explaining the benefits of water softeners, solar panels, and security systems. Marla gravitated toward the kitchen displays while Dalton paused at a section with barbecue grills. Pet products, flooring choices, and home lighting didn't interest her. Neither did massage chairs or laser peg toys, whatever those were. Something for older kids, she surmised. There wouldn't be much here for infants.

They collected information at several booths, rapidly filling the goody bag with more items. Marla liked the cell phone pad offered at one wireless carrier's spot. It would help protect her nightstand when she put her phone down at bedtime. A few pens went into her bag while she nibbled on milk chocolate kisses from another booth.

An air-conditioning company was giving away portable mini fans sporting their logo. She swiped a couple while the rep was talking to a potential customer. They'd be useful in case of a power failure during summer storms.

Their group split up to cover more ground in a shorter amount of time. Dalton went in search of the granite dealer's booth. Marla's assignment was to visit the exhibit for Amaze

Design Center. She handed the stroller over to Anita and Reed, who agreed to meet for lunch at the food court.

"Be careful, Ma," Marla warned her mother. "Remember that note I got at the salon? It threatened my family. That could mean all of you."

Anita's face puckered. "Don't worry about us. We'll be on the lookout. Just watch your own back."

Marla roamed off, checking the event brochure for the design company's location. It should be two aisles down and to her right.

As she neared her target, she was glad to note both Brad and Caroline manned the space for the design center. The company president shoved his eyeglasses further up the bridge of his nose as he conversed with a stocky fellow wearing a three-piece suit.

Marla gasped when he turned her way, and she glimpsed his bowtie. His features looked familiar, same as his style of dress. Was this the same man she'd spotted at Jack's funeral?

Whatever the man said to Brad next, it turned his face a purplish hue. He spat something back. Mr. Bowtie snickered, then turned on his heel and left.

Marla debated if she should go after him or stick with her original plan. Deciding upon the latter, she approached the booth.

"Hi, fancy seeing you here," she said to Caroline and Brad, as though she were surprised to come upon them.

Caroline put her hands on her hips. She wore her brown hair in soft waves and had on a slinky wrap dress that enhanced her hazel eyes. Marla recognized it as a Lilly Pulitzer design.

"Marla, what are you doing at the expo?" Caroline asked, her southern accent more pronounced.

"I'm here with my family. Who was the guy that just left your booth? I've seen him somewhere before."

"That's Oscar Fielding. He's Davinia's manager," Caroline blurted before Brad cast her a pointed stare.

Nancy J. Cohen

"Isn't Davinia your sister?" Marla said to him. "I'm hoping to meet her at the garlic festival. My stylists are doing the hair for the pageant contestants, and I understand Davinia is a judge."

"Who told you Davvy was my sister?" His lips thinned as he regarded her from behind his lenses.

Marla made a vague gesture. "I don't remember. I've been talking to a number of people lately."

"Yes, I heard you were still butting your nose into other people's affairs. I thought I'd told you to stop asking questions or you'll be sorry."

"Is that a threat?" Marla's blood chilled. His words sounded awfully similar to the note she'd received at the salon.

"Consider it a warning. You don't know who you might rile. We all have to be careful."

She refused to be intimidated. "I might be happy if you tell me what you did before establishing Amaze Design Center. Did you work for another company?" She bit her tongue to suppress what she knew about Brad's history as George Eustice's partner.

"That's not your concern."

"Should I go speak to your friend, Oscar?" she asked, hoping to taunt him into saying more. "Or perhaps your sister. Is she here, too? I would think she'd stop by to offer her support."

"Davvy could care less. As for Oscar, he's a pain in the ass."

Before Marla could hop on this trail, a visitor grabbed Brad's attention. The guy picked up a brochure and started a dialogue that Brad was all too glad to join in. He must have noted the gold watch the man flaunted on his wrist.

"What are you really doing at the show? Are you stalking us?" Caroline asked, her gaze glacial as she regarded Marla.

"Of course not. I'm here with my family. We love going to home shows. Besides, my mother needed to relax with all the grief she's been having over her remodel. She's here with her husband. They need their lives to return to normal."

"Don't we all," Caroline said with a sour expression. "But Brad was right. It isn't wise for you to pry into other people's affairs. As for your mom, we can finish her project once the police give us the go-ahead. Tell me, how is Detective Wanner's investigation going? Is he getting any closer to making an arrest?"

Is Caroline genuinely curious, or is she probing for information?

"He doesn't share his findings with us," Marla replied in a noncommittal tone.

"That's too bad. We'd like to put this whole thing behind us as well. Our reputation is at stake when our projects don't get completed on time."

Your company's reputation has already suffered because of Jack's poor communication skills. "Has Brad decided who to hire as project manager going forward?" she asked. "I don't imagine your crew can get back to work without someone in charge."

"He's had too much on his mind to do interviews just yet." Caroline's glower indicated Marla was partially at fault for that problem.

Maybe his creative bookkeeping is the issue that needs his attention.

The sister's manager might have answers. Clearly, Oscar had a beef against Brad for some reason. Had he come all the way to the show just to confront the man? He could have gone to their office during the week. Or perhaps he had shown up for support, and they'd gotten into an argument by chance. That seemed the more likely prospect.

"I have to go rejoin my family," she told Caroline, eager to seek the other guy out. If she offered a sympathetic ear, Oscar might be willing to talk.

She muttered a polite farewell and hurried off. Her trips up and down the aisles failed to produce results, however. Oscar Fielding must have left the premises or else the mob of people prevented her from finding him in the crowd.

Fortune brought her to Dalton, who was eyeing a collection of rock waterfalls. She sniffed a fresh-water scent with a hint of chlorine as she neared. She did like the one on the far right that looked the most natural with ferns peeking up from its crevices. Something similar might be a nice addition to their landscaping.

"Hi, hon. It's almost time to meet Ma and Reed," she said, tapping her watch for emphasis.

His eyes brightened and he grinned at her. "I spotted them over by a display for garage storage systems. Are they thinking of getting built-in shelves?"

Marla shrugged. "I have no idea, but they need better organization. Their garage is so crammed with stuff that they can only fit one car inside."

Dalton strode down the aisle alongside her. "How did your talk go with the design company people?" He cut a handsome figure with his broad shoulders encased in a polo shirt hanging loose over a pair of black jeans.

Marla felt a surge of pride as female eyes glanced his way. She related her observations from her stop at the company's booth.

"Obviously, Oscar knows Brad through his sister," she concluded. "But why would the actress's manager show up at Jack's funeral?"

"To pay his respects in Davinia's place? We won't really know more until we talk to the man. It's unclear how either one of them would be familiar with Jack unless he'd done work on Davinia's estate. He could have been the foreman in charge of the project that led to her testimonial."

"That's true. But then that begs the question, how long ago was her remodel? Was it before or after Brad established this design center? And speaking of Brad, he warned me off about snooping around. I'm wondering if he might be the sender of that message I got at the salon. Did you get any prints off it?"

"Afraid not, but the lab boys are still working on it for other clues."

"Caroline asked me about Detective Wanner's progress. I got the feeling she was pushing for info about his investigation."

Dalton's mouth compressed. "I expect she's nervous about his inquiries into their company. My chat with George Eustice was interesting. He had no qualms about warning me against Amaze Designs, saying they were late in paying their bills. He'd been in business with Brad before and wouldn't trust him beyond his nose."

"Did he give you more details about why they parted ways?"

"He'd learned Brad ignored shortcuts his work crew took, as long as they produced satisfactory results."

"What kind of shortcuts?" She could imagine a few of them, based on the reviews she'd read. Improper wiring, sloppy plumbing, cheaper grade of wood on the cabinetry.

"He wouldn't elaborate. I'm surprised he signed on to fill their granite orders if he didn't trust them. I mentioned what you'd told me about Jack eyeing his daughter. George looked like he was about to throw a fit. As a father myself, I can understand his rage."

"Do you think he hated Jack enough to kill him? If he was frightened for his child's safety, George might have thought he needed to protect her."

"He seemed more resentful of Brad. I wonder what Detective Wanner has on their prior partnership."

Marla snorted. "I'll bet you have more information than he does. You should call him and fill him in on what we know. It might take the heat off Reed."

"We'll see. Let's go retrieve Ryder. Your mother probably wants a break by now."

As they strolled down the aisle, Marla sniffed the scents of coconut and vanilla. They passed an aromatherapy display with oil lamps, room fragrance, diffusers, and wax melts.

The aroma of roasted coffee drew her toward the food

court at the rear of the exhibit hall. Marla spied Anita and Reed seated at a table. They waved to catch her attention.

After greetings all around and a fast check on the baby who smiled and gurgled at her arrival, Marla addressed the elder couple. "Thanks for watching Ryder. We can hold down the fort if you guys want to get something to eat."

They took turns ordering food. Meanwhile, Marla set up the baby's tray, popped the lid on his lunch container, and gave him his milk.

Once they'd all finished eating, Marla and Dalton shared what they'd learned.

"Oscar Fielding, Davinia's manager, was speaking to Brad when I approached the design company booth. He was angry about something the manager said."

Anita perked up. "Isn't Davinia the celebrity actress who endorsed Amaze Designs?"

"Yes, that's correct," Marla replied.

"I still don't understand why her review made a difference to you in choosing this company," Anita told her husband.

His eyes blazed. "Since you all seem set on prying into my life today, I'll tell you. Davinia did me a favor a long time ago. I owed her one, so I figured I would support her brother's enterprise. I had no idea Jack Laredo worked for their company."

What? He'd known Davinia personally? What else wasn't he sharing with them?

"What sort of favor?" Dalton asked, pouncing on Reed's words. His brows knitted together as he regarded his stepfather-in-law.

"It's a private matter."

"You do know we're trying to help? That can't happen unless you tell us everything."

"You're as bad as Wanner with your questions. I've had enough." Reed shot to his feet and collected their trash.

Marla felt the heavy mantle of disappointment. Clearly,

Reed wasn't done keeping secrets from them, and now he'd insulted Dalton. How could they trust him under these circumstances?

"Oh look," she told her mother, who sat by in stony silence. "Ryder is throwing his diced cucumber on the floor and laughing at us. He's making a mess."

"I'll get it," Dalton offered, rising so quickly he almost knocked his chair over. "See if he'll drink more milk."

"Today is National Hairstylist Appreciation Day," Marla mentioned, hoping to lift her mother's spirits. "We're celebrating at the salon on Tuesday. I've placed an order with Arnie's deli for lunch to be delivered. It's my treat to the staff."

"That's generous of you." Anita's eyes glistened as she glanced up and offered a small smile at Marla's change of topic. "How is the dear man? Is his wife pregnant yet?"

"With two school-age children from his previous marriage, he may not have that on his agenda. I need to give his wife a call to see how she's doing. We haven't touched base in a while."

Anita paid attention to Ryder during the drive home while Reed stared grim-faced out his window. Marla twisted her hands in her lap. Instead of smoothing things between the elder couple, she'd only succeeded in widening the wedge between them.

"Do you think Reed's sons would know any more about his connection to Brad's sister?" she asked Dalton once they were back home and had settled Ryder in for a nap. Marla stood by the sink washing the baby's lunch dish and bottles while Dalton put away the rest of their gear. Anita and Reed had already left.

"I'm not asking the boys behind his back. If he isn't going to come clean, his dirt will wash out in the end. What's on your agenda for tomorrow?"

"I'm meeting Tally for lunch," she said. "Maybe she'll have some fresh insights. I don't feel as though we're getting anywhere on this case. We open one door, and another one slams in our face. We're not any closer to nailing a particular suspect, although the granite guy still tops my list."

He came over and tickled her arm. "Hey, where's my spirited sleuth who won't let anything get in the way of justice?"

"She needs to retire." When her husband stepped away, she dried her hands on a towel and spun to face him. "I'm limited in the amount of time I can spend looking into things, and so are you. This case isn't even your jurisdiction."

"No, but it involves my family. That's enough for me."

"Can you do anything to light a fire under Wanner?"

"He's probably just as frustrated as we are. Everything seems connected and yet the facts don't add up. I'll keep digging further into these people."

"Okay. Tally always has good ideas when it comes to catching bad guys, so I'll see what she says. In the meantime, we need to tread carefully because someone is watching."

Chapter Fifteen

The next morning, Marla stepped inside Dressed to Kill boutique and paused to gawk at the racks of glittering evening gowns. She never tired of admiring the beautiful creations with colors ranging from sexy black to tropical turquoise, royal blue, and claret red. Sequins, seed pearls, and beads reflected light from the crystal chandeliers hanging overhead.

Off to the right stood a counter with bar stools and a refrigerated display case offering sandwiches and snacks for sale. The aroma of fresh pastries permeated the air along with a faint citrus scent.

A seating arrangement with couches tempted shoppers to linger in the elegant setting. Usually Marla gravitated toward the section with high-end daywear as well as the handbag and shoe collections. Her fingers itched to pull out her wallet and buy something. Maybe a pair of crystal earrings? That wouldn't add too much to her credit card balance.

"Marla, it's great to see you!" Tally bustled over to embrace her in a tight hug.

"Likewise." She withdrew to regard her friend. Tally wore a teal twist dress that looked great on her slim figure, but then she could wear anything and pass muster as a model. "I love coming here. It makes me wish I had an occasion to wear one of these gowns."

"Hah. Then you'd have to get a babysitter for Ryder. It's not easy having a social life with a toddler," Tally said in a wry tone.

"Hey, speak for yourself. Ryder is only turning one this June."

"I know. I miss the little guy. He's so cute."

"I can say the same for Luke. Do you want to eat in or go out?" Marla asked, okay with either choice.

"Let's go to Lara's on the corner. I feel like being served. Hold on a sec while I close up for lunch." Tally grabbed her purse, set the alarm, and locked the door. "Remind me to show you our new stock," she said as they headed toward the restaurant anchoring the end of the shopping strip. "There's a skirt you're going to love, and I have the perfect poppy-colored top to match it."

Marla gave a rueful chuckle. "If I didn't have to go into the salon every day, I'd probably hang out in my pajamas."

"Ugh, I remember that feeling. The first year with a baby is so exhausting. It goes by in a blur."

At the restaurant, they requested a quiet table at the opposite end from the bar. Marla appreciated the modern ambiance with recessed ceiling lights and an open kitchen. Potted plants softened the cavernous room while soft jazz music played in the background.

They commiserated over the responsibilities of motherhood until the waitress brought their drinks along with a basket of warm bread. She took their meal order and left them alone.

"Tell me what's been going on with your mom," Tally said, spreading a napkin over her lap.

Marla took a sip of her iced coffee then filled Tally in on recent events.

"I'm still wondering why the killer wrapped Reed's tie around the foreman's neck," Marla concluded. "It had to be meant as a message to Reed or as a distraction for the cops."

"What kind of message?"

"A warning, perhaps. Like, he'd better stay silent about what he knows, or else."

"That sounds scary."

"I know. However, Reed seems just as confused as we are about what it means. That leads me to believe the tie was used to throw suspicion his way."

"What did it look like? That might have bearing on the killer's intent, unless it was a random choice from his closet." Tally buttered a piece of bread as she spoke. She'd always had a wholesome appetite. Her tall, lithe frame allowed her to eat more calories than Marla without adding to her weight.

Tally's gaze wandered to a group of businessmen striding past. They cut handsome figures in their suits.

Marla lifted her brows. Tally hadn't been actively seeking to date since her husband Ken's death over two years ago, but perhaps she was ready for that step now.

"Reed confirmed the tie belonged to him, but he didn't give us a description," she said in response to Tally's question.

"So you don't know the pattern or colors?"

"No. I hadn't thought to ask." Marla tamped her urge to call Dalton with this inquiry and settled for eating a bite of buttered bread instead. "I'll ask Ma for more information next time I talk to her. She organizes the stuff in their closet. Reed has kept all his neckties and work clothes even though he's retired."

"Old habits die hard. So who's on your suspect list? Have you eliminated anyone else since our last chat?"

"Pete and Juan are the general contractors. Juan has a verifiable alibi so he's off the list. Before Jack's death, they'd completed the demolition and installed the cabinets. Ma is happy with the finished look."

"Are they done, or do they have to come back?"

"They still have work to do. I'm hoping to talk to one of them and ask about Reed's prior connection to Jack." She described the incident with Jack's son when he was a college student.

Tally's mouth rounded in an "O" sign. "Holy smokes, no

wonder the detective is interested in Reed. He had a personal connection to the victim."

Marla's glance rose to her friend's hair. Was that a streak of gray on top? This was new since they'd last met. A natural blonde, Tally had a thick head of wavy hair other women would dye for... so to speak.

"I wish Detective Wanner would regard the other people involved with as much interest," she said. "Lenny Brooks, the tile guy, is the person who found the body. He still has to finish the shower seat. Lenny didn't appreciate how Jack treated customers. He also said the design company hadn't paid him for his last two jobs. The granite dealer complained about the same issue."

"What's the holdup with the money?"

"Brad funds the payroll, but Jack was the one who handed out the checks. The problem could stem from either one of them. I'm wondering about Brad's bookkeeping. Did Jack suspect him of withholding money on purpose and confronted him about it? Or did the opposite happen? Brad issued the funds that his crew and suppliers never received."

"Sounds like they both could be rotten apples. If someone suspected Jack of stealing their paychecks, they might have decided to get rid of him."

"True, but is that a strong enough motive for murder?" Marla spied the waitress heading their way and fell silent until she'd delivered their entrees. The grilled salmon salad looked divine. She dug in, savoring the teriyaki flavor on the moist fish. Tally had ordered a turkey burger with sweet potato fries.

"George Eustice, the granite guy, had the best reason to want Jack gone," Marla continued. "He's still number one on my list."

"Yes, you told me about him. Jack had inappropriately propositioned his daughter." Tally took a big bite of her turkey burger and then wiped her greasy fingers on her napkin. "I agree he's a viable candidate. Who else have you got?" she said between bites.

Marla speared a piece of fish with her fork. "I met Hannah

at the funeral. She's Jack's ex-girlfriend. Her brother wasn't happy about their relationship. I don't know anything about the guy, but he's worth a follow-up. Maybe he wanted Jack permanently out of his sister's life."

Tally's brow creased. "It doesn't seem reasonable that the brother would resort to murder to get rid of him. He could have paid Jack to bug off."

Marla considered this suggestion. "Good point. Jack did appear to be the type to take the money and run. Meanwhile, there's Caroline who works at the design center's office. She approves the subcontractors. Her friend Jodi, who came into my salon, hinted that she takes kickbacks from applicants. I don't think she did it, but she might be covering up for Brad."

"How so?"

"If he's doctoring their accounts and Jack found out about it, Brad would have had a reason to do away with him. Plus, Brad threatened me at the home expo. His words echoed the warning note I received at the salon."

Tally pursed her lips. "It sounds as though he should top your list along with the granite guy."

Marla ate for a few moments in silence. "I spoke to Tobias Banyan, the permit inspector. He acted defensive when I questioned the design center's ethics and his role in approving their work. It's possible Tobias may have known Brad before he established Amaze Design Center."

"Didn't you ask Dalton to trace Brad's background?"

Marla lifted a forkful of salad. "Yes, and he's a ghost. There's no record of what he did before he set up this company. The granite dealer gave us a lead, however. Apparently, George Eustice was a former business partner of Brad's. George said he dissolved their partnership upon learning Brad overlooked shortcuts by their workers."

"What does that mean? Are you implying they did slipshod construction? That could involve those two contractors you'd mentioned."

"Pete and Juan? Yes, I suppose so, but I don't see how it would benefit them. If Jack was supposed to bring in licensed operators such as an electrician, and he let his general contractors do the job instead, he could have been pocketing the difference in their pay scale."

"That makes you wonder about the inspector's role," Tally pointed out.

"One customer, whose review I'd read, indicated Tobias might be taking bribes." Marla chewed and swallowed another bite. "I'm hoping to meet Brad's sister at the garlic festival. Maybe she can tell me more about her brother's history."

Tally dipped a sweet potato fry into the sauce that came with her dish and popped it in her mouth. "Oh, I forgot to tell you. Davinia came into my shop the other day along with her manager. She ordered a dress for the garlic festival. She's on the judge's panel, and as their headliner guest, she'll be announcing the winner at the grand finale. It's amazing how celebrities won't be seen in the same outfit twice, although it's great for my business."

"You should start a consignment section for their castoff gowns, unless you're afraid it would cannibalize sales from the full price racks."

Tally chuckled. "Rich people will still pay retail."

"True, but it might make your shop more affordable for us average folks."

Like me, she thought but didn't say aloud. She supported Tally's shop by buying a new outfit each season. Tally had an uncanny eye for pointing out what would look great on her. She may not have her friend's enviable figure, but she appreciated clothes that flattered her five-foot-six frame. Plus, Tally gave her a discount.

"I haven't bought anything new since I had Ryder," she confessed. "Aside from work, I don't go anywhere special to warrant shopping for myself. I'd rather get more baby clothes."

"I can't resist buying things for Luke, either. Once he turns three in August, at least he'll be able to stay in the same toddler size until next year."

"What else did Davinia say when she was in your shop?" Marla asked, eager for any tidbit that might help the case.

"She was excited about the festival, but that awful manager tried to convince her to withdraw. He said it was a demeaning role in such a provincial venue. She replied that the publicity would enhance her image of a hometown girl who had become famous. Davinia reminded him that she had gotten her start there when she'd been crowned queen."

Marla wrinkled her nose. "I spotted the manager talking to Brad at the home expo. Whatever the guy said, it made Brad angry. I had wondered why Davinia didn't stop by to greet her brother, but maybe she stayed home to avoid the paparazzi."

"Davinia never brings a friend into the store when she comes," Tally remarked. "It's always the manager who accompanies her. I couldn't stand having that man hanging around and watching my every move."

"I don't like him either. If I can get Davinia alone at the garlic festival, I'll ask her about Brad."

"Good luck with that."

Tally flagged down the waitress to order dessert once they'd finished their meals. She couldn't pass up a chocolate opportunity, while Marla settled for a refill on her iced coffee.

"How's your mom holding up?" Tally asked, leaning back in her chair.

"She's doing okay, but she's worried about Reed. He admitted that he chose the design company as a show of support for Davinia's brother. Davinia had done him a favor in the past, and he wanted to return the good deed. But he wouldn't elaborate any further."

"Does Detective Wanner have any other suspects besides Reed?"

"I imagine so, but it's been three weeks already, and he doesn't seem to be getting anywhere. I wish he would accept

Dalton's input, but Wanner won't involve him due to a conflict of interest. We're grateful for whatever details he does share."

"I'm sorry for your mom. This must be terribly frustrating for her."

"Yes, it's been stressful. I wish I could do more to help her and Reed."

"Remember to ask her for a description of the necktie at the crime scene. Maybe it'll ring a bell for someone." Tally's face brightened. "Yum, here comes my chocolate brownie sundae. I asked for two spoons. You have to taste it."

Marla indulged herself in a spoonful of the gooey dessert while asking about her friend's life and Luke's activities.

She'd just requested the bill and plucked a credit card from her purse when her cell phone rang. "Oh, it's Dalton. Excuse me for a moment," she said to Tally. "Hi, hon. I'm at lunch. What's up?"

"I have news about Jack Laredo," he said in his deep voice.

"Yes, what about him?" Her heart thumped in sudden alarm at his clipped tone of voice.

"The man had a rap sheet. Evidently, he'd been involved in one of those copper-robber rings. They got caught and he spent time in prison."

"No way. Wait, what do you mean by copper robber?" Marla's heart raced at the realization that a convicted criminal had been inside her mother's house.

"He and his gang stripped copper wiring from air-conditioning units and stole underground pipes from homes, including your mom's development. They'd operated for quite a while in the area until an anonymous tip led to Laredo's arrest."

Chapter Sixteen

"Do you think Jack went straight after his release from prison, or did he resume his former role as a thief?" Marla asked. She glanced at Tally, who appeared to be enthralled by her water glass. Doubtless her friend was listening to every word.

"I don't know enough to make an informed guess," Dalton said. "That type of crime would be handled by a different division. I've left Detective Wanner a voicemail message to call me. He might have more details."

"Who else was in this alleged thievery ring? Did your research turn up any other names?"

"I'm still working on it. I don't want to alarm your mother, but Jack's associates may be involved. Ask her if the former owners of her house did any remodels. That could be useful to know in case any of the workers were involved in this gang."

After he hung up, Marla told Tally what she'd learned. "What if Pete, one of the general contractors, found out about Jack's criminal past and threatened to expose him to Brad? That could have gotten Jack fired."

Tally pursed her lips. "Then Pete would be the dead guy and not Jack. Besides, doesn't Brad do background checks on the people he hires?"

"That would be Caroline's responsibility. Remember how her friend Jodi—my new client—hinted that Caroline might be taking kickbacks from the vendors she approves? If Jack greased her palm, Caroline might have slipped him through regardless of his history."

"Or Jack lied on his application where it asks if you've ever been convicted of a felony."

"Stealing copper may not be considered a serious crime," Marla suggested. "Dalton told me the classifications. If I recall, they include felonies, misdemeanors, and infractions."

"I've heard about copper thefts," Tally said, her eyes gleaming. She loved a mystery as much as Nicole at work, who devoured whodunit novels as though they were candy. "It's a valuable commodity, along with other metals. Crooks sell it to scrap dealers for a high price."

Marla wondered how this issue related to the project at her mother's place. "Wouldn't the thieves favor construction sites? They'd have plenty of time after workers left for the day to sneak in and strip out whatever they wanted. Abandoned buildings would offer the same opportunities."

Tally nodded. "True, and they can cause a lot of harm at those sites. In one article I'd read, crooks ripped open the walls on a building scheduled for demolition. They cut out the copper piping and wires. Unfortunately, they didn't turn off the main water valve, and the construction company had to pay an enormous water bill."

Marla had never realized developers had to deal with these types of problems. "I imagine builders have to balance the cost of security against the potential replacement of stolen materials, not to mention damage repairs. Either way, they'd lose money."

The waitress trundled their way and left the bill on the table. Marla grabbed it, glanced over the charges, and put her credit card down. "This is my treat," she told Tally. "It's been too long since we've gotten together."

"Thanks. It'll be my turn next time." Tally's demeanor sobered. "It's awful how bad guys have no regard for other people's lives. A friend of mine once had her jewelry stolen. It hurt more for the sentimental value of the items lost than the money involved."

"Thieves have been around since the dawn of time," Marla

said with a cynical twist to her lips. "But why steal copper? What makes that particular metal so valuable?"

Tally got out her cell phone and did some research. "Copper is used in critical infrastructures such as electrical substations, cell towers and telephone lines. It ensures reliable connections and is corrosion resistant. Thieves can make thousands of dollars per month from selling copper parts to scrap metal dealers."

"How does that affect the average homeowner?" Marla got a whiff of barbecued beef as the waitress strode past carrying a tray piled high with burgers and fries.

Tally snorted. "For one thing, your power can go out when they steal a transformer. Your central air-conditioning units are another target with their copper piping. If the thieves did their job, you could come home one day and find your cooling system didn't work. Your electrical systems and plumbing might also have copper components."

The waitress returned their way to take the payment. "I didn't realize copper was so prevalent," Marla said after the server left them.

Tally's eyes widened. "Listen to this. Copper can also be found on propane tanks. Thieves cut the pipes at ground level near the meters and then rip away as much piping as they can reach. It can result in a home losing its gas supply. Can you imagine how annoying that would be? You turn on the range and nothing happens."

"I'd be more afraid of a dangerous leak caused by a cut pipe. Doesn't a security system protect against people stealing this stuff outside your house?" Marla asked, thinking of the video cameras and exterior lighting around her place.

"Nope. Here's one case where a man took ten minutes to crawl beneath a house and cut out a hundred feet of piping using a plumber's tool. They're fast, so by the time you receive an alert, they're already gone. Nothing is ever secure to a determined criminal."

"You're right." Marla had learned the sad reality of Tally's statement through the cases Dalton had shared. "It makes me wonder if Jack had truly given up his activities as a copper thief, or if he'd resumed his former practice. Either way, it might have led to his death. Hopefully, Dalton can uncover more information."

"Keep me posted on what you learn," Tally said, gathering her purse. "You do realize I'm the Watson to your Holmes, yes?"

Marla laughed, and she was still chuckling on her way home. But her mood sobered that night when she brought up the subject again to Dalton after they'd put Ryder to bed. She repeated what Tally had told her.

"I never realized copper was a target for criminals. What can be done to stop these thieves?" Having finished her other chores, she was brushing her hair in front of the dresser mirror.

Dalton lay on the bed with his book resting open on his lap. "That's a tough one," he said, folding his arms behind his head. "Some states have passed laws to ensure better record-keeping by the scrap metal dealers and penalties for noncompliance. It doesn't help that only a small percentage of the crooks are arrested and convicted of a misdemeanor. They pay a low fine or serve a short prison term. It doesn't deter them from striking again."

"That doesn't sound too effective. What other options are available?"

Dalton's brows lifted. "The dealers could record the photo IDs of sellers with each transaction. They could request payment by check to establish a paper trail. Or they could refuse to accept the goods unless the seller proves legitimate ownership. These guys will steal anything, even commemorative statues and cemetery ornaments. It's a billion-dollar industry."

"So the scrap metal dealers are the key to stopping them?"

"Exactly. The only thing we can do as average citizens is

to be watchful. Keep the bushes trimmed around your house and install exterior lighting and cameras."

"We already do that much. Do you suppose it's worth the effort to talk to any of the scrap metal buyers in the area? You could show them Jack's picture and ask if he'd stopped by in recent times."

"I'll suggest it to Wanner whenever he calls me back. He might already have that covered. It's his locale, not mine."

Marla tried to shut out these unpleasant issues as she settled down for the night and drifted toward sleep. Elusive dreams created a restless slumber. Thoughts flashed and fled before she could register them. She awoke startled, as though a cry had wakened her.

Ryder's wails sounded from his video monitor. He was wide awake, howling in his crib. Marla glanced at the empty spot beside her on the bed and at Dalton's rumpled pillow. He'd already gotten up. The bathroom light was on behind the closed door.

Great, she'd have to start Ryder's feeding. Still groggy, she proceeded through the morning routine while her brain went along by rote. Brianna added an extra mouth to feed, and the dogs scampered underfoot demanding attention. Dalton came into the kitchen, his hair still damp, and helped her pack Ryder's lunch kit. He took care of Spooks and Lucky while she dressed Ryder. It was her turn to drop him off at daycare.

Finally out the door, she remembered to call her mother once she hit the road. Since this might be the only free time she had all day, she let out a whoosh of relief when Ma answered.

"Good morning, *bubeleh*, what's going on? Is everything all right?" Anita's singsong voice came loud and clear over the car's speaker system.

"Yes, I'm taking Ryder to daycare. Hey, that's your grandma," she told her son, flicking a glance at his car seat through the rearview mirror.

"Eh," he said in response.

"Yes, it's my mother, sweetie. Hey, Ma. How are you doing?" she asked.

"I'm as good as I can be under the circumstances."

She heard the frustration in her mother's tone. "I have a question for you. Do you have the contact info for the sellers of your house?"

"Why would you ask?"

"Dalton has learned something about Jack that he wants to follow up on. Are you aware if the previous homeowners did any remodeling?"

"I believe so, but it was years ago. We don't have a forwarding address for them, but I can text you their real estate agent's name. She might be able to help."

"Thanks; that would be great."

They exchanged pleasantries before Marla got off the phone. At a stoplight, she forwarded Ma's information to Dalton. He replied with a terse thanks.

She didn't give the subject another thought as she dropped Ryder off at daycare and headed for the salon. Several hours passed until Arnie Hartman walked in bearing lunch platters for the staff. She'd cleared counter space in the rear storeroom and had the owner of Bagel Busters set the goods there.

After she added a placard that said, *Thank you for all you do*, she turned to him. He smelled like garlic and pickles and wore his customary apron over jeans and a tee shirt. His moustache quivered as he grinned at her.

"Happy belated National Hairstylist Appreciation Day," he announced in his New York accent.

"Thanks, Arnie. This looks great. The girls always love your food."

"I know. Robyn has been picking up the bagel order every morning for your clients. What's doing, *shaineh maidel*? Have you been avoiding me?"

She frowned. "Of course not. I've been busy. My mother is involved in a murder case."

"Oy vey. I thought you were occupied with the baby. Is Ryder okay?"

"He's fine, thanks." Her face dissolved into a smile as she showed him the latest photos on her cell phone.

"What's the deal with your mom?" Arnie asked finally, crossing his arms.

Marla gave him a brief rundown of what had been happening. His variety of expressions was almost comical as he regarded her during this recital.

"I'm sorry for your troubles. Is there anything I can do to help?" he asked, his face earnest.

"Not really, but thanks for the offer. How are Jill and the kids? Anything new with you guys?"

"We're doing well. Speaking of kids, tell me about Brianna. Doesn't she graduate next month?"

Marla clapped a hand to her face. "Oh gosh, yes. We still have to plan her graduation party. You're invited, of course. We have the date but not the place yet. Brianna promised to look into restaurants with private rooms, but I've forgotten to follow up."

Her cell phone played its melodic tune. Dalton's face showed on the screen.

"Excuse me, Arnie, but I'd better take this. Please give my regards to your wife. We'll have to make plans to get together soon."

Marla answered the phone as soon as Arnie left.

"Hi hon, what's up?" she said, holding the phone to her ear.

"Wanner returned my call, and he had unexpected news. You're not going to believe this, but Tobias Banyan is dead."

Chapter Seventeen

"What?" Marla gripped the phone closer to her ear. Had she heard correctly? She'd seen the man only recently. How could the permit inspector be dead?

"He died at home from carbon monoxide poisoning," Dalton added. "I don't have all the details yet, but this smells fishy to me, especially coming so soon after Jack Laredo's death."

"It could have been an accident," Marla said, her voice subdued. Still stunned, she stared at a smudge on the wall. What did this mean for their investigation? If it turned out to be a deliberate act, that would put a whole new spin on things.

"Tobias lived in West Boca," Dalton told her. "It's not my territory, but I know a guy there and have contacted him for more details. I've also left a message for that real estate agent you'd mentioned. I'll get back to you when I have news on either situation."

"I can't believe Tobias is gone. Dear Lord, didn't he have a wife and children?"

"They're safe. His family was out of town visiting the wife's mother. Tobias was alone in the house."

"Thank goodness for that much, but their poor family."

"We'll talk more about it later. Did Ryder make it to class okay?"

"He was clingy this morning. I hope he's not coming down with something." The baby caught colds nearly as often as she did the laundry.

"Maybe he's teething again."

"Let's hope so. I couldn't handle a call from his teacher on top of everything else today."

Marla emerged from the storeroom in a trance. She announced the complimentary lunch to her staff. Her mood dampened, she headed to her station to prepare for her next client.

"What's wrong?" Nicole asked, wandering over. Her raven hair tied in a high ponytail, she looked comfortable in a coral pants set.

Marla caught a whiff of strong chemicals from one of the manicurists who was doing acrylics. Sometimes she wondered about the fumes she breathed in all day. "Dalton had some shocking news to share."

Nicole gaped at her. "Don't tell me they've arrested Reed."

"No, it involves someone else. I'll explain later. My customer just walked in." Marla plastered a smile on her face and showered attention on the woman. It helped calm her nerves to focus on work.

The hours seemed to fly by as her staff enjoyed the food she'd provided. They greeted a steady influx of clients.

Marla never did resume her conversation with Nicole. Anxious to get home, she couldn't wait until the clock struck five and she completed her last wash and blowout.

Once she was on the way to pick up Ryder, she allowed herself to consider the dreadful tidings of the day. Who had discovered Tobias's body? Was it his wife coming home from her mother's house? A neighbor who'd smelled a strange odor outside? Or a housekeeper coming to clean on a regular rotation?

Horrifying images played in her mind of Tobias falling asleep and never awakening. How long did it take carbon monoxide to build to toxic levels? Several days or only a few hours?

Her temples throbbed as she considered the implications.

She resumed the subject with Dalton at home later that evening. Tobias's death plagued her on many levels.

"Was this an accident or a deliberate attempt to do away with the permit inspector?" she asked her husband in their bedroom. Ryder was peacefully asleep, and they'd completed their evening chores.

"It's too early to tell," Dalton said, combing his hair with his fingers. "If there's foul play involved, and this case is related to Jack's death, it doesn't fit the M.O. of a broken neck."

"What does that mean? That the first crime was one of opportunity?"

"Not unless the killer was among the expected work crew that day. Otherwise, who else would have known Jack meant to show up at your mother's job site?"

"Maybe someone followed him there. Or he could have had an appointment to meet somebody. Has Detective Wanner checked Jack's personal calendar?"

Dalton laid out his clothes for the next day on his wooden valet stand. "Wanner should have acquired Jack's cell phone records by now. He hasn't said anything about the victim's schedule. I can ask about it next time I talk to him."

Marla pulled her bed covers down, exposing the sheets. She slid inside their cool comfort and straightened her nightshirt. "It's possible Jack was bribing Tobias to give his crew a passing grade on inspections. Who would benefit from knocking off both of them?"

Dalton grunted. "Bradley Quinn comes to mind. His company's reputation would suffer if these allegations were true."

"So what's our next step?"

"First, we have to see if Tobias's death is ruled accidental or not. In the meantime, I'll wait to hear from the real estate agent who sold Anita and Reed their house. It would be helpful to talk to the former owners about their remodeling job. I'd like to know if it happened around the same time as the copper thefts."

"We should also ask them who was on their work crew. That could be relevant."

Marla had a restless sleep that night. Questions pummeled her about the case.

One response came when Dalton touched base with Wanner the next day and asked about Jack's schedule. Other than his work-related appointments, the foreman's cell phone hadn't indicated any other meetings. Nor did his phone records show any unrelated calls the morning of his death. Caroline at the office verified his assignments.

Dalton finally got a reply from the real estate agent later that afternoon.

"I have the address for the sellers," he told Marla on the phone. "Ellen and Max Haywood moved to a condo in Stuart. I spoke to the wife, and she said they'd be home tomorrow morning if we wanted to stop by. I'd like to run up there and interview them in person."

"I won't have to be at work until one o'clock, but that will cut it close." Marla stepped outside the salon for some privacy. She used her earpiece to talk and sat on the front bench. "Can't we discuss this with them over the phone?"

"I prefer to meet people face-to-face to gauge their reactions. I told them you're the buyer's daughter and that you'd like to pick up any appliance manuals or service records they forgot to leave in the house. You also had questions about the remodeling work they'd had done. Mrs. Haywood was curious to hear what your mom is doing to the place. The pair made many fond memories in that house."

"What time did you say we'd arrive?" she asked, mentally rearranging her schedule.

"Ten o'clock. It'll take us an hour and a half to get there."

"If we're done early, we can eat lunch in town. I know a good restaurant."

She reentered the salon after they'd disconnected. If one more thing crowded her schedule, her brain would explode. This trip had better be worth her time. She already had too much on her mind. Her family. Jack's murder. And now Tobias's death. Plus, this weekend was the garlic festival. Thank goodness Robyn was handling those details.

Fortunately, work occupied her attention throughout the rest of the day. During the early hours on Thursday, she performed her morning routine, catching up on chores while Dalton drove Ryder to daycare. Before he returned, she checked in with her mother.

"Hi, Ma. We heard back from that real estate lady. Dalton and I are going to speak to the sellers this morning."

"I hope you learn something useful," Anita said. "Detective Wanner stopped by again yesterday. He wanted to look in our garage."

Marla's breath hitched. "What for?"

"He didn't say. Probably looking for murder weapons, if you ask me. I really don't like that man."

"Jack's neck was broken. The killer didn't need any weapons. Did Detective Wanner ask you about anything in particular?"

"Yes, he wanted to know if we had gas or electrical appliances. Why would that matter?"

Marla drew in a deep breath. Her mother deserved to know. "There's been another death," she explained. "Tobias Banyan, the permit inspector, was found dead in his house from carbon monoxide poisoning."

Her mother gasped. "Oh no, how horrible. That poor man. But wait," Ma said as the wheels must have clicked in her mind. "What does that have to do with us?"

"It's possible his death, if not ruled an accident, is related to Jack's case." Now that she thought about it, if Wanner went to her mom's house to look for evidence, he might already suspect sabotage.

"Let's hope the detective is visiting all the other people involved in Jack's case. Do you believe these two incidents are related?"

"In my opinion, Ma, it's too coincidental for them not to be connected. Tell me, was Tobias the permit inspector on your job?"

"Who knows? Jack had all those papers. We won't get the final copy until the job is done. We signed the permit application, but that's all. The rest is up to the design company."

"Reed had no reason to meet with the permit guy in person?" If she could prove he had no connection to the man, that might get her stepdad off the hook, especially if both murders were linked. That's assuming Tobias didn't die by accident after all.

"I don't believe they've met." Anita paused. "Listen, you would tell me if you knew more, wouldn't you? I don't like being kept in the dark, and this latest death scares me. It's bad enough that Reed tries to protect me, but you don't usually hold back."

Marla compressed her lips. She was doing her best to keep things on an even keel, in her own life and for her mom. She had a fleeting thought that it would be nice if her brother got involved, but he had his own problems. She'd not forgotten about him but didn't have the energy to deal with anything else at the moment.

"I've told you what I know, Ma. How are things going between you and Reed?" she asked, concerned for their relationship. "I thought you two were on the mend."

Anita sighed. "He's still holding back. I can tell by the way his face tightens when I try to get answers. It has to do with that actress."

"Maybe he's protecting her the same as you." She, too, was curious about Reed's history with Davinia. That was something she hoped to learn more about at the garlic festival.

"It doesn't mean he has to act like a clam," Ma said in an

irritated tone. "Good luck with the former homeowners today. Give them our regards and tell them we love the house."

I hope you feel the same way once this case is cleared, Marla thought as she pressed the disconnect button.

Dalton arrived home and greeted her in the kitchen. "Are you ready to leave?" he asked. "We might hit rush hour traffic so we should get going."

Marla, hoping to relax in the car, hoisted her purse and followed him out the door.

"I have a theory about Tobias's death," Dalton said, once they hit the highway.

"Oh yeah? Did Wanner confirm it was a homicide?" She reported her conversation with her mother and that the detective had been asking about their appliances.

"Not yet, but he did mention Tobias's home had a propane tank. Propane gas is colorless and odorless. A chemical is added that gives off a bad smell so it's more detectable. However, if the piping is rusty or a leak occurs underground, this odor might not be present. In that case, you can look for patches of dead grass in the yard as a warning sign."

Marla was glad they had electrical appliances in their home. "How does the gas get into the house if the damage occurs outside?" She didn't understand what this had to do with Tobias's demise but was willing to hear him out. Clearly, he'd researched the topic.

Dalton gripped the steering wheel as they sped north on I-95. "Propane is lighter than water. After a heavy rainstorm, any propane leaking into the ground may be displaced by rainwater soaking into the soil. As a result, the propane surfaces and can seep into your house if you have cracks in your foundation."

"Wouldn't a leak cause an explosion?"

Dalton nodded, his gaze focused forward. "In some cases. Propane mixed with air is flammable. It can be ignited by an open flame, an electrical spark, or static electricity. That's why if you suspect a leak, you should get out of the house as quickly as possible. Don't turn on the lights, adjust the thermostat, or even use your cell phone. Once outside, you can turn off the gas at the tank."

"I'd stand clear and call for help." Marla stared at the palm trees lining the road. "Are there leak detectors you can buy for propane gas, like our combo alarms for smoke and carbon monoxide?"

"Yes, you can order them online. They're easy to plug into a wall outlet, but propane gas is heavier than air. It's best to put them lower to the ground."

"Aren't there any warning signs inside the house?"

He nodded. "Hissing noises near a gas appliance may be a sign. Your houseplants might die due to reduced oxygen. If you have a gas stove, the smell might linger longer than normal after you turn on the burner, or the color of the flame might change from blue to orange or yellow."

"Most people probably wouldn't notice those things," Marla said. "We're more familiar with the physical symptoms, such as dizziness, nausea, or headache. Anyway, I still don't understand how carbon monoxide poisoning relates to propane gas."

"If a pipe is damaged or an appliance vent gets clogged, incomplete combustion will occur. Carbon monoxide is a byproduct of this process," Dalton explained.

"Tally said propane tanks may have copper piping. If that's stripped out by thieves, would it cause a leak into the house?"

"It's possible. If a cut pipe is the source of the problem in Tobias's death, I'd suspect one of Jack's former associates might be involved."

"Do you think that's why Wanner was sniffing around my mother's house? He could have been looking for wire cutters or whatever else you need to sabotage a supply line. Their place doesn't have any gas appliances. Wanner asked about it, probably to determine if Reed had any familiarity with propane tanks."

"We need to determine who else was in that robbery ring," Dalton said, his brow creasing. "I have a feeling we'll find more answers in that direction. Let's see what we can learn at our next stop, and then I'll give Wanner a call to update him."

They got off the highway at Stuart and followed their GPS to the sellers' house. Ellen and Max Haywood lived in a high-rise condo by the beach. Marla and Dalton passed through security and took an elevator to the seventh floor. A long, carpeted hallway stretched before them in either direction.

As they ambled down the corridor, Marla sniffed cooking odors reminiscent of her grandmother's apartment in New York State. You could tell what people were having for dinner by the aromas emanating from their front doors.

She had reluctantly accompanied Ma on a dutiful visit once a month. Her nose wrinkled as she remembered the smell of cabbage soup simmering on her grandmother's gas stove and the inevitable tuna salad prepared for the visitors. Perhaps those memories were responsible for her aversion to a high-rise lifestyle. She didn't care to know what her neighbors were eating for each meal.

They rang the doorbell on the Haywoods' unit. A woman with layered honey-wheat hair opened the door with a friendly smile on her face. Younger than Marla had expected, she wore a caftan and had tied a bandana sixties-style around her head. Chunky turquoise jewelry adorned her neck and wrist. Scents of vanilla and cinnamon wafted from the kitchen.

"Something smells good," Dalton said after introductions were made.

"Please, come in. I'm baking banana bread. If you're still here when it's ready, you can have a slice."

Her husband Max was a tall guy with gray hair and a moustache. He had sunspots on his ruddy complexion that indicated time spent outdoors. He wore a button-down shirt tucked into belted trousers.

Inside the living room, souvenir plates took up space on a

wall unit along with Mexican onyx paperweights and southwestern pottery. An eclectic collection of paintings hung on the walls. Marla guessed the couple had acquired these on their travels.

She complimented the selection of art works, encouraging the pair to talk about their trips. A set of sliding glass doors led to a screened lanai with a view of the ocean. She glimpsed the brilliant blue sky and the waves below.

At Ellen's invitation, she and Dalton sat on the sofa. They declined an offer of coffee.

"Have you guys done much traveling?" Ellen asked, seated in an armchair opposite them.

Marla and Dalton exchanged glances. "We visited his family in Arizona," Marla replied, catching his signal that she should continue to take the lead. "We've only been married a few years, and we have a ten-month old son. Our trips now are limited to daycare and back, I'm afraid. Besides, I own a hair salon that keeps me busy," she said, handing over a business card.

"And you?" Max asked Dalton. "What do you do? With a baby at home, I gather you're not retired. Besides, you aren't old enough."

"I don't have to wait until I'm sixty-five," he retorted in a snippety tone that made Marla glare at him. What kind of response was that?

"He's in the security business," she told the couple hastily. "He loves his work and is great at what he does." She needed to steer the conversation toward their renovations to see if she and Dalton could connect the dots to the copper thefts. At the very least, Marla hoped to learn who'd been on the work crew at the couple's job site.

"I believe it was your mother who bought our house?" Ellen said, eyeing them curiously. "How does she like living there? We raised our two kids in that home. We could have used a bigger place, but we wanted to stay in the neighborhood."

The aroma of baking bread from the kitchen made Marla's stomach rumble. A breakfast bar and fruit cup hadn't been an adequate meal.

"My mother loves the house," Marla replied. "She especially likes the kitchen cabinets and the pullout drawers. Reed has made the front room into his home office. They've repainted and changed the carpets and now they're remodeling the master bathroom. I understand you'd made some changes during your time there."

Ellen bobbed her head, her hair swinging inward. "We bought a new vanity after the sink faucet sprang a leak. It had a stone countertop and double sinks, although I realize it would be too low by today's standards. We never updated the shower. It still had those tiny tiles that were in fashion when we bought the place."

"Did the same company do your bathroom as well as the kitchen?"

"Yes, it was Kingdom Kitchens. I looked up our records after your husband called. I had forgotten to leave them for the new owners. He said you also wanted any appliance manuals or other service receipts we might have packed by mistake. I'll go get them. Are you sure I can't bring you something to drink?"

At their refusal, Ellen bustled from the room. Dalton engaged Max in a talk about sports while Marla got up to admire the view. She studied the ebb and flow of the ocean below. People were out sunning on the beach and swimming in the current. They must be tourists, she figured. The water would be too chilly for her until mid-summer.

"I put the documents in here," Ellen announced, returning with a large manila envelope in hand. "Please give this to your mother."

"Thanks." Marla took it and resumed her seat. "Do you mind if I glance through the papers now?" At the woman's nod of approval, she withdrew the stack and shuffled through them. "You have a few business cards in here. One names a Ben

Brigham as the remodel company president, and another mentions a guy named Kyle as their designer. Do those names ring a bell?"

Max shook his head. "Not really, but I do recall Jack working for us as one of the construction guys. You know that old expression, 'You don't know Jack?' That's how I remember him. The fellow used every excuse in the book as to why things didn't happen on time. Brigham should have fired him but the two seemed as close as a kite to the wind."

Marla suppressed her excitement at this news. "Do you happen to recall Jack's last name?"

"Sorry, I'm lucky I remembered that much."

She riffled through the papers. No other business cards fell out, but she did catch a signature. Her heart skipped a beat as she nudged her husband and pointed to the fellow's name. Jack Laredo's scrawl was clearly identified.

"How did you come to hire Kingdom Kitchens?" Dalton asked, shifting his position.

Max grimaced. "A friend recommended them to us. I should have done more due diligence, but we weren't as well versed in online reviews as we are today. We called their references and verified that they filed the proper permits. Some people had complaints, but most were happy with the results. We had no qualms about going forward with them."

"Did they fulfill their contract?" Marla was curious to know.

"It took longer than we'd expected, but everything got done. We were fortunate. Do you know my cousin took a hit in one of those remodeling scams? Jimmy gave a deposit to a company that wanted fifty percent up front. After a few false starts, they disappeared into the night. He lost ten grand in a wire transfer to some dummy account."

"That's awful. I'm assuming he reported the theft."

"Yup, but it was too late. The scammers were already ghosts by then."

Ghosts. A chill crept up Marla's spine. Hadn't Dalton said the same thing about Brad's past? Brad... and Ben Brigham. What were the odds they were one and the same?

Dalton cleared his throat. "Do you recall who else worked with Jack?"

"It's been ten years since our remodel. Our memories aren't that good," Ellen said. A buzzer sounded from the kitchen. "That's my timer. The banana bread is done. Would you like a piece?"

"No thanks, we'll be going to lunch from here," Marla replied.

Dalton addressed Max after Ellen went into the kitchen. "Do you recall reading about a band of copper thieves in the area about the time you were doing your remodel?"

Max gave a vehement nod. "The newspaper had a big article on them. Those crooks stole everything from air-conditioning units to water pipes. They'd tear up your property to get at the metal. The scrap dealers never questioned the source."

"Were the thieves ever caught?"

Max's gaze darkened. "Jack was the only one apprehended. We were shocked when we heard he was involved."

Marla got out her cell phone and did a search for related articles in that time frame. "Here's a news item that mentions the thefts. It's dated ten years ago in March."

Max nodded. "That sounds about right."

She pointed to her cell screen. "One of the robbers was arrested and the other two fled into the wind. No names were given."

"Can you remember anything about the other contractors who'd worked with Jack?" Dalton inserted. "Were they tall or short? Dark hair or light?"

Max's face folded into a frown. "His pal had a tattoo of a sea serpent on his arm. I think he'd been in the Navy. He disappeared after Jack's arrest, so I gather they were in on it together. Imagine those two guys working jobs in the area and stealing copper on the side. Thank goodness they'd finished our project by then."

"What about the third man?" Marla asked, scouring her search listings. "Maybe he acted as the fence and sold their stolen goods to the scrap dealers."

"I have no idea. Why would this matter now?" Max asked, getting up to pace the room.

"After his release, Jack went back to work for another remodeling company as a project supervisor," Dalton informed him. "I'm sorry to tell you he's dead."

"Oh, dear," came Ellen's startled cry as she rejoined them. She wiped her hands on an apron. "How did it happen?"

Marla responded. "He died on my mother's property. Jack worked for the company my stepfather hired for a bathroom remodel. The tile installer found him dead in the shower. We're wondering if Jack's former associates might be involved."

"The permit inspector is another victim," Dalton added. "We don't know yet if his death is related to Jack's case."

Ellen's jaw dropped. "Are you thinking he was part of the robbery ring? If so, that would mean two members of their gang are dead. That leaves one of them still on the loose."

Chapter Eighteen

Dalton called Detective Wanner once they were in their car outside the condo building. He put the call on the vehicle's speaker system before filling the detective in on their findings.

"Pete Ferdinand has a tattoo like the one you've described," Wanner remarked.

"He's the same fellow who's been working at my in-laws' house," Dalton said. "If I recall, his pal Juan had a verifiable alibi, but Pete did not."

"That's correct. We've confirmed Ferdinand was a member of this robbery ring. Unfortunately, he's flown the coop. I've put out an alert for him."

"Have you identified the third copper thief?" Marla asked. "We're thinking it might have been Tobias Banyan, the permit inspector."

"I'm looking into it, ma'am. In the meantime, I'd suggest you don't make any conjectures unless they're based on facts."

"Wait, you were at my mother's house inquiring about gas appliances. Is there something about Tobias's death that led you there?"

A silence met their ears, followed by a resigned grunt. "We're calling it a homicide. There was evidence of tampering to his propane system. Please keep this information to yourselves."

"Why would you question my stepfather? As far as I know, Reed had no connection to Tobias."

"We'll see." Wanner didn't have anything else to add and hung up.

Marla regarded her husband. "Do you think Pete killed his partners in crime after all these years? I mean, why else would he run unless he's guilty?"

"We won't know his role until Wanner finds and questions him."

"How about Tobias? We need to learn if he was part of the robbery ring," Marla said.

"Those thefts took place in Boynton Beach. I can ask our team at the burglary desk to contact their colleagues in the area and inquire about the case."

"I'll do more research on the newspaper angle," Marla suggested. "It would be helpful to find an article that mentions the third person's name. One thing puzzles me, though. If Pete is the killer, why would he go after his associates now?"

"Maybe Pete and Jack went back into business together and Tobias threatened to blow the whistle on them."

"So why would Pete kill Jack?"

"Possibly because Pete wanted all the money for himself. Who knows? Let's relax and focus on lunch."

At the restaurant, they climbed a set of wooden steps and entered the seasoned structure with an ocean view at the rear. Marla loved the nautical ambiance with fishing nets and lanterns strung overhead and seaside décor on the walls. The smell of ale hung in the air, possibly from the beer-battered fried shrimp as advertised on a wall poster.

They got a quiet table with a view. Happy to cool off inside with the air-conditioning, Marla ordered an iced coffee while Dalton got a soft drink. They both had to go back to work so cocktails were out of the question.

"Are you all set for the garlic festival this weekend?" Dalton asked after their drinks arrived and they'd given their meal orders. Marla had selected grilled butterflied shrimp with fries and coleslaw. She liked Dalton's choice, too, but felt pecan-crusted mahi mahi and a loaded baked potato would be too heavy for lunch.

"We'll be ready when the time comes," she said, slathering a warm roll with butter. The bread melted in her mouth. It was so good that she couldn't resist another piece. Two were her limit, or she wouldn't have room left for her meal.

"It's the first time your staff has done a pageant, isn't it?" Dalton inquired, his brows lifting. His molten gray eyes regarded her as his shoulders relaxed and the tension visibly ebbed from his face.

Marla sagged back in her seat, grateful for a respite from their worries. "It'll be our first time involved in a competition," she acknowledged. "It's not really a beauty pageant. The girls are evaluated based on their talents. I imagine the backstage work will be similar to the fashion show we did for that Las Olas dress designer."

Hopefully, it won't end in a similar disaster with a dead body, she thought.

"How long will it take?" Dalton observed the waitress walk past with a steaming platter.

"We'll have two hours tops to prep twelve contestants. That's four girls per stylist. Nicole and Zoey have signed on, along with Robyn. She'll watch the clock for us. Once we're finished, we'll be free for the day."

"What time does this start?"

"Our check-in time is noon, but I plan to get there earlier to eat lunch and look around. The finale begins at two o'clock. I'd like to watch the show until the winner is announced."

"You said Davinia was one of the judges? It would be helpful if you could meet her to ask about Brad. She might reveal how she knows Reed and what favor she did for him."

"That's the plan. George Eustice's daughter will be there, too. I'll make sure to do her hair myself."

He gave her a wicked grin. "Hey, is there a costume award at this shindig? We could dress up. I can be the bulb and you can be the head."

A different sort of head came to mind, and she felt heat

rise into her cheeks. "Don't you have that reversed? But no thanks. I'm looking forward to the food. Maybe I'll find some new recipes or even a cookbook for sale. I hope Ma and Reed are still planning to join us. You'll need help with Ryder while I'm occupied."

With pleasant anticipation of the festival ahead, they enjoyed their lunch. Marla took a bite of the grilled shrimp and savored its buttery taste. They made idle chitchat for the rest of the meal.

During the drive home, she didn't feel like talking about anything serious and stuck to topics involving Ryder and the conversations she'd had with other mothers. Teething and food introductions and sleep regressions had become Marla's world now.

"Brianna found a restaurant for her graduation party," she mentioned, almost forgetting to tell him. "Kiki's by the Ocean has private rooms. They still have availability for lunch on Sunday, June the Sixth. I think we'll need a larger room between Brie's guest list and ours."

He gave a grunt of agreement. "Isn't her prom first on the calendar?"

"Yes, and she needs outfits for both occasions. I need to take her to Tally's store. Dressed to Kill is bound to have something she likes. Her cap and robe haven't come in either, but we still have time."

Dalton shook his head. "I can't believe these events are coming up so fast."

"I know." Senior prom, graduation, then college. Hopefully, only happy occasions would follow. Marla had never envisioned her life turning in this direction, but she appreciated every minute. Her heart filled and she fell silent, rejoicing in her blessings.

****

On Friday, Marla managed to do the research on the copper robbers as promised. However, she failed to discover any mention of the third member's name. His identity had remained elusive to the police even back then.

They got a break on Saturday afternoon when Dalton left her a text message to call him. She phoned him from the salon storeroom for privacy.

"What's going on?" she asked, anxious to hear his news.

"Pete Ferdinand has been arrested," he said into her earpiece. "He's being charged with Tobias Banyan's murder. Wanner found tools in his work shed along with evidence that he'd sabotaged the permit inspector's house and caused a propane gas leak."

"Did he confess?"

"He's claiming innocence. However, he did admit that Tobias was a member of their robbery ring."

"Is Wanner also accusing Pete of murdering Jack? That would clear Reed's name from the case." Unable to stay idle, Marla put away a few developers that other stylists had taken down from the shelves and not replaced.

"Not yet." Dalton paused. "I'm wondering if Jack was the fence rather than Tobias. Jack could have accumulated the cash, paid off his buddies, and secretly kept aside a bigger stash for himself. If he got a hunch that things were about to blow, he might have hidden the goods. What better place than inside the wall at his latest job?"

"Are you kidding? That's preposterous." How did Dalton come up with this crazy theory?

"Jack figured he'd come back later when the heat was off and tell the homeowners he had to do repairs," Dalton continued. "Remember that Chinese drywall scandal? People will believe anything."

"All right, but then what?"

"He got caught and went to prison. After he was released, he had to wait a while before returning to the site. His former pals might be watching him, same as the cops. Hey, did you know that term derives from coppers, and I don't mean the metal. It's an English derivative. To cop means to capture or to arrest. A copper is a noun, as in one who cops. In those days, criminals used it in a derogatory manner."

"O-kay. I think you're stretching things, but I can dig deeper into the newspaper archives to look for mentions of missing money."

Marla emptied the coffee pot she kept in the storeroom for her staff and rinsed it out. She put it on a paper towel to dry and stashed the creamers in the fridge. It was nearly day's end. Cleaning up now would allow her to leave right after her last client.

Dalton spoke to someone in the background and then addressed her. "I have to go. We can talk more about this later."

"All right. Love you."

Marla mulled over their conversation as she went back to work. It couldn't be a coincidence that both Jack and Pete had ended up at the same house where they'd done work before. The garlic festival would give her the opportunity to learn more. Amaze Design Center had a booth there. If either Nadia or Caroline were present, she could ask if the contractors had requested this assignment in particular.

****

Marla bounced out of bed early on Sunday morning to tend to the baby and to prepare for the day's excursion. The garlic festival was being held at a popular plant nursery that had a gift shop with fun novelty items, a café, a gourmet food shop, and an elevated stage for local bands to play during weekend festivities.

She kept her work tools in a bag inside her car, so she didn't need to pack them. She did add a kit with makeup supplies, though. Dalton would drive separately with Ryder, while Anita and Reed would meet them there.

"Are you sure you don't want to come?" she asked Brianna at the breakfast table.

Still in her pajamas, the teen shook her head. She'd fastened her long hair into a ponytail and looked much younger without any makeup. "No, thanks. I'm going to the beach with my friends. I'll miss that when I'm in Boston, so I have to go now while I can. Leave the dogs to me. I'll take them for a walk and make sure their dishes are filled before I go."

Brianna offered to wash their empty plates along with the baby bottles from last night, so Marla left her to it. Glad to get out of the house, she headed off in her SUV while Dalton was still packing Ryder's gear into his sedan.

The paved front parking lot was full by the time Marla arrived at the festival grounds. She'd been given a VIP pass, so she got directed to a dirt lot closest to the entrance. Other cars zoomed past in a cloud of dust, forced into a single line toward a more distant section. Everyone would need a car wash after this event.

Outside, the sun streamed down from a cloudless sky on a perfect day in May. She grabbed her tool kits, locked the car, and headed across the grass toward the center of activity. Naturally, the only way to enter the grounds was through the gift shop. She showed her pass to the ticket attendant, collected a festival brochure, and exited through another door.

She texted Dalton and her mom that she'd arrived and then consulted the map provided. Exhibitors included local businesses, a health care clinic, a fitness club, charitable organizations, and service clubs. She located Amaze Design Center at the number twelve spot not far from the food vendors.

A smile curved her lips as she noticed her salon mentioned in the credits. Davinia's name was prominent as the special guest celebrity.

Aware that her time was limited, she stuffed the brochure into her handbag and hurried forward. A band had started playing at ten o'clock. Loud rock music competed with the boisterous laughter of children and the chatter of adults as she traipsed along a concrete path. She found the backstage green room and entered to check in.

Nobody was there yet. Tables and chairs had been set up along with mirrors and electrical outlets. Careful not to trip over a wire trailing across the ground, she stashed her bags under a covered table and headed out to find her family. They were supposed to meet at eleven for lunch. It would upset Ryder's schedule, but hopefully he'd get tired out enough to nap at his usual time.

Colorful flowers beckoned to her from the nursery section. Potted green plants covered the area along with statuary, garden ornaments, rock waterfalls, and faux boulders. Wind chimes tinkled in a floral-scented breeze.

A text came through from Dalton. "I'm with Anita and Reed over at the south side."

Eager to meet up with them, she headed through the throng toward the food stands set up in a row along the walkway. The scent of garlic permeated the area. Oh, yum. Should she get the garlic crab cakes or the jerk chicken? There was the Argentine beef that Dalton wanted to try. It came with black beans and rice. She walked past a set of portable bars selling a variety of drinks, including garlic-flavored beer.

"Hi, guys." She tickled Ryder under the chin. He sat in his stroller, his eyes wide as he regarded the bustling activity around them. She grinned at his expression of wonder before greeting Anita and Reed with warm hugs.

Her mother had made up her eyes in a hue to match her royal blue top. She wore a silver necklace around her neck with "Grandma" written on it that Marla had given her after Ryder was born. Hoop earrings adorned her ears. She looked happy to be there.

Reed wore a polo shirt in light blue along with navy trousers. With his white beard, he fit the image of a distinguished professor, even in casual clothes.

Questions about the murders burned the tip of Marla's tongue, but she didn't care to dampen their pleasant mood. She'd wait for the right opening later on.

"We should grab a picnic table before they're all gone," she suggested. "I'll sit with Ryder while you get something to eat."

Dalton claimed a seat. "No, I'll watch him. You go first since your time is short. What are you thinking of getting?"

"I might try the chicken shawarma," she said. "It's chicken thighs baked with spices. It comes with toum, a Lebanese garlic sauce, plus pita bread and cold tabbouleh." Since the portions were larger than she'd expected, she had decided to pass on the crab cakes and jerk chicken in favor of tasting something new.

"Sounds good," Dalton said, getting out Ryder's tray. "I'll start Ryder's lunch in the meantime. It's early for him but maybe he'll eat something."

"Okay." Marla walked off with Anita and Reed. They passed displays of Cajun specialties, taco bowls, and Asian hibachi grill. Reed went to the booth selling garlic chicken shish kebabs, while Anita decided on a garlicky portabella burger.

Laden with their meals, they returned to the picnic table. Marla cut a piece of chicken and stuck it in her mouth. She rolled her eyes heavenward as she chewed. The flavor of the tender meat was addictive.

Ryder popped a piece of diced cantaloupe into his mouth and chewed while watching her. He grinned and reached for another bite. Glad he was eating, Marla concentrated on her meal. Dalton had gone off to get his selection and came back with a sizzling platter.

A cooking show finished at a demo stage set up nearby with rows of folding chairs on the grass. Now a tall fellow took the mic, speaking loudly to be heard over the live music thumping in the background.

"I'm from Castle Growers and I am here to tell you about garlic," the man said, dressed as a garlic bulb with white pants and an inflated top. His head sported a flat cap to match the theme.

"Garlic, or *allium sativum*, has been grown as far back as ancient Egypt. It's used for both culinary and medicinal purposes. Close relatives are onions, shallots, leeks, and chives. The familiar odor is produced as part of the plant's defense mechanism. When a pest invades its cell wall, the plant releases certain substances that react to form allicin. This compound is responsible for the smell we know."

"Is that why we're supposed to crush garlic before cooking?" blurted one fellow in a front seat. He wasn't as polite as others who raised their hands.

"That's correct. The amount of allicin created depends upon the number of cell walls that are breached. Chopping or crushing will stimulate a reaction. But if you boil or roast the bulb instead, you'll cause the breakdown of other compounds that produce a different flavor."

Marla tapped Dalton on his arm. "I didn't know that, did you?"

He was entertaining Ryder with a toy and didn't respond.

The speaker pointed to a woman waving her hand. "Yes, ma'am?"

"How can we clear our breath after eating garlic?" she shouted from a few rows back.

"Chew on some greens, such as parsley or basil, although you're probably better off using a minty mouthwash." He chuckled and went on to the next question.

The imagery of those colors raised an issue in Marla's mind. She wondered how to tactfully approach the subject but decided on a direct attack. "Reed, I hate to bring this up when we're having fun, but the mention of green brought to mind a question I have for you. Can you describe the tie that was taken from your closet?"

A flush stole over Reed's features, and he lifted his chin. "If you must know, it was emerald-green with diagonal red stripes. I'd wear it at Christmas. Why does it matter?"

"I'm not sure it does, but it's possible the killer picked that particular necktie for a reason."

Anita stared at her. "However did you get that idea?"

"Tally suggested I ask what it looked like in case the tie was meant as a message."

Reed snorted. "The only message it means to Wanner is that I'm guilty."

"Those colors or pattern don't hold any special significance for you?"

"Not really."

Marla swallowed her disappointment. Probably every guy who celebrated the holiday had a similar tie in his wardrobe.

"You and Ma have your own closets. How do you suppose the killer found this item? Was it hanging on a tie rack, or did he have to rummage through your belongings?"

Reed gazed at her as though she'd sprouted horns. "I assumed he grabbed whatever was handy. All of my ties are well organized. Anita goes in there to straighten things up. She has them on those fancy hangars for that purpose."

This still didn't tell them if the killer had picked this garment on purpose. She supposed they would never know until the cops caught the guy. How did Reed feel about Pete being the focus of Wanner's attention now? It would certainly alleviate their anxieties if Pete confessed to Jack's murder.

Reed cleared his throat. "Isn't it getting near the time when you have to assume your duties?" he asked Marla.

Aware that he was changing the subject, she glanced at her watch. "You're right. I'd better get going. The contestants and my other stylists should have arrived by now." She blew a kiss to the baby. "Bye, bye, Ryder. Mommy will see you later."

"I'll take him to the kid zone," Dalton said, gathering their trash. "I don't know if we'll be able to hang around all afternoon. It depends on Ryder and if he naps in his stroller or not. Send me a text when you're done."

"I will. Ma, do you want to come with me?" she asked, in case her mother wanted to talk in private.

"No, thanks. We need more flowers in front of our house,

so I'd like to see what the place has to offer. Then I want to visit the food shop for a jar of olive tapenade. We'll probably hook up again with Dalton at that point and take a turn in watching our grandson."

Anita stroked the baby's arm and made cooing noises to him. He smiled in response, eliciting a collective grin from his elders.

Marla had to force herself to turn away. She headed in the opposite direction down the path but then came upon a vendor selling garlic-flavored condiments. It wouldn't hurt to take a quick look, would it?

She asked about prices and then zeroed in on a basketful of fresh bulbs. "You don't have any jars of peeled cloves, do you? I forgot to buy it the last time I went to the supermarket."

The wizened guy wagged a finger at her. "It's better you peel them yourself, lady. Or at least read the labels. Don't buy any peeled garlic that originates abroad."

"Why not?"

"Most of the world's garlic supply comes from China. It's been known in some instances to be processed by prisoners," he said, distaste evident in his downturned mouth. "The acidic content dissolves their fingernails, and they end up biting off the skins with their teeth."

"Eww, that's gross." Marla's stomach turned at the notion.

"Also, imported garlic can be contaminated by heavy metal pollutants or pests. There was one case in Australia where a woman in the food industry imported garlic from another country. She told her online suppliers to label the packages as office supplies to avoid getting a permit. This meant those bulbs weren't fumigated at entry. They carried a nasty plant pathogen that could have wiped out the entire country's agriculture. That's why you should buy fresh garlic grown and processed in our country." He held up a netted bundle as an example.

"Thanks, I'll be more careful next time," Marla promised, making a purchase and hurrying on before he could start another lecture.

She passed the restrooms, roped off for the festival due to renovations. A sign from Amaze Design Center claimed credit for the job.

Now that's interesting. They have their hands in this pie, too?

She'd find their booth later. For now, she had a job to do.

Her other stylists had arrived along with the pageant contestants by the time she reached the prep tent. After waving to Nicole and Zoey, Marla hastily retrieved her tool bags from under the table where she'd left them.

Robyn, the salon receptionist, stood by holding a clipboard. She gestured Marla over to an attractive middle-aged blonde who wore a starred nametag on a lanyard around her neck. It rested on her chest over a glittery black gown.

"I'm Gladys Atkinson, pageant director," the woman said, sticking out her hand for a firm shake. "We're so pleased you're donating your time for this worthy cause. These girls are amazing. You should have seen their talent show. Each one of them deserves to win."

"I imagine it's a tough choice for the judges."

Gladys leaned inward, a wave of lily-scented perfume accompanying her action. "The remaining finalists do get a valuable consolation prize, though."

"Oh? What's that?" Marla asked, sensing it was expected of her.

"A generous gift from one of our sponsors will award them each a laptop and a year of free technical assistance."

Marla gazed at her in wonder. "You know, I have a stepdaughter who's about to graduate. I'd been thinking of getting her a piece of jewelry, but maybe she'd prefer a new laptop, too." Either way, Marla had better get on it. Graduation was almost upon them.

"The kids like tech these days. Or consider a Smartwatch if she doesn't have one."

"That's a good idea, also. Anyway, we need to get started

if we're to get the girls ready in time. Robyn, do you have our assignments?"

Robyn consulted her notes. "Yes. You can start with Amelia," the receptionist said aloud as though they hadn't planned this beforehand.

Marla nodded and turned toward the granite dealer's daughter. Here was her chance to gain more insight into his confrontation with Jack. Although it appeared Pete was guilty of the murders, she shouldn't rule out the other possibilities. George Eustice still had a very clear motive to have wanted Jack dead.

Chapter Nineteen

Amelia Eustice looked the same as Marla remembered from their brief encounter at the granite yard. She had wide almond-shaped eyes and straight black hair that flowed down her back like a Tahitian dancer's. If this contest were judged on beauty, she would win without a doubt.

Marla led the girl to one of the chairs in front of a mirror and dumped her bags on the table. She laid out her tools as she sought an opener for their conversation.

"It's nice to see you again, hon. If you remember, we met briefly at your dad's granite yard."

Amelia gave her a startled glance. "Oh yeah, now that you mention it… that must be why you look familiar."

Marla chuckled. "I hadn't realized there were so many different types of stone until I saw those slabs."

"Are you having work done on your house?"

"No, but my mother is doing a remodel." Marla changed the subject, not wishing to go down that road, at least not yet. "Do you have any ideas on how you want your hair done?" she asked in a breezy tone.

Amelia shrugged. "Not really. If my hair is too heavy to put up, you can leave some of it down my back."

Marla studied the teen's facial structure and felt her hair texture. A vision came to mind of the perfect updo with tendrils of hair framing Amelia's face. She described what she had in mind.

"That sounds perfect," Amelia said, her shoulders visibly relaxing.

Marla plugged in her curling iron. "What made you enter the contest?" From the corner of her eye, she noted Nicole and Zoey taking their clients to the prep tables. The other contestants chatted together by a rack of evening gowns.

"I really want the scholarship." Amelia spoke in a sweet, soft voice. "It's the only way I'll be able to afford going out of state."

"It's a terrific prize. What did you do in the talent portion?" Marla spritzed her hair to give it some lift. Extensions would have added volume, but they weren't allowed. Nor did Amelia need them with her gorgeous locks.

"I played the flute. I've taken lessons since I was eight."

"Did that show take place here? I didn't see any notices for it."

"It was held in the community college auditorium. Only members of the press were invited, along with our families, the pageant personnel and judges."

"Do you already know which schools you're interested in?" She wondered how to touch upon the girl's experience with Jack but would have to tread carefully. Marla didn't want to upset the teen right before the pageant's grand finale. Maybe she could steer their talk toward her father's reaction instead.

"I'd like to go to New York and study music at Juilliard."

"That would be fantastic. Your dad must be excited for you."

Amelia's face pinched. "He's not very supportive."

"Oh, no. Why is that?"

"He wants me to stay in Florida and study something practical."

"I know that feeling. My mother wanted me to become a teacher. Maybe your dad will change his tune if you win the scholarship. Is he here today to watch the final event?"

Amelia glanced away. "He's somewhere outside."

Marla sectioned off pieces of her hair with large clips. "All dads are afraid to lose their little girls," she said with a sympathetic smile. "My stepdaughter, Brianna, is a senior in high school. She's been accepted at Boston University. My husband is still coming to terms with her leaving. Tell me, is there anyone else in your family?"

"My mother died two years ago from cancer," Amelia said in a matter-of-fact tone, but her eyes relayed her pain. "I don't have any sisters or brothers."

Marla paused, curling iron in hand. "I can understand why your father is so protective, then. He wants to keep you safe. However, I'm surprised he let you enter the contest." *Especially because he knew you'd be on display in front of an audience.*

"The only reason was for the scholarship. He won't admit it to me, but I'm aware of how the big chains have affected his business." She met Marla's gaze in the mirror. "You look surprised that I would know, but I'm good with math. Dad lets me help him in the office."

"Still, he had to pay your entry fees, not to mention your gown and other necessities. He may not verbalize his support, but he's there for you."

"You're right, and it's been a great experience, even if I don't win."

"Have faith in yourself. The competition isn't over yet." Marla fell silent as she curled each strand and pinned it in place. When she was nearly done, she dove into the topic she meant to address. "Speaking of competition, my mother chose Amaze Design Center for her renovations. Or rather, my stepfather selected them based on their reviews. Does your dad do business with this company often?"

Amelia's expression soured. "They're one of his best referrals, but I'd be careful around them... well, except for Nadia. She's always been nice to me. Dad shouldn't have agreed to work with those people again. That was a mistake."

"Your father mentioned that he'd known Brad, the company president, in the past?" Marla stood back to study her artistry. The upsweep was elegant and yet softly feminine at the same time. She only had to loosen a few tendrils to complete the look.

"They were business partners until they split up. Dad doesn't like me to talk about it."

Why is that? Do you know about the shortcuts Brad took to save money?

She tried a sympathetic tact. "I understand. My stepdaughter, Brianna, hears about her father's cases. He's a police detective. She can't discuss what she learns, either. I'm concerned for my mother, though. She was aggravated when their project manager didn't communicate things well. The old adage is true about being careful what you wish for. The man is dead."

Amelia jerked upright. "Was that Jack Laredo?"

"Yes, the very same. Had you met him?"

The girl's eyes took on a hunted glaze. "He was a bad person. Whenever he came to my dad's place and I was there, he gave me this creepy look. And when he suggested—" She broke off, pressing her lips together.

"You're a beautiful girl, honey. Did he make inappropriate advances?" Marla asked quietly so no one else could hear. She felt bad about pressing the young woman for answers, but a man had been murdered. She couldn't pass up this opportunity to learn more.

Amelia nodded, remaining mute.

"Did you tell your father?"

"Yes. I figured he'd ask the man not to come by anymore." The girl spoke in such a low tone that Marla had to strain to hear her.

"Is that what happened?"

"I really can't say."

Marla patted her shoulder. "I know it's hard to talk about things that trouble us, but it helps to get them out in the open. My stepdaughter tells me things all the time. You remind me of her in some ways." Her heart went out to Amelia who didn't have a mother to confide in.

It must be tearing her apart to keep this stuff bottled inside her.

Marla's kindly tone broke Amelia's barriers. The teen

covered her face with her hands and murmured, "Dad threatened to kill Jack. I'm afraid he did it."

"Your father may have been angry, but that doesn't mean he acted on it," she suggested with a hopeful note.

Oh yeah? If anybody made lurid remarks to Brianna, Dalton would go after them for sure. But not to murder them. How far had George gone?

Maybe he'd accosted Jack and they'd struggled. George might have broken Jack's neck by accident. But then, would he still be complaining about not being paid by their company? He'd been pretty verbal about it when she'd met him. A guilty man would keep silent so as not to draw attention to himself.

"What exactly do you believe your dad did to Jack?" she asked in an undertone.

Amelia glanced at her through teary eyes. "Dad said he was going to make sure Jack never looked at me again. He went off in a rage."

"How long ago was this?"

"It's been a month or so."

Marla did a rapid mental calculation. Tomorrow would be one month since Jack had died.

"That doesn't mean your father had anything to do with what happened to the man," Marla said, hoping for the girl's sake that she was right. "Or did he say something—"

"He came home and said Jack wouldn't bother me anymore. I got scared when I saw the bruise on his face. When I asked him what he'd done, he said Jack had taken a swing at him. My dad knew things that could get Jack in trouble, and Dad threatened to expose him if Jack didn't leave me alone. That's when Jack hit him."

"So Jack was alive when George last saw him?" Marla wanted to delve deeper into Amelia's statements but didn't dare upset her further. Besides, the next contestant was hovering nearby, impatient for her turn.

"I suppose," Amelia said in a doubtful voice.

"Maybe you should ask your father for the truth. He only wants to protect you. You need to clear the air and regain the trust in your relationship. Now go join your friends. I'll touch up your makeup later."

"Thanks for listening, Marla. Your stepdaughter is lucky to have you for a mom."

Marla blinked away a sudden surge of moisture on her lashes. She covered her emotion by polishing off the session with a generous spritz of holding spray.

As she worked on the next girl, she mulled over their conversation.

Without knowing exactly what had happened between Jack and George during their confrontation, she couldn't remove the latter from her suspect list. However, with his daughter being his sole responsibility, would George really have committed murder in a fit of rage and risked going to jail?

Nicole kept glancing at her from the next chair over. They were spaced adequately apart to give each stylist enough room. No doubt Nicole was dying to hear what Marla had learned.

They didn't have time to chat, because as soon as the young ladies were ready, they donned their gowns and lined up for their stage appearance. Marla collected her bags and hurried outside to watch the show.

Gladys, the pageant director, made a few announcements into the microphone, her voice booming to the crowd. She credited the sponsors and then turned on some lively background music while introducing each of the contestants. The regular band was taking a break during the competition.

Marla stood behind several rows of occupied chairs to watch the evening gown procession. Pride swelled her chest at each girl's appearance. Their hair and makeup looked great and their walk down the makeshift runway ran as smooth as mousse. They were a well-poised group of young women.

Their glances at the judges' table drew her attention over there. In the front row facing the stage sat three people at a special table festooned with ropes of garlic. They took notes as each girl did her strut. One was a guest chef as evidenced by his white outfit and the toque on his head. Another guy in a suit must be the mayor whom Marla had seen listed in the brochure.

That left the lone woman as Davinia Quincy, the actress and Brad's sister. Marla would have to meet her later to strike up a conversation.

As the girls lined up on stage to await the judges' verdict, Marla glanced at the crowd. Amelia's father sat off to the right. The big fellow clenched his hands in his lap. Had he murdered Jack with those meaty fists? Or had he merely confronted the man and warned him off his daughter in a skirmish that left him bruised and Jack still alive?

Right now, George was probably hoping his daughter would win. If his business had lost money to the chains as Amelia suggested, how else could he afford to send her to college? It didn't matter if she went out of state or not. They needed the scholarship to fund her education.

Marla's glance roamed to the stocky man in a suit sitting directly behind Davinia. She recognized him as the actress's manager, Oscar Fielding. He leaned forward and whispered into her ear. What was it he'd said that put a frown on her face?

A momentary shadow made Marla's head turn. Brad was sauntering their way.

He must be on a break from the design company booth.

Oscar wasn't happy to see him from the grimace on his face. And judging by Davinia's taut features, neither was she. Oscar got up to intercept Brad, and they exchanged a few words that brought a snarl to the manager's mouth. Brad spat something back and hoofed off in the opposite direction.

While Marla wondered what they might have said to each other, the pageant director consulted with the judges. Gladys accepted a sealed envelope from the mayor and returned to the stage. Marla focused her attention forward in anticipation of hearing the winner's name.

"Ladies and gentlemen, our judges have selected a festival queen. But first, can our esteemed guests please join me on stage."

Gladys handed each judge a gift bag. "These are items contributed by our sponsors and various vendors. It's a small token of our thanks for your participation. Folks, you all know Mayor Gentry. We are honored by your presence, sir. Chef Maurice, we're delighted you could join us. The chef has a demonstration in the theater kitchen at three o'clock. Otherwise, you can find him at his restaurant, Chez Maurice. And finally, allow me to welcome the fabulous and beautiful Davinia Quincy, star of the popular TV hit, *Family and Friends*."

Loud applause sounded as Davinia stepped toward the mic. Marla envied her perfect figure in an emerald gown sparkling with sequins. Her bosom nearly spilled from its low neckline. Crystal chandelier earrings dangled from her lobes partially hidden by a mass of golden hair.

In contrast to her pale complexion, she wore a heavy application of eye makeup and blood red lipstick on her wide lips. Her stunning appearance reminded Marla of a cross between Sophia Vergara and a younger Dolly Parton. No wonder the daytime soap audiences loved her.

Davinia took the envelope from Glady's hands and spoke in a throaty voice to the crowd.

"I am honored to be here and to have the opportunity to meet these lovely young ladies. Each one of them is smart and talented and deserves the prize." She beamed at the contestants and then returned her attention to the assembly. The mayor and chef resumed their seats, and the pageant director moved to the side to give the actress the spotlight.

"You know, I got my start here many years ago," Davinia said, clasping a hand to her chest. "I won this very same competition and didn't realize that in the audience was a talent scout for a casting agency. The rest, as they say, is history. That makes this pageant incredibly meaningful to me. And now for the moment you've all been anticipating."

Marla held her breath as Davinia slit open the envelope with a long fingernail. She admired all the girls but fervently hoped Amelia would win.

Davinia pronounced the words she wanted to hear. "Let's clap our hands for Amelia Eustice, our new Garlic Queen! Congratulations, my dear."

Amelia gasped and clapped her hands to her face. The other girls surrounded her with their congratulations and good wishes.

George jumped up and shouted. "You did it, baby girl!" He pumped his fist in the air. The crowd rose to join him in cheering. Marla whooped her approval and clapped her hands.

Davinia drew Amelia forward and bedecked her with a crimson sash and a headdress of spring flowers. Braids of garlic hung down on either side of the head piece. A stagehand brought over a necklace of strung bulbs with which Davinia adorned Amelia's neck.

The other girls exchanged hugs and accepted certificates for their consolation prizes. A photographer herded them together for pictures, snapping photos of the judges as well. Davinia did a series of practiced poses in between the chef and the mayor.

As soon as she was free, Davinia headed toward the judges' table to collect her purse. Marla, torn between congratulating George on his daughter's win or engaging Davinia for a brief chat, chose the latter. This might be the only chance she'd get. The woman's manager was occupied elsewhere. Marla knew that wouldn't last.

"Excuse me." She rushed forward on the grass to accost the actress. "I'm Marla Vail, owner of Cut 'N Dye Salon," she said in haste, so the actress wouldn't consider her a rabid fan. "My stylists did the girls' backstage hair and makeup. I've been wanting to meet you to discuss a personal issue."

Davinia gave her an assessing glance. "Well, here I am."

Marla floundered for what to say. "My stepfather, Reed Westmore, is a fan of yours. In fact, he chose Amaze Design Center to do his bathroom based on your endorsement."

The actress's face flushed. "That was merely a promotional quote. I didn't have any work done by them myself, you understand."

"Oh, I didn't realize that. But I do know the company president is your brother."

Davinia glanced at her manager, who was busy speaking to the photographer. "I gave a quote because I thought it might help his business. Now if you'll pardon me, I have an interview with the Gazette reporter."

Appealing to her ego might get her to stay, Marla thought. She needed to gain information on Brad's background.

"Didn't you grow up in this area?" she asked. "I heard you say you'd won this contest in your early days and it jumpstarted your career."

"Yes, I had my lucky break at this festival. It means a lot to me." Davinia's gaze darted past her as though she were looking for an excuse to break off their conversation.

"Did you want to become an actress even then?"

Davinia chuckled, making her bosom jiggle. "I'd always loved putting on a performance. My parents had to watch me put on endless shows at home."

"They must be very proud of you."

"Sadly, they're both gone. My dad died of a heart attack and my mother got pneumonia after a bout with the flu."

"I'm sorry. So it's just you and Brad now?" At the woman's terse nod, Marla went on. "I think it's fascinating how a local woman became a star."

"I was lucky, that's all. Talent is only half the battle. Speaking of which, I loved the way your stylists fixed the girls' hair. If you give me your card, I'll be happy to pass your name along to my friends."

"Thanks. I'd like to do more work for local celebrities. Tell me, did you stay in the area after you signed on with the talent scout?" Marla asked, handing over her business card.

Davinia nodded. "I started with commercials until I graduated high school. Then a big role came along with a major studio. I moved to California and used the scholarship I'd won to attend college out there."

"Did you family move with you?" This was her chance to steer the conversation to Brad.

"No, they stayed here. My brother was only a sophomore then."

So Davinia was the older sibling. "What did Brad do after he graduated?"

The actress grimaced. "Nothing good. I'd hoped he would—"

"Davinia, what are you doing?" Oscar loomed into view and tapped her arm. "You'll be late for your interview, and you promised the reporter a half hour."

"Oscar, dear, this is Marla Vail. She's the salon owner whose stylists did the girls' hair. She'd like to do more work with actors, so maybe we can put in a good word for her."

He raked Marla over, his beady eyes cool as obsidian. His stocky body was encased in an impeccably tailored suit with a crimson bowtie. He sweated under the sun while she wondered why he would dress so formally for an outdoor festival.

"It's nice to meet you," he said, his voice as curt as his manner. "Come on, Davvy. We have to go. Remember what I told you to say to this journalist."

They strolled off without so much as a goodbye. Marla stared after them, taken aback by the manager's rudeness. Davinia seemed to allow him to push her around. Then again, he was responsible for her schedule. Apparently, he also advised her on how to relate to the press. Marla couldn't fault him for doing his job, but he could have been more polite.

He'd cut off what Davinia had been about to say regarding

Brad's life after high school. Frustrated that she'd been so close to gaining new information, Marla turned away.

A brief flash hurt her eyes and made her wince. *What's that?* Something gleamed in the grass.

It was a diamond tennis bracelet with rocks half the size of her fingernails. As Marla stooped to pick it up, she noted the clasp was open. It must have slipped from Davinia's wrist.

She peered around but didn't see the actress in the milling throng. Unfortunately, while Marla had given Davinia her business card, the woman hadn't shared her contact info.

Reluctant to place such a valuable object in the festival's Lost and Found, Marla stuck it in her purse and vowed to return it later. Perhaps she'd run into Davinia again on the nursery grounds. Or she might find the pageant director who would have the woman's number.

She texted Dalton her whereabouts and was glad to hear Ryder had fallen asleep in his stroller.

Pleased she could spare a few more minutes, she headed over to the design company booth. Caroline sat at their table alone and looking forlorn. After exchanging greetings, Marla asked where Brad had gone and if it was only the two of them there. This was a good chance to delve into the goings-on at the company if she could get Caroline to talk.

"Brad went to say hello to his sister. Nadia couldn't come today. She had no one to babysit for her son who has a cold." A soft Southern accent inflected her words. She stood to face Marla, who admired her orchid dress and amethyst necklace with earrings to match.

"When your child is sick, you have to do what's best for him," Marla said. She dug into her purse and retrieved her sunglasses. Her tool bags were getting heavy to carry. She should stash them in her car.

"Is your baby here? I'd love to see him." Caroline craned her neck to peer around Marla.

"My husband is watching him. Even when he works, we

have two grandmothers in the area who can help. What does Nadia do when she has an appointment on a weekend? Does she bring her child along? It must be difficult being a single mother."

Caroline wrinkled her nose. "Her boyfriend, Zerkov, used to babysit. But when he left, she didn't have anyone else. She has no relatives nearby."

"That's too bad." Since Caroline seemed willing to talk, Marla would take advantage. The crowds had started to thin, so it was less likely they'd be interrupted. People were heading to the guest chef's cooking demonstration.

"It's worse because Zerkov took his car that Nadia was using," Caroline added. "Her old Dodge broke down and she didn't have the cash to fix it, so she sold it to the mechanic."

"That's awful. How does she get to work?"

"She uses public transportation. Poor thing can barely pay her rent and certainly can't afford any new car payments, not that she'd get approved for a loan. She's scared Yanni will discover her financial situation and will sue for custody."

"Yanni? I thought you said Zerkov was her boyfriend?"

"Yanni is her ex-husband. He's been nothing but trouble." Caroline wagged a finger at Marla. "Nadia won't let anyone take her son away. That boy means the world to her. There's nothing she wouldn't do to keep him."

Chapter Twenty

Marla pondered Caroline's last remark. How far would Nadia go to preserve her family? Maybe Jack had discovered the architect had a live-in boyfriend and threatened to tell her ex-spouse. He might even have demanded payments to keep quiet.

Nadia was already cash-strapped, and that would have been the last straw. Had she been so desperate that she'd asked her boyfriend to eliminate Jack?

"If you don't mind my asking, why does Nadia stay with your firm if she could make more money elsewhere?" Marla asked. "It's obvious she's a skilled architect."

Caroline pursed her lips. "Nadia won't leave because she's afraid she would be unable to find another position. Plus, Brad does offer benefits like sick days and health insurance."

"I can understand the need for job security. However, I visited the granite yard the other day and met George Eustice. He said the design company owed him money. Maybe Nadia should start looking for other opportunities."

"Nonsense. Our accounts are caught up, thanks to a substantial deposit on a new job." Carolyn darted a glance over her shoulder. Did she regret sharing that detail?

Why would Brad use a deposit from a new job to pay his debts? Perhaps their company was having cash flow problems after all.

"I'm a bit confused," Marla said. "Did Brad issue the checks, or did Jack write them from a company account?"

Caroline gave her a hard stare. "I don't believe that's your concern."

"Maybe not, but my mother would like to get her bathroom done as quickly as possible. If people aren't getting paid, that could adversely affect her project."

Tired of the sun beating down on her head, Marla stepped into the shade and plopped her bags on the grass. Caroline was being conveniently chatty, she thought. Was the woman bored, or did she have an ulterior motive in talking to Marla?

"We should be back on track soon. Tell me, how's the investigation going?" Caroline asked, confirming Marla's suspicions. "Does the detective have any leads that are panning out?"

"You must know Pete Ferdinand was arrested for the murder of Tobias Banyan, the permit inspector," Marla told her.

"Yes. We were shocked by the news. What have you heard about it?"

"Apparently, they were involved in a copper theft ring in the past. Jack was part of their operation. I thought you vetted these people before accepting them onto your vendor list."

Caroline winced. "Jack hadn't committed a felony. His conviction was for a misdemeanor. Brad found out about it at one point, and they had words. But Brad valued Jack's skills and kept him on."

Was that the only reason Brad didn't fire him?

"How did Pete and Juan get assigned to my mother's house?" she asked. "I realize Jack was foreman on all your projects, but don't you have other contractors who do the general labor?"

Caroline smoothed the soft waves of hair framing her face. "Pete and Juan had an opening in their schedule when your stepfather signed the contract. We have two other guys, but one was out sick and the other on vacation." Her eyes saddened. "Now we'll have to find someone to replace Pete as well as Jack."

"How did Brad take the news? He must have been upset to lose another worker."

Caroline peered past Marla. "You could ask him yourself if he'd return. He should have come back by now."

A young couple stopped by to inquire about the company's services. As Caroline launched into her sales pitch, Marla glanced at her watch and grunted. She hadn't realized so much time had passed. Wishing she could stay to chat further, she excused herself and moved on to find her family. The aisles had gotten more crowded, and she dodged people on both sides of the path.

A bump jarred her elbow. "Marla, is that you?" cried a familiar female voice.

She spun to regard Jackie Petronis, the wife of one of Dalton's colleagues. An ash-blond swirl of hair framed the woman's petite face as she regarded Marla with a broad grin. She stood a good foot shorter than Marla's five-foot-six-inch height.

"Hey, Jackie, it's nice to see you. Is Cabbie here?" Cabbie was her husband's work nickname because he held the record for bringing in bad guys in the back of his patrol vehicle.

"He's over by the garden ornaments. How about Dalton? Is he with your son? I'd love to see the baby."

"They're at the kid zone. My stylists just did the hair for the pageant contestants. Did you see the finale? The girls were spectacular."

"Sorry, I missed it. Hey, are you guys going to the Memorial Day picnic? I'm on the committee and didn't see your names on the reservation list."

Marla frowned. "Dalton said he would contact Betsy about it. Maybe he forgot. I'll remind him to get our tickets before the deadline."

"Okay. I'd thought maybe he didn't want to come because—" Her cell phone rang, and she fumbled to answer. "Hi sweetie. Guess who I found wandering through the crowd? Marla and Dalton are here... Yup, I'll be right there. Bye."

She gazed at Marla with regret. "I have to go. Charles needs my decision on a decoration for our front lawn. I already told him I liked the flamingo, but he's not into it."

Jackie headed off before Marla could say farewell. What did she mean about Dalton not wanting to come to the police picnic? Nicole's barbecue was that same weekend. Had he gotten the dates mixed up, thinking they were on the same day?

They'd discuss it later. Meanwhile, she headed toward the kid's play area, lost in thought until a scream ripped through the air. It seemed to come from the restroom vicinity only a few feet ahead.

She loped in that direction, lugging her bags that got heavier by the minute. Upon rounding the corner of the facility that was roped off due to renovations, she halted with a gasp.

Bradley Quinn lay on the ground, his body sprawled between the rear of the lavatory facility and a grove of bamboo trees. He stared up at the sky, a garlic garland wrapped around his neck.

Marla clapped a hand to her mouth, bile rising in her stomach. No, this couldn't be real. Unfortunately, the longer she stared, the longer the seconds ticked by, and Brad didn't move.

One of the guests, a matronly woman, must have been the person who'd screamed. From the pallor on her face, she looked about to topple over.

Marla's wits returned. "Did you call for help?" she asked, crouching to feel for a pulse. Nothing. Brad's pupils were dilated, and his chest didn't move.

"No, I-I didn't think of it. I was taking a shortcut to the exhibit area and came upon him lying there. Is he dead?"

"It looks that way." Marla straightened, took out her phone, and punched in the emergency code. As the dispatcher took her information, people hurried over.

"What's going on?" Dalton asked from behind.

Marla almost swooned with relief. She disconnected the call and whirled around. Her husband's appearance had an instant calming effect on her. "Where's Ryder?" she croaked, her throat suddenly dry. She didn't see his stroller anywhere.

"Your mother is watching him. They're looking at the flowers. What happened here?"

"This lady walked by and found Brad on the ground. I was the next person to arrive. I couldn't feel a pulse, so I called nine-one-one."

She stuck the phone in her purse and folded her arms across her chest to keep from trembling. This couldn't be happening. Not here. Not now.

"All right, people, move back. We need to secure the area. I'm with the police," Dalton informed the crowd. He retrieved his phone, dialed a number, and barked orders at the recipient. "I'm going to be needed here," he told Marla when done. "You'll have to take Ryder home. I can get your formal statement later. Did you notice anyone else in the vicinity?"

"I did." The witness pointed a finger at the crowd. "I saw that fellow talking to the dead man earlier by the ice cream stand. I couldn't hear what they said, but they both looked angry."

Shock turned Marla's blood to ice. Reed stood there, a grim expression on his face as all eyes turned his way.

The retired professor spread his hands. "Hey, I was only asking Brad when our bathroom might be finished. He wouldn't give me a straight reply. If they weren't going to complete the job, I wanted a refund."

Marla made a motion for him to zip his lips, but everyone had heard him. Dalton called him over. "Stand there, Reed. We'll need to get a statement from you." He addressed the witness. "Ma'am, did you notice anything else when you arrived?"

"No, sir." The lady clasped her hands together, a distraught expression on her face.

Marla narrowed her eyes at the woman. Was she for real, or had someone paid her to implicate Reed? Maybe she'd seen him talking to Brad earlier or maybe not. But the woman wouldn't risk getting caught in a lie on record, would she?

209

If her testimony was genuine, how did Reed get there so fast? Had he heard the woman's screams? And where were Ma and Ryder?

She considered what it meant that Brad had a garlic garland wrapped around his neck. Somebody had put it there. With Pete in jail, another person had to have murdered Brad. Did the garland serve as a signature by the killer, like the tie around Jack's neck? If so, what about Tobias, who'd died from carbon monoxide poisoning? Was he not part of the same cycle?

Nothing could be determined until Brad's exact means of death was recorded by the medical examiner. This homicide had landed in Dalton's territory, meaning now he'd have a justifiable interest in Wanner's cases. Perhaps they could finally share the details of their investigations.

She scanned the grass, looking for clues. Footprints trampled the area, but probably lots of people had come this way. Dalton's team would do a more thorough search.

Festival officials arrived along with first aid personnel. The latter, once they'd determined their services weren't needed, took charge of the witness who quivered in place. They managed to retrieve a folding chair and sat her on it.

Marla thought of Caroline's reaction when she heard the news. She'd be upset if she had truly cared for Brad.

With the company president dead, what would happen to the firm? Had Brad named a successor in his estate documents?

Davinia, as next of kin, might have that information. Dalton would have the sad duty of notifying the actress about her brother's death.

She got her husband's permission to depart and left the scene. How would this news affect Ma? It was yet another blow to compound a series of traumatic events.

She spied her mother pushing Ryder's stroller on the concrete path among brightly colored flower beds. Nobody in this area seemed concerned. They must not have heard the commotion at the far end of the festival.

"Marla, there you are," Anita said upon spotting her. "Ryder adores the flowers. I have to stop him from picking them. How did the pageant go?"

"The girls looked beautiful in their evening gowns. You would have enjoyed it." She motioned to a nearby bench. "Listen, I have some news. Let's sit a minute."

Marla was grateful to rest her arms from holding her bags. Anita joined her, turning the stroller around so they could see the baby. Marla spent a few minutes talking to her son, comforted by his tiny face. Her heart softened as his big round eyes peered at her.

Wishing she could stay in the bubble, she pierced it to address the issue in front of them. "Something has happened," she told her mother. "You're not going to like it."

"Uh-oh. What now?"

"I'm afraid Bradley Quinn has been found dead behind the restroom facility."

"What? Brad Quinn from the design center? Oh, my God."

"There's more. A witness said she'd spotted Reed arguing with him earlier. Were you with him then?"

"No, he said he was going to get some garlic ice cream." Anita wrung her hands in her lap. "I don't believe it. Why does this keep happening to us?" Her mouth trembled. "You don't think Reed did it, do you?"

Marla gazed at her aghast. "Ma, how can you say such a thing?" But even as she said it, her own doubts niggled at her.

Anita shook her head. "I don't know him anymore. I fear there's more to his business with these design center people than he's telling us."

Marla agreed but didn't say so aloud. Instead, she patted Ma's shoulder. "We need to have faith in him. He's part of our family, and he'll need our support now more than ever."

"You're right, but we'll be unsettled until this case is solved."

"You can come home with me and Ryder. Dalton will be stuck here for a while. He said he'd bring Reed back with him."

"Okay, we should get going. I'm exhausted."

Sirens sounded in the distance, coming closer. Marla stood and stuffed her bags into the back of the stroller. Her feet dragged as they headed toward the exit. She had to prepare Ryder's next meal and entertain him at home while he expended his energy. Regardless of what happened, she couldn't deviate from her routine.

Anita trudged alongside her as guests fled to their cars. Word must have finally spread. Marla was grateful the pageant finale had taken place at least. Amelia and the other girls had deserved their moment of glory.

Where had George gone after the award ceremony? Had he stayed with his daughter? Caroline had been on the grounds as well as Davinia and her manager. They'd all had a connection to Brad. Where had he gone after his brief encounter with Davinia's manager?

Dalton should speak to the people on either side of their company's booth and across the aisle. They might have seen or heard something significant. He should also get a list of ticket holders and exhibitors, but he'd know to request these items from event organizers.

Her thoughts tumbled and coagulated into a mental mass like a rubber band ball until Ryder's whimper drew her attention.

"Do you want some milk?" she asked. She withdrew his bottle from their baby care bag and handed it to him. He grabbed it eagerly and brought it to his mouth.

Once they reached her car, Anita settled into the passenger seat without saying a word. Marla secured Ryder, got in the front, and started the engine. A welcome blast of air-conditioning cooled her skin.

She didn't feel like talking, either, so she focused on getting them home safe. There would be plenty of time to discuss things later. Maybe Anita and Reed should stay the night. That is, if Reed didn't end up at police headquarters as a murder suspect.

Chapter Twenty-One

Reed came home along with Dalton, and he and Anita accepted the invitation to stay the night. They were both too sapped of energy to drive to Boynton Beach. Besides, Dalton needed Reed to come into the station on Monday morning to give a formal statement.

Marla felt better about keeping her mother under her watchful eye. Anita was nervous enough already, and this latest incident would only make matters worse.

The next day, nobody spoke about the elephant in the room. Anita and Reed delighted in Ryder's antics as Marla got the baby dressed and fed. She hustled him into her car to take him to daycare, promising to call Anita later.

The older couple planned to stop by Dalton's office so Reed could sign his statement before they headed home. They'd leave the house at the same time as Dalton and follow him there.

Marla ran errands until Dalton texted her that he was done with Reed, and she should head over to the station. It was her turn to state her observations for the record.

"I don't have much to add," Marla told her husband, seated alone with him in his office. "I heard screams and rushed over to the site where Brad lay on the ground. The lady who'd raised the ruckus was there and no one else."

Dalton adjusted his recorder to catch her words. "Please describe your observations when you noticed the victim."

Marla cleared her throat. "Bradley Quinn lay face-up on

the ground with a garlic garland wrapped around his neck. He was unresponsive and had no pulse. I called nine-one-one."

"To your knowledge, was anyone else present at the festival who knew the deceased?"

Marla named Reed, George, Caroline, Davinia and Oscar. "They were all there, but I didn't see any of them near Brad. Well, that is, until Reed showed up."

She answered more questions, growing more uncomfortable by the minute, until Dalton shut off his device.

As the tension in her shoulders relaxed, she surveyed the wilted plant on his windowsill, the dust on his bookshelves, and the stack of papers on top of his file cabinet. Usually he kept things fairly neat. Why did she get the impression he was letting things slide? Was work so overwhelming that he couldn't be bothered to straighten up?

"If I could speak to Amelia again," Marla told him off the record, "I might ask if George had stayed by her side. She would have been occupied with her duties as garlic queen, and he could have wandered off."

"It's best if you steer clear of the granite yard," Dalton said, his eyes boring into hers. "I'll be following up with these people from now on."

Marla mulled over the suspects. "I doubt Caroline did it. There's no way she could have lured Brad behind the restrooms and snapped his neck, if that's how he died." She gazed at her husband with a coaxing smile, hoping he'd confirm the manner of death.

Dalton tightened his mouth. "We know Pete Ferdinand isn't guilty. He's in jail. Maybe Wanner got the wrong man."

"If so, the evidence against him must have been planted," Marla pointed out.

"I sent Wanner a text to call me. Hopefully, he'll get back to me sooner rather than later." Dalton drummed his fingers on the desk pad. "Nadia and Caroline from the design center staff seem unlikely as suspects, but I can't eliminate them entirely."

"Why not? Nadia wasn't even there yesterday."

"Yes, but she had a boyfriend. Maybe she lied and didn't break up with him."

"And then what? She enlisted the guy's help to do away with Jack when he threatened to contact her ex-spouse?" Marla scoffed. "And then she did the same for Brad? She had no motive for knocking off her boss."

"We'll see." Dalton's brows drew together. "George Eustice is still at the top of my list. He had reason to eliminate Jack to protect his daughter."

Marla had told him what Amelia said about her dad's confrontation with Jack. It could be as the girl explained. The men had an angry clash and … Wait, didn't Amelia say George had something on Jack to make him back off?

My dad knew things that could get Jack in trouble, and Dad threatened to expose him if Jack didn't leave me alone.

She repeated these words to Dalton. "George could have known about the copper thefts and that Jack was doing it again," she suggested.

"That's possible. If Amelia told the truth, her dad left Jack when he was still alive. But that doesn't let George off the hook for Brad's murder. They'd been business partners. Perhaps there was still bad blood between them, and it boiled over."

Could they be dealing with two different killers? Marla voiced her idea aloud. "It would help if you could track Brad's history. George might be willing to supply more details now that the man is dead. Otherwise, have you given any more thought to Lenny Brooks? The tile guy claimed he'd gotten stuck in traffic and arrived late the day of Jack's death, but he was the one who found the body. And Brad's company owed him money."

"I'll take another look at the timing, but there's lack of motive where Brooks is concerned." He glanced at his watch. "What's on your agenda for the rest of the day?"

Marla got his signal. Time for her to leave. She collected

her purse and rose, wondering why something about his workplace continued to bother her.

"I figured I'd visit Davinia to return her bracelet. Do you have her address and phone number? I'd like to text her first to make sure she'll be there."

"What bracelet?" Dalton picked up a pen from his desk and twirled it in his fingers.

"I found a diamond tennis bracelet in the grass right after we met. I'd introduced myself once the pageant was over. Davinia's manager hustled her off for an interview, and I didn't see them again."

She frowned as a memory surfaced. "I did observe Brad talking to Oscar earlier. According to Caroline, he left the booth to go say hello to his sister. I saw him approach when she sat at the judge's table, but Oscar stopped him. They had a brief exchange that made them both look angry. Brad stomped off in the opposite direction."

"That makes two people who had words with Brad the day he died."

Right, Marla thought. *That would be Reed as well as Oscar.*

Her pulse thrummed. If Oscar became a suspect, this could provide a new angle to pursue that led away from her stepfather.

"I'll see if I can get Davinia to elaborate on Oscar's relationship to Brad," she offered.

"Her brother just died. It might be wise for you to wait."

"She'll be upset about losing this bracelet. It must have cost a fortune, assuming the stones are real." Marla dug the item from her purse and showed it to Dalton. "I know she's mourning her brother's loss, but it'll bring her a measure of relief to get this back."

He shook his head. "It's best for you to stay away until I've done my interviews."

"Is it? You know Davinia will be more willing to talk to me, and returning her jewelry gives me the perfect excuse."

"You do make a convincing argument." Dalton's lips twisted in wry acknowledgement as he wrote down the actress's address and phone number.

Marla's eyes widened when she noted the location. "She must live in one of those mansions by the water. I imagine it irked Brad that she had so much money while he was struggling."

"Possibly." Dalton wagged a finger at her. "Be careful what you say and don't share any details about my case."

"Mum's the word." She'd stop at the grocery store and pick up some pastries before heading over to Davinia's house. A quick text message verified the woman was home and would receive her.

****

The sun had risen higher in the sky by the time Marla arrived at the celebrity's impressive corner estate on the Intracoastal Waterway. She lived at Las Olas Isles, a community with multi-million-dollar mansions and mega-yachts moored at backyard docks.

Davinia's residence, a Mediterranean-style structure, looked palatial beyond a private iron gate. Thank goodness she'd called ahead, Marla thought, as she punched in the guest entry code she'd been given. She drove through and followed a palm-lined drive toward the main entrance. At least she'd chosen a royal blue dress to wear with wedge sandals. She would have felt out of place in these posh surroundings in jeans and a casual top.

She stepped outside of her parked car to survey the property. Multiple towers fronted the sand-painted façade, with marble steps leading up to a set of arched double doors. The second story boasted a balcony with a wrought iron railing. Tropical plants, colorful crotons, and royal palms graced a broad lawn, while the scent of gardenias filled the air.

A maid in a black uniform and white apron answered the doorbell and led her indoors. Marla paused inside a tiled foyer to gaze in rapture at the interior. Her entire dining room would fit inside this entryway lit by a crystal chandelier. Ahead was a spiral staircase with polished steps and a fancy handrail.

To the left was a parlor with contemporary furnishings. The formal dining room was on her right. It had a long, rich wood table that must have seated at least twenty people. Silver serving pieces gleamed at intervals on either side of a fresh flower arrangement.

"This way, please." The maid gestured for Marla to follow her toward a large open room in the rear. It had floor-to-ceiling windows and a water view. Marla's glance swept the cream-colored sofas, brick fireplace, and mahogany bar with a granite countertop.

She sat on one of the couches, careful not to dislodge the collection of throw pillows. Outside the window, she glimpsed a tour boat gliding past. She could imagine the onboard guide describing the residents in the lavish homes that lined the canal. She'd feel as though she were in a fishbowl living here. A rectangular swimming pool glistened off to the side, making Marla wonder where the dock was located. It must be around the corner at the other end.

Davinia breezed in amid a cloud of perfume. She wore a purple caftan and a turban with a jeweled feather perched atop her head. An amethyst necklace sparkled around her neck and on a large ring around her finger. She greeted Marla with outstretched arms and a grin on her heavily made-up face.

"Hello, darling, I didn't expect to see you again so soon."

That's for sure. The actress didn't look like a woman in mourning for her dead brother.

"I'm sorry for your loss." Marla handed over the bakery box in her hands. "Here, I brought you some sweets. I wouldn't have disturbed your privacy except my errand couldn't wait."

This excuse presented her with the perfect opportunity to ask about Brad's background and his relationship to Oscar. She'd have to be tactful when approaching the topic.

"Thank you, I appreciate your support." Davinia pawned her gift off on the maid and ordered coffee service for her guest. "You said on the phone that you had found my bracelet?"

Marla dug the item from her bag and handed it over. The diamonds glittered in the sunlight streaming in through the windows. "Is this yours? I found it in the grass after we met yesterday."

Davinia pressed a hand to her heart. "Oh Lordy, yes. I thought it was gone for good. You're an angel for finding it and returning it to me. What can I do to repay you?"

Tell me everything you know about your brother, Marla wanted to say but didn't. Instead, she tried a different tact.

"Like I'd said earlier, I would be interested in doing more work for celebrities. If you can mention my salon to your friends, I'll be happy. Meanwhile, please tell me about your house. It's magnificent."

The actress smiled, and two tiny dimples appeared in her cheeks. "Thank you. I knew I wanted a place on the water when I decided to move back home. This one became available just at the right time. It has eight full bedroom suites in addition to the master. Each one has its own bathroom, sitting area, and walk-in closet. Do you want a quick tour?"

"I'd love to see more of the place." Marla rose, eager for the opportunity to note any items of interest to her husband's case. Framed family photos, for example, could be revealing. So could a home office. Did Oscar work here, or did he have a place of business elsewhere? She supposed Dalton would be investigating him now and learning more about his background.

As they passed through various rooms, Davinia spiked the tour with commentary. Marla responded with complimentary remarks. She noted that childhood pictures of Davinia and Brad were disappointingly absent.

However, fresh flower bouquets decorated nearly every public room. They must account for the heavy floral scent that pervaded the house. Orchid, violet, and lavender blooms predominated. Marla glanced at Davinia's flowing purple garment. Obviously, she favored this color scheme.

They passed briefly into a study where cherry wood bookcases lined the walls. Here the actress displayed her trophies along with framed photos of herself on set and at various events. Oscar appeared in a number of them, evidently escorting her to award ceremonies and to premieres related to her acting career.

One item in a glass case caught her eye. "I can't believe you kept the red sash from your days as garlic festival queen," Marla said. "It's too bad you didn't get a tiara instead."

Davinia smiled. "Darling, I was happy to get that sash along with the ridiculous headdress. I've had plenty of other occasions to wear jewels."

They moved on to a cozy room with a huge television screen mounted on a wall, brown leather furniture, a wet bar, a billiards table and a fireplace. French doors led outside to a covered patio with a dining set and a complete outdoor kitchen. The open pool glistened off to the side and beyond flowed the Intracoastal Waterway.

"Your house is perfect for entertaining," Marla remarked. "Do you host parties often? Or do you prefer a quiet lifestyle when you're at home?"

Davinia cast her an amused glance. "I'm not a recluse, if that's what you mean. I enjoy having friends over."

They entered a tiled kitchen with white cabinetry. A stab of envy washed over her. Marla could easily picture herself working at the professional range and washing dishes at the enormous single sink. Tall windows by a breakfast nook would tempt her to linger and watch the boats sail by on the waterway.

The aroma of brewed coffee reached her nose. On a side counter, the maid placed two delicate bone china cups and saucers on a tray along with a crystal sugar bowl and creamer. Marla's blood sang for another jolt of caffeine.

"Come, let's sit down." Davinia signaled for Marla to follow her.

"Your home is gorgeous," Marla said, claiming her prior seat in the gathering room at the rear of the house. "I love the kitchen. It's so bright and airy with its water view." As she glanced out the window, the water taxi chugged past, crossing paths with a motorboat.

The maid delivered their coffee and a platter with snacks.

Marla pointed to the glittering garnish on the food. "Is that real gold?" she asked, never having seen such a thing.

Davinia laughed. "Of course, it is. We made these appetizers for my soiree Saturday evening. This is a fresh sample, though, so you needn't worry." Her face grew sad. "That was the night before... well, now I'll be having friends over for a different reason."

Marla assumed she meant condolence calls. At least she'd have friends to console her on her brother's death. Probably Oscar wouldn't care. He might be relieved the man was out of her hair, especially if the two guys didn't get along.

Marla transferred a smoked salmon roll with rice and avocado to her plate. It was coated with gold beads. "Is this safe to eat?" she asked, lifting a fork.

"Yes, it's quite all right. Haven't you heard of edible gold?" Davinia's eyes crinkled with mirth.

"Not really." Marla didn't socialize in the circles where they served such things.

"My former husband learned about it when he was stationed overseas in the army. After Craig came home, he started a manufacturing business in Naples. He says gold is biologically inert and doesn't break down during digestion."

"Oh, lovely." Marla had a distasteful image of the results, especially when she pictured one of Ryder's diapers with gold flake deposits.

Erasing that image from her mind, she took a tentative bite of the sushi roll. The beads tasted similar to those gelatinous pearls in fancy drinks. They had no flavor but were smooth on her tongue.

She passed on the other items. One piece was topped with a translucent white food and sprinkled with gold dust. Was that raw fish? She'd stick to the smoked salmon as a safer bet. Even the turkey mini wraps with fresh raspberries were decorated with gold crumbles. How bizarre. And how typical of the elite who went all out to impress their friends.

Anyway, she wasn't here to discuss food, she told herself as she added cream to her cup of coffee and took a sip. At least the drinks hadn't come with gold sprinkles.

How could she bring the conversation around to the questions she needed answered about Brad and the manager? She'd better start before they got interrupted. Davinia would still have to make final arrangements for her brother, unless she'd passed that duty along to Oscar.

The woman had shown few signs of grief during their conversation so far. Was she glad her brother was gone? Or was she still numb and suppressing her sadness through social niceties?

"I was honored to be part of the garlic festival pageant," Marla mentioned. "All of the girls were so deserving of the prize. You must have been so excited when you won the title as queen. How did Brad feel about his big sister moving to California when your career took off?"

Davinia shrugged. "He didn't care. We were never close. In fact, Brad always resented me because I was Mom and Dad's favorite. He did things to get attention, but it wasn't anything good. They tried hard to encourage him, but he was set on the wrong path from the start."

"What did he do after high school?"

"He didn't go to college. It wasn't the fast track to success that he wanted. He got odd jobs and ended up in construction."

"Is that what he did before establishing Amaze Design Center?"

"You could say that." Davinia plucked at her caftan, her face downcast.

"I have a confession to make. My mother is having her bathroom redone by his company. I did some research, and I couldn't find much on Brad before he started this business."

Marla didn't want to confess her husband was the detective investigating Brad's death, or Davinia might throw her out. This was an easier path, especially because it was true.

Davinia snorted. "You won't find anything since Brad changed his last name from Quincy to Quinn. He thought it would fool people. His dummy companies sure did."

Marla, who'd just taken a sip of coffee, put down her cup with a clatter. "Excuse me?"

"When things got too hot, Brad jumped ship. He thought I didn't know about his tricks, but I kept an eye on him. He promised me this time would be different. I should have listened when Oscar told me not to believe him."

"Did I hear my name?" The manager strode into the room, a scowl on his face as he took in the scene. "My dear, is this woman upsetting you?"

Chapter Twenty-Two

Startled by the manager's sudden appearance, Marla could only stare at him. When did he get there? And why would he assume she might be upsetting Davinia? Had he overheard the actress's comments about Brad?

She couldn't help her defensive reply. "I came here to return Davinia's bracelet that she lost at the pageant yesterday. It fell off and landed in the grass. If you recall, I was at the festival as a hairstylist for the contestants. Davinia mentioned the old days when she won the crown."

"Oh, well in that case…" He straightened the bowtie he wore with his slate gray suit. Although his jacket expertly fit his stocky build, in these elegant surroundings he looked more suited to a boxing ring than a drawing room.

Had Oscar stopped by to help Davinia make funeral arrangements for her brother? As her friend as well as her manager, Marla should have expected him to be there to offer support. If she recalled, he and Davinia had known each other since childhood.

That meant they hadn't met in Hollywood when Davinia lived in California. They must have reconnected when she moved back home. Did he have any other clients, or was Davinia his sole means of income?

"How are you doing, my dear?" he asked the actress. "I came by to assist you with Brad's memorial plans."

Davinia responded with a fond smile. "You're a sweetheart, Oscar, but I can manage on my own. I don't think reality has sunk in yet."

He moved behind her and placed his hands on her shoulders. "You may mourn your brother, but he was nothing but an albatross to you."

And it's good you're rid of him. Oscar didn't say it aloud, but Marla heard his message loud and clear.

"Poor Brad, all he ever wanted was our parents' approval. Being a success meant everything to him." Davinia's eyes filled with moisture.

Marla narrowed her gaze. Were those tears real? Davinia hadn't evidenced any sorrow during their earlier conversation.

"Your brother took the wrong path to get there," Oscar said. "You can forgive him in your heart, my dear. Meanwhile, why don't you let me save you the trouble of meeting with the mortician? I can handle everything. I've cleared your schedule, so you can stay home and avoid the paparazzi." He stroked her hair, his expression reflecting concern along with something more.

That's not all you want to handle, Marla realized. He was soft on his client. Did Davinia return his affection or even realize he felt that way?

At any rate, Marla's time here was finished. She wouldn't get any further information from Davinia with the manager present. The man raised her hackles. He was too much ingrained into Davinia's life. She seemed to appreciate his attention, but Marla would find his constant presence to be annoying.

Or was it the other way around? Perhaps Davinia recognized his affection and manipulated him into doing her bidding. Marla shouldn't discount either one of them from her suspect list.

She gathered her purse and rose. "Thank you for your hospitality. You know, it might be fun to serve these gold-flecked snacks at my next party. What's the name of your ex-husband's company? I'll look up his website."

"It's called Au-Some Eats." Davinia spelled it out. "The

'a-u' refers to gold's elemental symbol. Clever, isn't it? You can buy their products online."

"Got it, thanks." The name sounded rather plebian to her for a line of edible gold. It brought to mind a food truck, not a platter of glittering food for the elite.

Davinia wagged a finger at her. "If you talk to Craig, tell him I referred you. We still keep in touch."

"I'll do that. Meanwhile, I'd appreciate it if you could notify me about your brother's memorial service. I'd like to attend to pay my respects."

Oscar stiffened, his gaze growing cold. Uh-oh. Did he remember spotting her at Jack's funeral? "Wait a minute. Aren't you the woman whose mother is getting her bathroom redone?"

"That's right." Marla said it as though issuing a challenge. Why should that matter to him?

"I hope she's not going to post any bad reviews. The company is in enough trouble already. I've been hard-pressed to keep Davinia's name from being associated with them."

Marla stepped back from the sour expression on his face. "My mother will be happy once their project is finished. Any complaints have to do with the delays in getting the job done."

Oscar glowered at her. "Things should move along now that the bad eggs are out of the way. I'll have to ask you to leave. Davinia needs her rest. She has a delicate constitution."

Marla sneaked a glance at the actress who appeared anything but delicate. Her eyes held a hard resolve. Did she intend to honor her brother's memory despite the manager's enmity toward him? Or was she playing another game?

After bidding the duo a hasty farewell, Marla departed. She'd ask Dalton to look more closely into Oscar's affairs. If he'd put all his marbles into one basket, that meant trouble if Davinia's career faltered. How far would Oscar go to ensure that didn't happen?

Once in her car, Marla looked up the ex-husband's

company. His business was located in Naples on Florida's west coast. She put in a call and a masculine voice answered.

"Hi, are you Craig Vernon? My name is Marla Vail. I'm a friend of Davinia's."

"What can I do for you?" he asked in a wary tone.

"She served me some appetizers sprinkled with gold and said you manufacture the product. It's as awesome as your company name implies. Have you heard the news about her brother?"

"No. What about him?"

"I'm sorry to inform you that Brad has passed away."

Silence met her pronouncement, while Marla hoped she wasn't overstepping her boundaries by infringing on Dalton's investigation. Then again, he had no reason so far to talk to this guy.

"That's sad, but what do I have to do with it?" Craig asked, his voice gruff.

"I'd like to discuss his relationship to Davinia."

"Who did you say you were?"

Marla let out a frustrated breath. This would go better in person. Otherwise, he might hang up on her. Plus, she couldn't gauge his nonverbal cues over the phone.

"I'm a recent acquaintance of your ex-wife. Is it possible for us to meet today? I won't take up much of your time, and it's really important that I talk to you."

She did a quick mental calculation. If she left immediately, she'd cross Alligator Alley in an hour and a half. That meant three hours for travel and one to interview the guy. She should make it back in time to pick up Ryder at daycare. The trip wouldn't be practical unless she thought it worthwhile, but this guy might have the answers she needed to help clear Reed's name.

"I don't have much to say about Brad," the ex-husband remarked.

Marla hesitated, unwilling to provide too much

information. "There's a murder involved, and I'm married to the police detective who's on the case."

"Good God. Is the cop coming with you?"

She heard a note of panic in his voice. "No, it's just me. I want to chat about Brad, that's all. My mother is... well, I'll explain things when I'm there."

"All right. I'll talk to you for Davinia's sake. But I'm working, so you'll have to be quick."

Marla rang off, a triumphant smile on her face. Then her expression sobered. She'd have to make good time heading west but hated to go alone. Who could she get to accompany her? Dalton was busy processing Brad's murder. Tally was stuck at work in her dress shop. What about Robyn? The salon receptionist was off today and always game for an adventure.

"I'd love to come," Robyn said in response. "Give me fifteen minutes to get ready. You'll have to fill me in on everything. Is this guy single, by any chance?"

"He's divorced. I don't know anything about his current social life. He used to be married to Davinia Quincy, the actress."

"Oh, really? Then he must be good-looking. See you in a few!"

Marla stopped off at home to change into more comfortable clothes. She gave the dogs a brief run in the backyard before she picked up Robyn in the same neighborhood.

"I can't wait to see how this fellow makes edible gold," Robyn said in an eager tone. "If he has a factory, you'll have to promise me that we can take a quick tour."

"Okay, but I'll need to be back in time to get Ryder from daycare."

As they headed toward the highway, Marla brought Robyn up to date on recent events, relating as much as Dalton would allow her to tell.

"Who's your main suspect?" Robyn asked, adjusting her designer-brand sunglasses. She wore a spring green top with white Capri pants, perfect for an excursion on a warm Florida day.

Marla turned onto Alligator Alley. Clouds scudded overhead in an azure sky. On either side of the road, plains of sawgrass stretched to infinity as they sped west toward Naples at the other end. A white egret took flight, soaring gracefully into the air.

"Dalton is still placing his bet on George Eustice," she replied. "George was furious with Jack over his daughter. He was mad at Brad for not paying him. But Tobias? I can't figure out a motive for that one. George and Tobias may never have met, unless permit inspectors do granite countertops. I wouldn't think that's within their range of duties."

"So who's on the top of your list?"

"My guess was on Pete Ferdinand, one of the contractors," Marla said. "However, Pete was in custody when Brad died, so he's off the hook for that one… assuming it's a murder case. I'd say a garlic garland wrapped around the man's neck makes it a valid theory until we get confirmation from the medical examiner."

"Tell me again why we're traveling across the state to interview Davinia's ex-husband."

Marla shrugged. "I think Brad's sister fits into the picture somehow, and Craig might be able to tell me more about her."

Robyn glanced at her with a grin. "I'm glad you asked me to come along. I had laundry and food shopping on my agenda for today. This is much more fun."

"How was your date the other night with what's-his-name?" Marla asked, unable to keep the men straight in Robyn's life.

"Bor-ing. Anthony is a computer analyst, and all he talked about were scams and cybercrime," Robyn replied with a grimace.

"Lots of people fall victim to those scams or the crooks wouldn't keep doing it." Marla scrunched her forehead. Something niggled at her brain, but she couldn't grasp it.

"I know, but it wasn't what I wanted to hear all night." Robyn heaved a deep sigh. "It's impossible to meet anybody decent these days."

"Maybe you need to stop looking for Mr. Perfect."

Glad she wasn't single anymore, Marla focused on driving. They entered the cypress preserve where sturdy trees with bleached trunks lined the roadsides.

After taking the exit at Naples, Marla followed her GPS to the address Craig Vernon had supplied. She made a moue of disappointment as they passed Fifth Avenue with its boutique shops and restaurants.

"I wish we had time to go shopping, but I'm on a tight schedule. We'll have to grab fast food later on the way home," she told Robyn, who seemed content to be along for the ride.

The strip of warehouses where they ended up seemed to have full occupancy judging from the number of vehicles in the asphalt parking lot. Marla found a space, pulled in, and shut off the ignition.

A tall fellow answered her knock at the office door that led to Craig's factory. He wore a tee shirt over taut jeans, along with a pair of worn loafers. With his blond hair tousled on his brow, even features and a healthy tan, he appeared rakishly handsome. The scent of his spice cologne trailed them inside after they completed introductions.

Marla and Robyn took seats as indicated across from a scuffed wooden desk littered with papers. Peeling paint and dents along the baseboards cried out for refurbishment. A chemical smell added to the unsavory atmosphere. Marla resisted the urge to fan the air as dust motes sparkled in the sunlight trickling in from a single grimy window.

Unimpressed by the shabby surroundings, she wondered how well Craig's business was doing. Did he choose to remain here due to the cheap rent? Or was it all he could afford?

Robyn, on the other hand, couldn't get past Craig's striking good looks, judging from her blatant stare. Marla could imagine her assessment. If his company failed, this guy could get a job as a male model. Not only was his face straight off a billboard poster, but his broad shoulders and muscled arms fit the image as well. He didn't just sit in an office all day. Either his production process required strength, or he worked out.

"As I'd mentioned on the phone," she began, "I'm a recent friend of Davinia's. We met at the garlic festival. She was a judge for the pageant and I'm a hairstylist." She handed over a business card. "My staff did the contestants' hair for the grand finale. Davinia and I got to chat afterwards, and I paid her a visit this morning."

"Davvy always was fond of that festival. It's what gave her a start in show business."

"Yes, so I understand. How did you two meet each other?" Marla wondered if they'd hooked up when the actress lived out west.

His gaze took on a distant look. "We were at a party. She caught my attention right away. This woman with hair like gold cotton candy and eyes as blue as the sky walked into the room and the whole place lit up. I couldn't believe she'd look twice at me, but it happened."

"Were you in show business also?"

"Heck, no. I was the bartender. I'd just gotten out of the service and was living with a friend until I saved up enough money to rent my own place."

"Was this in Fort Lauderdale?"

He nodded, his fingers playing with a paper clip. "My dad sold insurance. I didn't want to go down that road, nor did I have a passion for anything in particular. My friends were all going to college. I didn't want to burden my folks with debt. Nor were my grades good enough for a scholarship. So I enlisted, figuring I could learn new skills in the army. I did, but not in the manner I'd expected."

"Davinia said you'd heard about edible gold while stationed overseas."

231

"That's right." His face broke into a lopsided smile that most women would find charming. Marla cast a side glance at her friend. Robyn appeared dazzled, her lips parted and her eyes fixed on the man. "The first time I saw people eating food coated with real gold," Craig said, "you could have bowled me over with a feather. My mouth must have opened so wide, a crow could have flown in."

"Where did you see this gold-decorated food?"

"Believe it or not, it was in India. After a tour in Afghanistan, I planned to quit. But then they offered me an assignment as an officer's aide because I'm good with languages. I could have made a career of it, but I can't stand bureaucracy." The brackets deepened beside his mouth. "One evening, I had guard duty at a dinner party my officer attended, and that's where I noticed the sparkling garnishes. The potential for manufacturing the stuff in the U.S. hit me right away. I could sell it to caterers who cooked for the rich and famous."

"So you didn't re-enlist when your tour of duty ended?"

"Nope. I went to live with a friend while figuring out how I could launch my new business. That's when I met Davvy. She was excited by the idea and offered to invest. I've already paid her back with interest."

Marla swept her arm at the surroundings. "I assume that means you've done well?"

He chuckled. "You can't tell from this place, right? In general, business has been good. I've been thinking of expanding and then I'd move to better quarters." His brow furrowed. "You're asking a lot of questions that have nothing to do with Davvy or Brad. I thought that's why you came to talk to me."

"True. Let's discuss their relationship. Brad's death happened at the festival. I visited Davinia the day afterward. She didn't appear to be overly upset by her loss."

"I'm not surprised. Brad always had one scheme or another in mind that would make him rich, and he enacted them at other people's expenses. I warned Davvy to disconnect herself from him, and Oscar backed me. But she had a soft heart where Brad was concerned."

"Do you know what Brad did before he started Amaze Design Center?"

"He had other firms that I always felt were shady. He promised Davvy that he was going straight with this company." Craig noted her questioning glance. "Yes, we've kept in touch. She still calls me sometimes."

"May I ask why you broke up? Did Brad cause a rift between the two of you?"

Craig dropped the paperclip and leaned forward. "We split up because of Oscar. I couldn't stand the guy. He was always around, and Davvy acted as though she wouldn't have a career without him. He'd only gotten involved after she moved back home from California. I do have to give him credit for looking out for her interests, though. Plus, he fended off that other guy who threatened her."

"What's this?" Marla asked, her breaths shallow. She exchanged a glance with Robyn, who sat listening intently.

"A man who worked for Brad recently approached Davvy and said he'd go public with things he knew about her that could cause a scandal unless she paid him. Oscar took charge and had a chat with Jack."

"Jack Laredo?" Marla sat up so straight that she dislodged her purse. She grabbed it by the strap and slung it back over her chair.

Craig's eyes narrowed. "Yup, that's his name. Oscar must have told Brad, because he was furious when he found out Jack had approached his sister. I'm surprised he didn't fire the guy, but who knows what they were covering up for each other? Anyway, Jack backed off. I don't know whether Brad or Oscar made the difference, but Davvy didn't care as long as that man kept his mouth shut."

Marla assumed Jack meant to expose Brad's unsavory

history and his connection to the actress. "I appreciate you sharing this information with us. As I said earlier, my husband is the police detective investigating Brad's death. Two other men who Brad knew are dead, too. Jack Laredo was one of them. The other was Tobias Banyan, the permit inspector who'd worked with Amaze Design Center."

"No kidding? Is Davvy safe?"

Was that real concern in his eyes? If Marla wasn't mistaken, her senses told her that Craig still harbored affection for his ex-wife.

"She has Oscar there. He'll watch over her." The man wouldn't let anything bad happen to his cash cow, that was certain. Not to mention that he practically drooled over her. If he cared about Davinia on a personal level, he'd have even more of an incentive to protect her.

Right now, Oscar topped her list of suspects. She could understand why he might want to get rid of Jack and Brad, but Tobias's death didn't fit into that picture. What was she missing?

Chapter Twenty-Three

"Has Davvy mentioned me at all?" Craig asked with a hopeful note.

"She recommended your business," Marla replied. "Davinia had served gold-decorated foods at a party Saturday night, and I tasted samples at her house this morning. I'd like to learn more about the product."

Craig whipped out a couple of brochures from a drawer. "These will tell you about our company. It gives the website URL along with the online store. Or you can call us direct to place an order."

Robyn stuffed a brochure into her purse. "Is it possible for us to get a peek at your factory? I'd love to see how you make gold flakes." She fluttered her lashes at him, clearly not getting the hint that he still had a flame for Davinia.

He gave her a kilowatt smile. "I'd be happy to show you around."

"Marla, we could sprinkle the food with gold at our next charity event," Robyn suggested. "Think what a sensation it would make. I can imagine the ad copy already." A dreamy look spread across her face, and she swept her hands in the air like a rainbow. "Our cause is pure gold and so are our desserts! Come try one and share the wealth."

"Let's not get carried away," Marla said as they both stood. Was Robyn serious, or was she suggesting a tour as a ploy to draw Craig out? If it were her choice, she'd leave for home, but she had promised Robyn a glimpse at the production process.

Craig stood, grabbed a toothpick from a box on his desk, and stuck it between his teeth. He chewed on it as he led them next door to a cavernous bay full of machinery.

"We start the process with the raw material," Craig explained as he began their tour. "This would be highly pure gold bars or gold grain mined in compliance with federal laws."

"What's gold grain?" Robyn asked, while Marla hoped the guy wouldn't be too long-winded. She had to get back in time to pick up Ryder at daycare.

"It's a small, round form similar to pellets."

"Do you store these materials on the premises?" Marla asked, glancing around for a safe. She hadn't noticed one in his front office.

"It's kept in a secure location," Craig said without further explanation. He tossed his toothpick into a trash can then indicated a furnace. A pair of tongs hung nearby. "Over here, we melt down the gold along with silver and copper. This compound makes it easier to produce gold leaf. Next we pour the molten alloy into a square mold."

Marla's ears perked up. Copper? Interesting that he used that particular metal in his production process.

Craig sauntered toward a big machine. "The squares go through these rollers where they're pressed into thin sheets. I'll sandwich these sheets between layers of special plastic to be compressed into thinner widths and longer strips until they're each point-zero-five millimeters thick."

"So gold leaf is essentially gold that has been stretched thin?" Robyn asked, holding her chin as she regarded the huge rollers.

Craig nodded. "It's a malleable metal. One gram can be stretched to three kilometers." He picked up a piece lying around and demonstrated its flexibility. "Over at this next table, we cut a long strip into six-centimeter squares. Each square goes between two sheets of specialty paper. This helps to keep the gold leaf at an even thickness. The next stage is to pound it repeatedly until it reaches a certain measurement. Finally, I'll trim the edges and it's done."

Robyn pointed to shelves holding labeled jars of gold flakes, shakers of gold crumbs, jars of gold powder, and boxes of gold sheets.

"You turn the gold into all of these products?" she asked while Marla noted another section with machinery for bottling and labeling.

"That's right. Gold doesn't only have edible properties, you know. It's also used in cosmetics as an anti-aging factor. But there aren't any true health benefits. Nonetheless, cosmetic companies are among my best customers, although the mainstay of my business comes from people in the food industry. For me, it's a win-win either way. Here's a shaker of gold crumbs for each of you."

"Thanks so much," Robyn said with a simpering look. "I can't wait to try this sample at home, although it would be more fun if I had company." Her glance dropped to his ringless left hand. "By the way, if you're ever on the east coast, look us up. We do men's haircuts in the salon and Marla offers a discount to new customers."

Marla snagged her elbow. "I'm sure Craig has his own barber, Robyn. Come on, we've taken up too much of his time, and I have to get back."

After they parted ways, Marla poked Robyn in the parking lot. "What were you doing in there? It's clear the man still has feelings for Davinia."

Robyn shot her a querulous glance. "Everyone is fair game if they're single. I hope you gained something useful from this visit."

"I did." Marla waited to discuss the murder cases until they were in the car. They stopped along the way to grab lunch at a fast-food place before heading east on Alligator Alley.

"I was interested in what Craig said about Jack and Brad," Marla stated, focused on the road as they passed through the cypress preserve.

"You mean how Jack tried to get money from Davinia? Who would have been madder about it—Craig, Brad, or Oscar?"

Marla considered the options. "Craig might have felt protective of his ex-wife, but Brad and Oscar had more to lose."

"Why do you suppose Brad didn't fire Jack at the time?"

"Probably because Jack knew Brad's secrets, and Brad didn't dare risk being exposed. Craig said Brad had owned other companies. I remember he'd used the name Brad Quincy when George Eustice partnered with him. It's likely he took on an alias as often as he changed his company name."

****

Marla got back in time to drop Robyn off at home and make it to daycare to retrieve her son. In the car, she debated whether to call Dalton or not. Instead, she texted him that she'd picked up Ryder and was headed home. They could talk later when they'd decompressed from the day.

Busy with the baby, Marla didn't have time to think twice about anything else until Anita called after dinner. Dalton wasn't home yet, having notified her he'd be working late. She was so tired, her eyelids drooped, but she still had to give Ryder his bath.

"Hi Ma," she said wearily into the phone. "What's up?"

"We have good news," Ma replied in a cheery tone. "Juan notified us that he's coming over tomorrow to finish his part of the bathroom, and Lenny will be doing the shower seat. The glass doors should arrive on Thursday."

"That's fantastic. I'm glad to hear it." Now that they'd been paid, the guys could finish this job and move on. Likely they'd seek work elsewhere if the design company folded.

"I just want to get it done at this point," Ma added, her voice determined.

"Yes, I agree. How's Reed? Has he said anything more

about what's on his mind?" *Oh, crap.* She'd forgotten to ask Davinia how she knew Reed and what so-called favor she'd done for him in the past.

Ma clucked her tongue. "He's still not talking. Nor have I heard from Michael. You'd think your brother would call to see how we're doing, but I suppose he's dealing with his own problems."

Marla should call Michael and suggest he phone Anita. She could detect the hurt in her mother's voice when she mentioned him.

"I have to get Ryder's bath ready," she said, glancing at him in his highchair. He was playing with his food and had pieces in his hair as well as on the floor. "I'll talk to you soon."

Ryder was already down by the time Dalton came home, but by then Marla was too exhausted to talk. She'd be more clear-minded in the morning to discuss things.

With the dawn came a new round of morning chores. Finally, Marla got caught up and told Dalton what she'd learned the day before. He acknowledged her report with a series of grunts and head nods.

"What's the matter with you? We've barely spoken since Brad was killed. I know you're busy with his case, but this news could be important."

He stuffed their son's bag with his daily essentials. It was his turn to drive Ryder to daycare. "Wanner is accusing Pete Ferdinand of killing Jack and Tobias. He isn't willing to believe Brad's death is related. I'm not so sure myself."

"It has to be, Dalton. They were all involved in something together. I could talk to his sister again—"

"No. You will not put yourself out there any further. This is sucking enough energy from us when our child should be the priority. It's *my* job to see that justice is done." He shook his head. "Not for much longer, thankfully."

Her shoulders tensed. "What does that mean?"

He stalked to the refrigerator and withdrew the baby's

prepared lunch. "Just that I hope to wrap this case soon," he muttered without meeting her gaze.

She glared at him. What was going on? She could demand an answer but didn't want to push him while he was working a case, so she let it go for now. Later, they'd be due for a heart-to-heart conversation.

After he departed along with Ryder, Marla called her brother to exchange news.

Charlene answered in a breezy voice. "Hi, Marla. You've just missed Michael. He's already left for the office."

Marla made a snap decision. "Actually, I really wanted to talk to you. Michael told me how you're not happy. He's upset that you want to leave and move back north."

Charlene gave a heavy sigh. "I don't want to leave *him*, but I'm looking for a better position than the jobs available in this area."

"I understand that becoming a school principal has been a lifelong dream, but isn't there anything in Florida that would suit you? Do you really have to move out of state, or are you homesick for your family there?"

"I've never been thrilled about living in Florida with the heat and humidity. But I wouldn't go if I could find a suitable offer."

"Is that the only reason? Or do you need a break from my brother?"

A brief silence ensued. "Michael spends so much time at work that we don't do things together as a family anymore. When I complain, he snaps back that he's earning a living so we can have a decent lifestyle."

"Status has always been important to him. I know you don't feel the same, but we'd hate for you to move away." She tried to sound supportive, but her voice came out with a tinge of resentment. Marla didn't like seeing her brother hurt.

"It'll only be a temporary separation, Marla. I'm not asking for a divorce."

"What about the children? Are you willing to uproot them from their friends?"

"They can stay here during the school year. I'll take them in the summer."

You're willing to leave your kids? Marla couldn't believe her ears. This wasn't the sweet and caring schoolteacher she'd known. What had caused Charlene to change?

"I'm sorry to hear this," Marla said, attempting to sound sympathetic but failing. "I can't believe you've exhausted all the possibilities in Florida. We'd miss you if you left. You're part of the family."

"It's my dream, Marla. I want to live it before I'm... too old. It's best this way."

Marla's throat clogged. Had Charlene been about to say something else? Good God, was there something wrong with her that she wasn't telling anyone?

Hoping she was being overly imaginative, she resolved to ask Michael to check Charlene's calendar. Maybe there were some unexplained appointments, such as doctor visits. Or maybe Charlene was having an affair. Marla didn't want to believe that explanation, but it would account for the disconnect between the couple.

Either way, maybe she could improve things for her brother if she advised him to spend more time with his family on weekends instead of going into work. She left him a text message to call her and proceeded to get on with her day.

****

It was mid-morning and Marla was at work when her phone rang, but it wasn't Michael. She answered the unknown call hesitantly, aware her next client was getting shampooed and would be at her chair within minutes.

"Hi, this is Hannah Brody," a woman's voice answered. "We met at Jack's funeral."

Good heavens, was this Jack's former girlfriend? Marla pictured the willowy brunette she'd briefly met on the cemetery grounds. "Oh, yes, I remember you."

"Can we talk? There's something I need to tell you."

Marla shot a frantic glance heavenward. Her busy schedule just got busier. "I could spare some time at lunch, but it'll have to be quick. Can you meet me on this side of town? There's a deli called Bagel Busters in my shopping strip. We could grab a bite to eat while we chat."

"Okay, I'll be there at noon. And Marla, please don't tell anyone about our meetup."

When the time came, Marla made her way over to her friend Arnie's restaurant. As she entered the deli, her nose picked up the scents of garlic, pickles, and freshly baked bagels. Her mouth watered, and she considered what to eat that would be quick.

Arnie left his cashier's post to give her a hug. His mustache quivered as he stepped back to regard her. He wore his customary apron over a tee shirt and jeans.

"Marla, it's good to see you. To what do I owe the honor?" His dark eyes twinkled with pleasure.

"I'm meeting a friend for lunch. Sorry I haven't stopped by more often."

"That's okay. I know you're busy." Arnie signaled to Ruth, a waitress. "Marla needs a table. Take good care of her, okay?"

Ruth winked at him. "You got it, boss. Come this way, please," she told Marla.

Arnie's eyes sparked with curiosity as she turned to go, but he didn't say another word and resumed his post. She knew he wanted the latest news on the murder cases, but she'd have to catch up with him later.

She studied the menu until Hannah arrived. When the woman showed up at the entrance, Marla stood and waved. The brunette gave a nervous glance over her shoulder before joining her. Was she afraid she'd been followed?

Hannah wore a loose-fitting top over stretch pants. Had she gotten a mite heavier in the midsection since they'd last met? Marla remembered her observation of Hannah rubbing her belly at the memorial service, and her theory about its meaning intensified.

She didn't let her notion show on her face. Instead, Marla greeted Hannah with a smile and inane chitchat to put her at ease.

Once they'd ordered their meals, she steered the conversation around to Hannah's request to see her.

"What's this about?" she asked, spreading a paper napkin on her lap.

Hannah picked up her spoon and twirled it in her hands. "I'd attended Jack's funeral to pay my respects, but my feelings were mixed about him. He wasn't always a good man."

"In what way?" Marla tilted her head, waiting patiently to hear what his former girlfriend had to say. Did she know about his activities regarding the copper ring?

"He had a temper. I know I provoked him to lash out at me. It wasn't his fault that I was so inept all the time."

Marla's mental antennae stood up. What was Hannah saying? That Jack had been abusive to her?

"Do you mean your boyfriend hit you?" she asked in a gentle tone.

Hannah put down the utensil in her hand and bowed her head. "Jack said I made him do it, but then he apologized afterward. I loved him and didn't mean to upset him. My brother didn't like Jack and urged me to walk out, but then I'd be alone."

"Yes, you'd mentioned your brother's disapproval of your relationship," Marla said, taking a sip of the hot coffee the waitress had poured.

"Stuart wasn't around at the start. He was finishing his tour of duty overseas. After his discharge, he got a job nearby. He said he'd take care of me if I left Jack."

Marla rolled this information through her mind. "What brought about your decision to break things off?"

"Jack forbade me to see my brother. He knew Stuart didn't like him. It got to the point where I was caught in the middle." She held her belly and regarded Marla with sad eyes. "When I learned I was carrying Jack's baby, I had a hard choice to make. Jack had a mean streak, and I was afraid of what he'd do to hurt me if he got angry."

"I thought you might be pregnant," Marla said in a soft tone. "So you decided to heed your brother's advice and told Jack you were leaving him?" From news articles she'd read, this could be a dangerous stage with an abusive partner that led to domestic violence.

Hannah nodded, a pained expression on her face. "Stuart promised to protect me from Jack. I... I'm afraid he's carried through on his words."

Marla gaped at her. "Surely you don't mean...?" Was Hannah saying she thought her brother had murdered Jack to get rid of him?

"I don't know what Stuart did to get Jack off my back, but he promised Jack wouldn't bother me anymore."

Hannah didn't speak as the waitress approached with their lunch. The young woman didn't make a move to pick up her fork. Marla, short on time, wanted to eat but didn't dare disrupt the flow of their conversation.

"Are you living with Stuart now?" Marla asked, attempting to comprehend the woman's situation.

Hannah took a sip of water. "Yes, and he's been wonderful to me. I'm just terrified he's done something bad for my sake."

"You do know I'm married to a police detective, right?" Marla asked, unable to stave off her hunger any longer. She took a bite of her grilled cheese and tomato sandwich. As its savory flavor met her tongue, she squirted some ketchup from a container onto her plate and dipped a French fry in it.

"That's why I wanted to talk to you," Hannah said. "This

doubt is killing me, and stress isn't good for my condition. I need to know if Stuart had anything to do with Jack's death."

"Has he said or done anything in particular to raise your suspicions?"

Hannah's shoulders lifted and fell. "Not really, but then I overheard someone say Jack had died from a broken neck. That narrows down the people who could have done it."

"Where did you hear this?"

"I don't remember. But Stuart had military training. Your average person wouldn't know how to kill someone with their bare hands." She spoke in an undertone, darting anxious glances at the other patrons.

"This may be true, but it doesn't mean your brother was involved," Marla said, admiring the girl's thought processes. She thought of Craig who'd also served in the military. And hadn't Pete acquired his tattoo while in the service? "If you don't mind, I'll pass this information along to my husband. Do you live in town?"

"Stuart's place is located in west Boca."

"All right." Marla hesitated, debating how much to reveal. "I'm tending to believe the design center people are involved in Jack's death. A couple of other men he knew from work have also met suspicious ends." She didn't mention how the permit inspector's manner of death didn't match the others. That is, assuming Brad had been killed the same way as Jack. She needed to ask Dalton for confirmation.

Hannah shook her head. "That's horrible, but it also makes me feel better if there are other possibilities." She took a bite of her turkey and avocado wrap and proceeded to devour her lunch with a healthy appetite. Maybe getting this off her chest had helped to relieve her fears.

Marla delved into baby topics and offered her advice to the mother-to-be. She was careful not to offer too much personal information. Even though Hannah's visit seemed forthright, she couldn't fully trust anyone until the murderer was found.

On her way back to the salon, she paused outside to call Dalton and fill him in on Hannah's revelations.

"That's interesting, especially in light of my news," he said. "I was going to notify you. We've received the M.E.'s report. Brad's neck was broken, same as Jack's."

Chapter Twenty-Four

Marla's lunch churned in her stomach. She sank onto the bench in front of her salon, absorbing this information.

"Tobias's death has to be related to the others," she said, adjusting her earpiece. "Did he have anything wrapped around his neck?"

"Not to my knowledge. There has to be something we're missing to tie these cases together," Dalton agreed.

"What does Wanner say?"

"He's still convinced Pete is guilty of the two crimes in his territory. However, Pete was in custody when Brad was murdered."

"You should check into the suspects with military or martial arts backgrounds," Marla said, reflecting on her conversation with Hannah.

"Good idea. We'll talk later. Stay safe."

Marla entered the salon, pushing aside these issues to focus on work. Ryder occupied her mind for the rest of the day after she left. Dalton worked late again, grumbling that he was missing out on playing with his son.

"Have you progressed at all on the case?" she asked him after they were both in bed.

He gave her a morose glance, his hair still damp from the shower. "Brad didn't have any family members other than Davinia. I doubt she'd be capable of breaking a man's neck, unless she'd had fight training for her acting roles. Or, she could have convinced her manager to do it for her. He's a possibility on his own, but I can't figure a motive for him other than protecting his client. As for the office staff, I've pretty much eliminated Nadia, who wasn't present that day."

"How about Lenny, the tile guy? Did you interview him?"

"He has an alibi. It's been verified."

"Is George Eustice still high on your list?"

He nodded. "Brad was late on his payments for two granite orders with installs. Plus, he covered for Jack, which might have fueled George's anger. But the daughter says her father didn't leave her side at the festival, even when she performed her duties as garlic queen. The pageant director vouched for him."

She cleared her throat. "There's one person you're not mentioning. I'll go visit my mother tomorrow morning. Reed needs to come clean about his role."

****

Anita greeted Marla with a bright smile when she opened the door to her home in Boynton Beach. She wore an apricot top over a pair of cocoa Capri pants, the casual clothes reflecting the relaxed look on her face. A gold chain around her neck was paired with hoop earrings, and her white hair appeared freshly styled although in need of a cut. It was getting long now that Marla noticed. Not that Anita had any time for a visit to the salon with all that had been going on.

Ma hooked a red-painted fingernail, signaling for Marla to follow her inside.

"Come and take a look at the bathroom. It's all done except for the shower doors, and they're being installed this afternoon."

Marla followed her with trepidation, remembering her first peek at the remodel. At the threshold of the master bath, she paused. It was like night had turned into day.

The shower gleamed with its finished seat, gray tile

248

design, and generous alcove. Her gaze swept the white cabinetry with dual porcelain sinks, the granite countertop, decorative mirrors, and new vanity lighting. The room looked elegant and yet practical at the same time.

"It's beautiful," she said, while her mother beamed with pleasure.

"It came out wonderfully, didn't it?" Anita glanced at Marla in the mirror. "I'll never be able to forget what happened here, but now we can move on. I've made sure the shower has been completely disinfected."

"I would hope so," Marla murmured, not sure she'd be able to get past the image in her mind.

"I want a change, Marla."

She gave her mother a startled glance. "Huh? What do you mean?"

"I'm tired of my hairstyle. Don't get me wrong. The pixie cut is a cute look for me, but it's time for a makeover. I've been growing my hair and want to become a blonde."

"Whoa, that is a big change."

"I feel as though I have a new lease on life. Reed finally told me what's been bothering him."

"Is that right?" No wonder Ma looked so perky. "What did he say?" She leaned forward, eager to hear his admission.

"For one thing, he's relieved Pete Ferdinand is behind bars. The rest isn't my story to tell. He's willing to talk to you about it now. Would you like me to make you a plate of gefilte fish with a slice of challah while you're busy? Or I could fix some tuna salad and sliced tomatoes."

"I'll have the gefilte fish for a snack, thanks. It'll be too early for lunch."

"All right. Come into the kitchen when you're done."

Marla wandered into Reed's office where he'd sequestered himself, allowing Marla and her mother some privacy. But now she looked forward to having a long-awaited frank conversation with him.

Reed wore a sky-blue polo shirt over navy trousers and looked relaxed for the first time since their ordeal had started. He rose at her entrance, nodding a greeting, and gestured toward the leather chair opposite his desk.

His green eyes met hers with solemnity. "How much has your mother told you?"

"She said you're relieved Pete is behind bars. How did you know him aside from his job here? There was some history between you and the people at the design center, wasn't there?"

"Not with the company. With Jack and Brad." Reed picked up a silver and black ballpoint pen and clicked it on and off. "Brad was a scam artist who would open a company, steal money from customers, and then disappear. He'd establish another firm under a different name and do it again. Mostly, they'd take a fifty percent deposit from customers and then either complete part of the work or vanish altogether."

Marla sat forward, clasping her hands in her lap. "How did you know this?"

His face reddened. "I'm ashamed to admit I was one of their victims. During my previous marriage, I signed the contract on a remodel and handed over a ten-thousand-dollar deposit to the salesman who'd given me the estimate. I even visited their showroom and met the president. It all looked legit, but that was the last I heard from them. When I drove by their office to ask why they weren't answering my calls, I was astonished to see the place closed up."

"Did you report your loss to the police?"

"Yes, of course, not that it did any good. They were fly-by-night operators. Then the weirdest thing happened. I was contacted by a woman who claimed to be related to the company president. She offered to make amends and gave me a refund."

Marla raised her forefinger. "Don't tell me. That was Davinia."

Reed nodded and put down his pen. "I didn't ask why she

had gotten involved. By then, Theresa—my first wife—wasn't feeling well. I thought the money would help pay for her medical care and didn't care how I got it."

"Is that why you chose Amaze Design Center?" Marla guessed. "Because Davinia had endorsed the company?"

"I figured she would offer an honest opinion, but I couldn't have been more wrong. When I realized my mistake, it was too late. I'd signed the contract after meeting with Nadia and Caroline. I never came into contact with Brad or Jack during those initial meetings." He scrubbed a hand over his face. "I should have been smarter after I'd been duped once before and read more about the company."

"Then what happened?"

"Jack came by one day, and I recognized him. He'd been the sales rep who'd taken my phony deposit years ago."

Ice water sluiced through her veins. "You do realize this gives you a motive for Jack and Brad's murders, right? What happened when you realized Jack's identity?"

"I marched down to their office and told Brad I knew all about them. Brad promised he'd gone legit and wasn't lying. He wanted to make his sister proud and was sorry for the grief he'd caused everyone. But then I wondered...." A hint of fear entered his expression.

"What?"

"Jack was the rotten cog in the wheel. Perhaps Brad decided to rid himself of the liability."

Her mouth gaped. "You believed Brad killed Jack?"

"If so, then he might come after me next. I knew all about his crooked deals. And by association, that would put your mom in danger. I couldn't say a thing, no matter what Detective Wanner believed about me."

"Why did you argue with Brad at the garlic festival? That still makes you a suspect in his murder investigation."

"I told him I wouldn't reveal what I knew about his past if he'd finish our remodeling job. Then Anita and I could move

251

on and forget about all this stuff. It was stressing her out too much."

"Why would you confront him like that if you felt he posed a threat?"

"I realized Jack's death might have had nothing to do with Brad. I'd heard about how Jack and Pete had been stealing copper. I thought the other guy who died, the permit inspector, might also be involved."

"So you suspected Pete of doing in his partners in crime?"

"That's right. I'd been wrong to suspect Brad of killing Jack."

Marla shook her head. "This is confusing. With Pete in custody, who did you think was responsible for Brad's death? Was it someone who might still come after you?"

Reed spread his hands. "What for? Brad's history has come to light. I can't add anymore that Dalton hasn't already learned."

Except for Davinia's involvement, perhaps. But what had she done other than make restitution for her brother's bad dealings?

Marla's mind reeled as she got up to rejoin her mother in the kitchen. The different cases had to be connected, but she still couldn't grasp the critical link.

After expressing her relief over Reed's admissions, she pushed aside her musings about the murders. Their conversation centered on Charlene and Michael.

"Charlene appears to be going through a midlife crisis," Marla said. "She could get a job in Florida if she looked harder, but she insists on moving up north. She knows Michael's business is here. He can't uproot himself and start over. She'd have to leave him to get her dream job, at least in her view."

Anita placed a plate on the table and indicated they should sit. "She's not interested in the alternatives if you ask me. There has to be some position in this state that would satisfy her."

"Maybe she'll come to her senses." Marla cut a piece of

gefilte fish with her fork and dipped it into a dab of red horseradish. It chilled her tongue as she chewed.

"Has Michael suggested counseling? It could be helpful," Anita said with a frown.

"I don't know if he'd agree. He's upset by Charlene's attitude."

"He should have confided in me. At least I could offer support."

"You guys have your own problems." Marla hesitated. "I've gotten the feeling something is on Dalton's mind, too. I don't want to ask him about it when he's on a case. I'm hoping he isn't feeling overwhelmed at having a child this late in life."

"That man dotes on his son. I doubt that's his problem. You should talk to him."

"We'll see." Marla buttered a slice of challah and took a bite. The soft bread gave her a sense of comfort as it resonated with her heritage.

"I miss Ryder," her mother said, clucking her tongue. "You didn't send me any pictures yesterday."

"Here's the latest one his teacher sent us." Marla showed Anita the photo on her phone. "Did I tell you we made a reservation for Brianna's graduation party?"

They discussed upcoming family events until Marla made her departure. She wanted to share her news with Dalton, but first she planned to visit the design center. She needed to have another chat with Caroline.

Brad's killer was still out there, she reminded herself as she headed onto a main road. Aware she'd been neglectful of her own security, she checked her rearview mirror to make sure no one followed her.

Thankfully, the design center office was still open. Marla hadn't been sure what would happen after the company president's death.

"We have an obligation to our clients," Caroline explained when Marla asked her why they hadn't closed. The brunette manned her position at the front of the store. "Besides, the cops cleared the scene. They took what they needed from Brad's office on Monday."

"Have you heard anything about a memorial service? I spoke to Davinia earlier this week, but she hadn't made arrangements yet."

"It's likely she'll hold a private service to avoid the press," Caroline suggested.

"Wouldn't she invite you and Nadia since you worked with Brad so closely?"

"I don't know about Nadia, but Davinia looked down her nose at me. As far as she was concerned, I sucked up to my boss. It never crossed her mind that I might have real feelings for him. At any rate, she might not want either of us to be present at his funeral."

"I'm sorry for your loss. What will happen to the company now?"

Caroline's gaze skittered away. "That will depend on what he stipulated in his will."

Marla noted the place seemed hauntingly quiet. She heard nothing except the hum of the air-conditioning unit. Nadia must have taken time off or quit to search for another job.

"Is there a particular reason why you came by today?" Caroline asked her. "I'm trying to get all our projects finished up. I don't like to leave customers hanging. Our reputation still matters. Since Nadia and I may both have to apply for new jobs, we'll need this place to look good on our resumes."

Marla folded her arms across her chest. "It would help if Brad's murder was solved. Who do you think is guilty? It wasn't Pete since he's in custody."

"How did Brad die? No one has told me."

Marla noticed that Caroline's blouse wasn't buttoned correctly. She'd missed the top row with the one on the right. Perhaps she wasn't as composed as she wanted others to believe.

"I'm not privileged to reveal that information. But it would have to be someone strong enough to overpower the man, same as Jack."

Caroline's eyes narrowed. "Was Lenny at the garlic festival? He had planned to go to college on the GI bill, but then his father died, and he had to earn a living. He lifts those heavy piles of tile all day, and he's the one who found Jack's body. Plus, he's one of the subcontractors whose payments got delayed. He might have blamed Brad for withholding the money."

"Lenny had an alibi, and so did Juan. Neither one of them was at the festival."

"How about your stepfather?" Caroline said, pointing a finger at her. "He's been complaining about the delays on their project and Jack's body was found on his premises."

Was Caroline truly grasping at straws, or was she diverting Marla's attention on purpose?

"Reed isn't a killer," Marla stated. "He knew Brad and Jack had swindled customers in the past. They changed names and companies until Brad decided to go legit. You could be implicated if he's been lying. I'd suggest you come clean, or my husband will bring you into the station to find out what you know. He might even regard you as an accomplice in Brad's murder."

Caroline glared at her. "I cared for Brad. I would never have hurt him. I'll tell you what I know if you mention to your husband that I've been cooperative."

"I will." Marla realized the killer might also take an interest in what Brad had told Caroline. If she wasn't guilty, was she in danger?

Caroline glanced at a smudge on the floor. "Brad lied to Jack about going straight. He had an almost pathological need to succeed, and his symbol of success was money. Brad took the final payment from customers and wired the money to his personal offshore account. He told me that once he had enough, he'd close the company and retire. We'd get married and go to live on one of the islands."

So Caroline had known about his schemes. Did she really believe his promises?

"How could Brad pay his crew or his suppliers if he stole their money?" she asked.

"He'd use the next deposit to pay off the suppliers from the last job. But he fell behind when we had a dry spell. That's why he missed a couple of payments. He got caught up once we landed a major new project and received the deposit."

"Did Jack catch on? If so, he must have been upset that Brad had cut him out."

"Jack was furious," Caroline said, wrapping her hands together. Her fingernail polish was chipped, confirming Marla's opinion that the woman was more distraught than she let on. "In retaliation, he pocketed a share of the cash that Brad deposited in the company account for the paychecks."

"Whose idea was it to bribe the permit inspector? Was it Jack or Brad who ordered inferior materials on purpose to save money?"

"That was Jack on both counts."

"His interference couldn't have pleased your boss," Marla said, tilting her head. Was Caroline speaking the truth? Or was she misleading her?

Caroline studied a speck on her desk pad. "I was afraid Brad considered Jack to be a liability and had killed him. He made me send you a warning note after you came snooping."

Ah, so that explained the mysterious message she'd received at work.

"If Brad murdered the foreman to silence him, then who killed your boss?"

Caroline's shoulders slumped. "I wish I knew. What does the investigation show? Is your husband close to an arrest?"

Here it comes. Caroline is trying to get inside my head. Was this entire confession a ruse to get Marla to lower her guard?

"I'm afraid he doesn't share those details with me. You'd better tell the truth," Marla insisted. "Otherwise, I'll suggest to Dalton that you were complicit with Brad in altering his bookkeeping records. It might even be a case of tax evasion along with murder. Keeping silent is one thing, but actively covering up a crime is another."

Defeat etched Caroline's features. "All right. There wasn't any new project. Davinia approached me privately and offered money to restore her brother's reputation. She made me promise I wouldn't tell Brad. I wrote up a false contract to fool him."

"So if his debts were paid, who would still want to kill him?" Marla asked, feeling something was missing.

"Beats me. I've told you all I know. I'm hoping your husband can solve this fast so we can get past this mess."

"Are you nearly finished with all the projects on the slate?"

"Yes, thank goodness. But there's one problem. I don't have access to write checks from the company account. I'm thinking Brad might have added his sister as a signatory, but I haven't gotten around to contacting her."

"Davinia might have access to his will, if he'd filed one," Marla suggested. "His estate plans could include the company assets. Maybe I'll visit her to see what I can learn."

Caroline's face brightened. "Would you? Nadia and I are anxious to know what's going to happen. If the business is sold, maybe we can keep our jobs."

Marla stared at Caroline, while thoughts tumbled in her mind. Davinia was definitely the nexus to which all trails led. But she still wasn't sure which role the actress played, or how much influence Oscar had over her. Marla would have to pay her a visit and pronto. The actress needed to take steps to ensure her safety before she became the next target.

257

Chapter Twenty-Five

Marla texted Dalton her plans and then headed east toward the Intracoastal Waterway. He'd be along to join her shortly, but she wasn't about to delay her visit to wait for him. Thankfully, the same guest entry code worked at the private gate. She'd given it to Dalton as well.

The maid answered the door and ushered Marla inside to await Davinia's arrival. After a brief interval, the celebrity breezed into the foyer in a cloud of perfume.

"Marla, darling, this is a convenient surprise. I meant to call you."

"Oh, really?" Was Davinia ready to come clean about her connection to Reed?

Davinia straightened the scarf-like drape that covered her shoulders over a plum top and palazzo pants. She had piled her blond hair atop her head without a hair out of place. Marla scrutinized the woman's hairline, or rather the lack of one. Was she wearing a wig?

"I'd like to hire you to do my hair for the upcoming soaps award ceremony," Davinia said.

"Excuse me?" Marla gave her a startled glance. That wasn't the topic she'd been expecting.

"I was impressed by the job you did at the garlic festival, and you mentioned you'd like to do more work with celebrities. It's a local event so you wouldn't have to travel far."

Recovering her wits, Marla grinned at the prospect. "I'd be delighted. Thank you for considering me."

Davinia patted her hair. "You might have guessed this isn't mine. It's easier to throw on a wig or a turban to meet company when I'm at home. But my hairstyle isn't why you came by."

"No, it's not. I wanted to know if you'd made plans for Brad's memorial service yet." Numerous other questions hovered on her tongue. She glanced at the rear of the house. Were they alone, aside from the maid?

"Come, let's go into the front parlor to talk." Davinia led her to a comfortably furnished room smelling faintly of wood polish and then faced her. "We've decided upon a cremation. Those were Brad's wishes in his estate documents. Oscar is dealing with it. But you could have asked me about this in a phone call. Why the personal visit?"

Marla debated which thread to follow first and chose to follow up on her most recent conversation. "I had a chat with Caroline at the design center. She's worried about her job, and so is Nadia. They're concerned about what will happen to the business."

Davinia's lips formed a pout and her forehead creased. "I'll have to get in touch with them. Brad left small bequests for both women. Everything else goes to me. I'm not sure yet what I'll do with the company. Oscar says it's a burden I don't need. He's probably right."

I would agree, but do you accept everything your manager tells you?

Marla walked over to the marble mantelpiece adorning a brick fireplace. Framed signed photos of celebrities graced its surface. Friends of the actress? She hadn't heard of most of them, but then she never watched daytime television.

"Amaze Design Center had a lot of suppliers," she mentioned. "As Brad's beneficiary, would you be responsible for any debts he left? I don't understand the legalities."

"There shouldn't be any unpaid bills," Davinia retorted, her voice bitter. "I made sure of that."

"Oh yes. I heard about your secret donation from Caroline. I also learned how you repaid my stepfather when he lost money to Brad and Jack's scam in the past. It was generous of you to help your brother make amends each time."

Marla figured a personal story might help to ease the sudden tension that had sprung up between them. "I helped my own brother once when he ran into financial problems. He'd made some bad investment choices, and his clients wanted to cash out. I gave him the means to make restitution. He's been doing well ever since."

Davinia moved over to stroke a statue on a pedestal. It looked to be an Asian figurine cast in jade. "Brad promised me he would go straight. Oscar warned me not to believe him, and I should have listened."

Marla nodded her agreement with this advice. "Caroline told me Brad was running another scam with Amaze Design Center. He took the final payment from customers and wired the money to his personal offshore account. Then he'd use the next deposit to cover his bills. If his dirty dealings came to light, it could have dragged your name through the scandal sheets. Who might have wanted to stop him to protect you?"

Davinia pressed a hand over her chest. "What are you saying?"

"There's one person who is always looking out for you. It must irk him that you keep shelling out money to save your brother."

"I hope you're not implying Oscar had anything to do with Brad's death. If so, that's the most preposterous thing I've ever heard."

"Is it? How well do you truly know him?"

Davinia glared at her. "Oscar wouldn't do anything to hurt me. I might not have approved of Brad's ways, but he was still family."

Something clicked in Marla's mind as her gaze came to rest on the statue Davinia had touched earlier. The jade statue.

Its green shade was a mite duller than the gown Davinia had worn when she'd won the pageant. Marla recalled the photo in the actress's study. A red sash of honor had been draped over her sequined emerald evening gown. Christmas colors… same as Reed's necktie fastened around Jack's throat.

"Did I hear my name?" Oscar strode into the room, a scowl on his face. He wore his customary bowtie with a suit that stretched across his stocky form.

What's he doing here? Has he been eavesdropping? Marla's hackles rose even as warning bells clamored in her mind.

She glanced toward the front door, hoping Dalton would get there soon. The maid seemed to have vanished, and the three of them appeared to be alone.

"Marla has said the most ridiculous things," Davinia told him. "She implied you did away with Brad to avoid a scandal."

Oscar's lip curled. "You're too soft, Davvy. We've been down this path before. It was in your brother's nature to scheme and exploit people's weaknesses. He lied to you about going straight."

"That's not true. He only needed another chance."

"Come now, surely you aren't so naïve. He'd always be a blight on your life. I took care of him for you."

Davinia gasped. "What are you saying?"

Marla pointed at him. "You're the person responsible, aren't you? You killed Brad."

Oscar swung his gaze her way and snarled. "Of course, it was me. Who else did you think would protect Davvy's career?"

How would he react if his client appeared unappreciative? Marla stepped back, not wanting to find out. Would Oscar hurt the woman he loved? How about her?

She scanned the room for an escape route. Oscar stood between her position and the door.

"You're not leaving. You know too much," he told her,

apparently guessing her intent. "You should have stopped asking questions when you had the chance."

He returned his attention to Davinia. "I thought the garlic garland around Brad's neck was a nice touch, didn't you? I'd meant it to remind you of your reign as festival queen."

Davinia's face paled. "How could you? Brad was my brother."

"Someone had to look out for you. It wasn't the first time, either. You should be grateful, my dear. I've always had your best interests at heart."

Davinia recoiled from him as she would from a snake. "W-What do you mean that it wasn't the first time?"

While his focus centered on Davinia, Marla considered what she might use as a weapon. She could swing her cross-body purse at him if she had the opportunity. Was there anything inside she could use to defend herself? She had a mini can of holding spray and the jar of gold crumbs Craig had given her. But she'd have to get close enough to Oscar to aim at his eyes with either one.

Meanwhile, another idea came to mind, and she fumbled in her bag for her cell phone. She speed-dialed Dalton's number and left her purse partially open.

"Tobias became a liability," Oscar admitted to Davinia. "You do know why, don't you?"

"Who?" Davinia shook her head, confusion mixed with horror in her eyes.

"The guy who worked as a permit inspector for your brother's company. He was taking bribes from Jack Laredo. I knew him from way back in high school. Don't you remember him? Tobias was on the city council then. He was the special guest of honor when you entered the pageant that started your career. Even then, he was amenable to making a quick buck."

Davinia gasped. "No, Oscar. You couldn't have—"

"I was in love with you, you know. So I did what I had to do for you to be happy. Tobias was the person who tabulated the ballots and announced the winner. Tears came to my eyes as I watched you accept the crown. Do you recall the emerald gown you wore? I'll never forget how regal you looked."

"You bribed Tobias to announce me as the winner? You *cheated?*" Davinia shouted. "How could you betray me like that? You're worse than my brother. At least he tried to do better!"

Oscar stiffened as he faced her. "You never got the message I meant for you after I got rid of Jack." He reached for Davinia, but she eluded his grasp. "The tie I wrapped around Jack's neck was emerald, like your gown that day. The color brought out the beautiful Irish green of your eyes. The red stripes represented the royal sash you wore as garlic queen."

Marla couldn't help the inadvertent cry that left her lips. "So I was right to relate the tie to the beauty pageant. You'd hoped to catch Davinia's attention, while at the same time casting blame on my stepfather."

Oscar rounded on her, his muscles budging inside his suit. Marla realized the killer didn't need military training or martial arts schooling to learn how to kill someone with his hands. There was probably a video online. They'd been looking at all the wrong places for the murderer.

His mouth twisted into a sneer as he regarded her, his eyes filled with malice. "I meant it as a message to Davvy, but nobody released that detail from the detective's office. Same as the garlic garland. I'd hoped Davvy would remember how I had supported her at the festival. Maybe she'd appreciate me more if she knew how hard I worked behind the scenes to keep her safe."

"I don't understand. Why kill Jack?" Marla asked, needing to understand his motives. She wished Davinia would edge toward the exit while she kept Oscar talking, but the actress seemed frozen in place. Davinia stared at Oscar with a horrified glaze in her eyes.

Oscar shrugged as though telling Marla anything at this point wouldn't matter. "Jack found out about the bribe when Tobias blabbed about his connection to a famous actress.

Tobias knew she was judging the upcoming contest and that it was a big deal to the town. Jack used this information to attempt to blackmail Davvy. When she told me about it, I knew I couldn't let him threaten her future. Her entire career had been based on a lie."

"So you did away with Jack?" Marla said to keep him talking until Dalton had time to get there. She hoped he could hear their conversation and had called for backup.

"I followed him that morning. When I realized where he was headed, I parked around the corner and waited for him in your mother's backyard."

"What about Tobias? Did you kill him too?" She cast a glance at Davinia, who looked about to pass out. Could she rouse the woman enough to resist Oscar if he attacked one of them?

Oscar snarled. "Tobias was a loose end. Not only had he been bragging about his role in Davvy's success, but he'd kept the original ballots from the contest she had won. He could prove she wasn't the winner and might get the same idea as Jack to extort money from her. It was convenient how he had a propane gas tank at his home and mentioned his family would be out of town for a few days."

"So it was you who planted evidence in Pete Ferdinand's work shed?" she said.

His chest puffed out. "That's right."

"I can understand you going after Tobias and Jack, but not Brad," she said, wishing the maid would return. Oscar might decide to spring at her at any moment. She edged toward the door, but he still blocked the exit.

"Unfortunately, Brad's latest scam would have caused a scandal if it came to light. Davvy kept providing funds to bail him out. It had to end."

"So you killed him, too? You figured to get rid of all the bad eggs so you and Davinia could live happily ever after?"

Davinia finally recovered her composure to respond.

"Oscar, how can you think I'd condone these horrible things you've done? You may have been my friend, but there can never be anything more between us."

His narrowed gaze swung toward her. "You don't know your own heart, my dear."

"On the contrary, my eyes have been opened. Please get out of here. Now." Her voice trembled and her lower lip quivered but she stood her ground.

Oscar's gaze darkened, and he stepped toward her. "You ungrateful bitch. If I can't have you, no one will. Especially after all I've done for you..."

In two long strides, he reached Davinia's side. He grasped her arm, twirled her around, and caught her in a choke hold.

Davinia lifted her foot to stomp on his instep, but he was too far back. She gave Marla a wild-eyed glance. Marla stood paralyzed, afraid in the next instant he'd snap Davinia's neck.

Regret enveloped her for not listening to Dalton. Surely, she'd be next.

Or not. She wasn't about to leave her son without a mother. Determination flooded her and gave her strength.

She grabbed the jade statue Davinia had touched earlier, bounded toward Oscar, and smashed the weighty object down on his head with all her might.

A crunch sounded, followed by a grunt. Oscar tumbled to the floor.

Davinia spun away, doubling over with gasping breaths. Marla stood there holding the jagged remains of the statue while Oscar moaned on the floor.

Banging noises sounded from the front door followed by repeated rings of the doorbell. Marla heard footsteps as the maid rushed to answer. Where had she been when Oscar threatened them?

Marla's knees buckled as Dalton's familiar voice answered. "Police. Open up! Keep your hands in front where I can see them and stand aside."

A moment later, Dalton burst into view, his gun drawn. Upon spying the scene, he stashed his weapon and cuffed the man down.

"Are you alright?" he asked, casting Marla a frantic glance.

"Yes, I'm fine. Did you hear our conversation?" Marla remembered her cell phone and pushed the end button to disconnect their call. Sirens sounded in the distance.

"I did, but I'll still need your formal statements. Backup is on the way. We'll get this guy secured and then you and I will have a talk."

Marla swallowed, imagining his admonishment that she should have waited for him to join her before entering the house. But all was well. She and Davinia were alive. The bad guy was caught. What else mattered?

Chapter Twenty-Six

Marla couldn't believe it was Mother's Day. So much had happened recently that she had trouble keeping the dates straight. But here she was, on the way to Anita's house for a catered brunch with the entire family. As Dalton drove, she twisted her neck to regard Brianna in the back seat playing with Ryder. She'd miss the teen when Brie left for college at Boston. They only had a couple of precious months together before her departure.

She'd suggested they all meet at a restaurant, but with the baby, this was actually easier. She could put Ryder down for a nap at her mom's place after lunch. And Michael's two kids would have somewhere to run around.

Once they arrived, Dalton carried their gear into the house while Marla began a round of greetings. She gave her mother a tight embrace. In the interim, Anita had come down to the salon for a makeover. She'd wanted to change her white pixie cut for a longer, layered style with a golden blond tint. Marla loved the results and knew it reflected Ma's lightened heart.

Reed gave her a tight squeeze and murmured words of gratitude into her ear. He smelled of musk aftershave and wool.

"Now we can move on and celebrate all the good things coming up," he said as they stepped apart. He smiled at her with fond affection, and her heart warmed. She hoped Reed, once he felt fully integrated into the family, would become a mentor to her.

His sons had joined them for the occasion. She greeted the guys, whom she'd met at several family events. Only one of them was married with kids, and Marla waved to the wife who sat on the floor watching their children, including Marla's niece and nephew. She eased Ryder from her arms so he could join them on the carpet strewn with toys and building blocks.

Michael and Charlene came over to exchange hugs. She'd expected the latter to be aloof, but Charlene's embrace was warm and friendly. Michael gave his sister an extra pat on the back. His broad grin made her wonder what had transpired between them. She wouldn't get the chance to ask until later, after she'd put Ryder down for his nap.

Everyone took seats at the extended dining table at mealtime and dug into the food that had been delivered. Marla fed Ryder in his highchair.

"Your bathroom looks great," Michael told their mother, spearing a tomato slice with his fork.

"Thanks, we love the results." Anita scraped polish-tipped fingers through her hair. Marla still wasn't used to her new look but really liked it.

"Despite the problems, I think the shower came out well," Marla said. "That tile guy is very talented."

"Lenny Brooks was glad to finish this job and run off to his next project. Did I tell you I hired my former rabbi to come by and say a prayer for the dead man's soul?" Anita passed the potato salad to Reed. "It was the only way I'd feel comfortable using the shower. Now with a blessing given to send Jack's spirit on its way, we can go back to normal."

"Jack should be at peace now that we've identified his killer," Reed remarked, his appetite obviously not affected as evidenced by his hearty portions.

"Nice tie." Marla pointed to his blue and red accessory.

His mouth twisted. "I can't believe Davinia's manager used my necktie as a message of devotion to her."

Dalton jabbed a finger in the air. "Oscar was delusional about her feelings for him. He claimed he did it all out of love to protect her, but she didn't return his affection that way."

"I can see how it would cause a scandal to reveal she'd never truly won the pageant," Brianna piped in. "Daddy discovered a manilla envelope in Tobias's belongings with the original ballots. Would you believe he'd held onto them after all this time?"

"Davinia must be upset," Anita said, her tone sympathetic as she brushed a strand of hair off her face. "Her brother is dead. Her manager is in jail. And she wasn't the real winner of the contest that launched her career. What will she do now?"

"Her show is still popular. She wasn't to blame for anything that happened," Marla said. "The worst of it might be a swell of publicity. Isn't that what celebrities want, whether good or bad? Nonetheless, she must feel lonely. Did I tell you she asked me to do her hair for an upcoming awards ceremony? Maybe I'll send her a gift certificate to our day spa."

"That would be generous of you," Dalton said with an approving nod.

"I spoke to Hannah, who was Jack's ex-girlfriend. She was relieved to know an arrest had been made. Her brother Stuart admitted he'd had words with Jack, threatening to expose his criminal past unless he left Hannah alone. She'd been afraid Stuart had done something violent but that wasn't the case."

"Isn't she pregnant?" Dalton asked.

"Yes, and she has come to terms with it. She's happy to have Jack's child and considers it a legacy to remember him by. She loved him despite his flaws."

Brianna stuffed a piece of spinach and cheese quiche into her mouth. "Enough about killers and their motives already. Let's change the subject. I can't wait until school is over. In the meantime, prom is next weekend."

"She's going with Jason," Marla told the crowd, wagging her eyebrows. "You should see her dress. It's absolutely gorgeous. She'll look like a dream in that gown."

"Aren't you doing her friends' hair at your salon?" Anita asked, lifting her penciled brows.

"Yes, that's right. Then the following Friday is her final class."

"We've reserved the dates for her graduation and Ryder's birthday party." Anita clapped her hands. "It's about time we can celebrate happy occasions together."

"Can we be excused?" one of Reed's grandchildren asked. At his nod of approval, they scrambled from the table. Michael's kids followed.

"Don't you have events over Memorial Day weekend?" Anita asked, spreading cream cheese on a bagel. She had been so busy setting things out that she hadn't had a chance to eat yet. She helped herself to some smoked salmon and sliced onions.

Marla nodded after taking a sip of hot coffee. "Nicole is having us over on that Saturday. Then Sunday is the police picnic. Thank goodness we have a babysitter lined up."

Ryder, seated in his highchair, babbled his opinion. Marla beamed at him and offered him a bite of cut-up strawberry. He took it and popped it in his mouth.

Dalton cleared his throat. "Um, about the picnic this year. It might be my last one."

Rendered speechless, Marla gaped at him.

He gave her a sheepish grin. "I was going to break the news in private, but this is as good an opening as I'm going to get. It's my twenty-fifth year at the department. I'm eligible for retirement with full benefits."

"No way." Marla's heart thudded in her chest. Surely, he didn't mean what she thought he meant?

"Yes, way," he said in teen-speak. "I put in my notice to retire as of September the first. I could have quit immediately with two weeks warning, but I hope to train my successor and not leave everyone hanging. That's the least I can do."

Marla's thoughts about his workplace gelled, and she realized why she'd sensed something was off. He'd removed his personal photos, including pictures of Ryder that he'd kept on his desk. He must have packed them away so as not to lose anything during the transition.

"I'm sorry I didn't tell you sooner, but I wanted to make sure we'd be all right financially," he said, giving her hand a squeeze. "I'll be able to spend more time with Ryder and can help around the house while you're at work."

"What will you do all day?" Brianna cried. "You can't leave your job."

Marla flashed his daughter a grateful glance. She'd been thinking the same thing.

"Listen, muffin. It'll be safer this way. With a new child to raise, I don't want to keep putting my life in jeopardy. Even though my position is mostly administrative, I do follow up on things in person. I need to think about our family now that we have a little one in our care."

"I thought you loved field work," Marla said in a petulant tone. Unable to wrap her mind around his announcement, she resented that he hadn't discussed this decision with her. No, she more than resented it. It made her heart pound and her teeth grind together.

"I do love the investigative part. I've been toying with the idea of becoming a private security consultant, and maybe I can teach at the law enforcement academy. I've been looking into their requirements."

"I'd bet you'd been good at teaching," Marla grudgingly admitted. At least he was considering his options.

At forty-eight, Dalton still had many years ahead of him. Would his pension be enough to cover Ryder's schooling and his daughter's college? They had Marla's income, but she counted on his share. Part-time work would be helpful in that regard.

More importantly, she'd be relieved of the worry that he might get shot in the line of duty. That factor alone should erase her concerns.

He gave her a broad grin. "You know about my interest in

history. This would give us a chance to attend one of the local battle reenactments. It could be fun."

Marla swallowed her doubts. "Oh, joy. You could even volunteer at the local history museum. You already know the curator. She was a suspect in one of your cases."

"That's right. Don't worry. I'll find things to keep myself occupied."

Marla remembered in vivid detail how Dalton's mother had felt when his dad retired. Kate had required a long period of adjustment and had resented his desire to travel to art shows. She'd finally learned how to compromise to meet both their needs, but it hadn't been an easy journey. Too bad the couple was out of town this weekend, or Marla could have asked Kate for advice.

Her gut churned at the potential problems ahead. *Let's stay positive*, she thought. It might be handy to have Dalton around. When Ryder got sick or the daycare center closed for holidays, he could take charge of their son while she went to work. But the best thing would be the extra time they'd have to spend together.

"I have news, too," Charlene blurted, folding her hands on the table. "I've accepted a position as elementary school principal at a private academy in West Palm Beach. It pays more than the other job openings and they want me to start in August."

Marla's lips parted. "What? I thought you were homesick for up north."

Charlene gave her a frank stare. "I am, but I realized my life is here with Michael and the kids. I was scared because I'm becoming more forgetful. I didn't want to lose my mind before I achieved my dream."

"Is that what's been bothering you? You hinted during our last phone conversation that something was wrong. I was afraid you had an illness you were hiding from us."

Charlene's eyes moistened. "I'm worried that it's

Alzheimer's. A cousin of mine had it, and in the end, she didn't know her own children. I wouldn't want you to see me that way."

Understanding dawned. Charlene was afraid she'd lose herself and wanted to spare her immediate family the pain. Even if she'd moved up north and the kids visited during the summers, she might have told them to stay home if her condition deteriorated. But that would be avoiding the problem, not confronting it with the full support of her loved ones.

"Everyone forgets things as they get older," she told her sister-in-law. "It doesn't mean you have a serious problem, but you can always get it checked out. We're here for you no matter what happens."

"I know. You've reminded me that family is everything. I want to stay through the good as well as the bad." She grasped Michael's hand and gave him a teary smile.

"And I've promised to set aside Saturdays for family day," he responded with a fond glance at his wife. "Work will have to wait. We need to spend time with our children before they grow up and leave the house. It'll happen in the blink of an eye."

"I hope not." Marla gazed at Ryder, playing with his food while seated in his highchair. He threw a piece of melon on the floor and grinned when he noticed her looking at him. She shook her head, unable to imagine him as an adult. Time was already passing by too fast.

Dalton took her hand and squeezed it, enjoying the moment with her. It would be good to have him home to share each milestone.

Marla's heart filled with love as she regarded the familiar faces around the table. "Being together is all that matters. We may not know what tomorrow will bring, but we have each other and that makes us stronger. Here's to more happy events in the future."

The others raised their glasses in acknowledgment and offered hearty cheers.

Family Brunch Menu

MENU
Zucchini, Eggs and Cheese
Smoked Salmon
Bagels and Cream Cheese
Cheesy Hash Brown Casserole
Sliced Tomatoes and Onions
Peach Cobbler

ZUCCHINI, EGGS AND CHEESE

Ingredients
1 cup biscuit mix
½ cup grated Parmesan cheese
½ cup vegetable oil
1 Tbsp. chopped fresh dill
6 eggs, beaten
32 oz. sliced zucchini
8 oz. chopped onions
4 oz. chopped tomatoes

Directions
Preheat oven to 375 degrees. Combine all ingredients except tomatoes in a large bowl. Pour into greased 9x13x2 inch baking dish. Sprinkle tomatoes on top. Bake for 30 minutes or until golden brown. Serves 4 to 6.

CHEESY HASH BROWN CASSEROLE

Ingredients

15 oz. can cream of celery soup
1 cup reduced fat sour cream
1 Tbsp. flour
½ tsp. garlic powder
24 to 30 oz. package frozen hash brown potatoes
2 cups reduced fat shredded cheddar cheese
⅓ cup grated Parmesan cheese
Paprika

Directions

Preheat oven to 350 degrees. In a bowl, combine soup, sour cream, flour, and garlic powder. Stir in potatoes and cheddar cheese. Pour into a greased 9x13x2 inch baking dish. Sprinkle Parmesan cheese and paprika on top. Bake uncovered for 50 to 60 minutes or until browned and bubbly. Serves 6 to 8.

PEACH COBBLER

Ingredients

¼ cup unsalted butter
1 ½ cups biscuit mix
1 cup sugar
⅔ cup reduced fat milk
21 oz. can peach pie filling
Cinnamon

Directions

Preheat oven to 400 degrees. Melt the butter and spread it on the bottom of a 9x13x2 inch baking pan. In a bowl, whisk together the biscuit mix, sugar, and milk. Pour batter into pan. Drop the fruit to cover batter evenly. Sprinkle cinnamon on top. Bake for 30 minutes or until browned and bubbly.

Acknowledgments

It takes a village to produce a book, and such is the case with *Styled for Murder*. I would like to express my gratitude to the following members of my team who helped make this book possible:

Ann Meier and **Janice Hardy** – You welcomed me to the Orlando area and invited me to join your critique group. This made me feel so very welcome after relocating to a new town where I'd be starting all over. Our Zoom meetings gave me the incentive to get back to work after a long dry spell due to the pandemic and a major move. I never would have finished this book without your encouragement. Your perceptive comments made the story stronger and helped me get this book ready for publication.

Jan Klein, Taryn Lee, and **Sally Schmidt** – I rely on my beta readers to read my book cover to cover while watching diligently for typos, inconsistencies, repetitions, and plot holes. I value your reports and set upon any corrections as soon as you suggest them. I need your sets of eyes and am deeply grateful you're willing to spend time on my behalf. Your opinions as readers are incredibly helpful.

Deni Dietz – You've been my editor since my books were published by Five Star, and I am grateful you're still willing to work with me. Your comments are always right on the mark.

Kat Sheridan from BlurbWriter.com – Kat comes up with the most pun-ilicious story blurbs with puns galore. You make my book descriptions so much fun to share.

Kim Killion from The Killion Group, Inc. – I adore this cover that is absolutely perfect for the story. I appreciate your willingness to make changes until the cover art is just right.

Judi Fennell from formatting4u.com – Your expertise in layout design ensures my book has a professional polish. Your attention to detail in getting my work ready for the market is much appreciated.

Author's Note

Thank you for taking the time to read *Styled for Murder*. The inspiration for this story came from my own remodeling woes. We loved the finished product, but there was a lot of aggravation along the way same as in this story. Regarding the garlic festival, I modeled it after the South Florida Garlic Fest. Regretfully, I didn't get the chance to attend before we moved away from the area. The house where we relocated has a propane gas tank, so I was glad to learn about the leak detectors during my research. As for edible gold, I haven't tried this delicacy yet but will be on the lookout for gold-sprinkled foods.

If you enjoyed this book, please write a review at your favorite online bookstore. Reader recommendations are critically important in helping new readers find my work.

For updates on my new releases, giveaways, special offers and events, join my reader list at https://nancyjcohen.com/ newsletter. Free Book Sampler for new subscribers.

Nancy J. Cohen

About the Author

As a former registered nurse, Nancy J. Cohen helped people with their physical aches and pains, but she longed to soothe their troubles in a different way. The siren call of storytelling lured her from nursing into the exciting world of fiction. Wishing she could wield a curling iron with the same skill as crafting a story, she created hairdresser Marla Vail as a stylist with a nose for crime and a knack for exposing people's secrets.

Titles in the Bad Hair Day Mysteries have been named Best Cozy Mystery by *Suspense Magazine*, won a Readers' Favorite gold medal and a RONE Award, placed first in the Chanticleer International Book Awards and third in the Arizona Literary Awards.

Her nonfiction titles, *Writing the Cozy Mystery* and *A Bad Hair Day Cookbook,* have won gold medals in the FAPA President's Book Awards and the Royal Palm Literary Awards, First Place in the IAN Book of the Year Awards and the *Topshelf Magazine* Book Awards. *Writing the Cozy Mystery* was also an Agatha Award Finalist.

Nancy's imaginative romances have proven popular with fans as well. These books have won the HOLT Medallion and Best Book in Romantic SciFi/Fantasy at *The Romance Reviews*.

A featured speaker at libraries, conferences, and community events, Nancy is listed in *Contemporary Authors, Poets & Writers*, and *Who's Who in U.S. Writers, Editors, & Poets*. She is a past president of Florida Romance Writers and Mystery Writers of America, Florida Chapter. When not busy writing, Nancy enjoys reading, fine dining, cruising, and visiting Disney World.

280

Follow Nancy Online

Email – nancy@nancyjcohen.com
Website – https://nancyjcohen.com
Blog – https://nancyjcohen.com/blog
Twitter – https://www.twitter.com/nancyjcohen
Facebook – https://www.facebook.com/NancyJCohenAuthor
LinkedIn – https://www.linkedin.com/in/nancyjcohen
Goodreads – https://www.goodreads.com/nancyjcohen
Pinterest – https://pinterest.com/njcohen/
Instagram – https://instagram.com/nancyjcohen
BookBub – https://www.bookbub.com/authors/nancy-j-cohen

Books by Nancy J. Cohen

The Bad Hair Day Mysteries
Permed to Death
Hair Raiser
Murder by Manicure
Body Wave
Highlights to Heaven
Died Blonde
Dead Roots
Perish by Pedicure
Killer Knots
Shear Murder
Hanging by a Hair
Peril by Ponytail
Haunted Hair Nights (Novella)
Facials Can Be Fatal
Hair Brained
Hairball Hijinks (Short Story)
Trimmed to Death
Easter Hair Hunt
Styled for Murder

Anthology
"Three Men and a Body" in Wicked Women Whodunit

The Drift Lords Series
Warrior Prince
Warrior Rogue
Warrior Lord

Science Fiction Romances
Keeper of the Rings
Silver Serenade

The Light-Years Series
Circle of Light
Moonlight Rhapsody
Starlight Child

Nonfiction
Writing the Cozy Mystery
A Bad Hair Day Cookbook

Order Now at https://nancyjcohen.com/books/

CPSIA information can be obtained
at www.ICGtesting.com
Printed in the USA
LVHW050311251121
704427LV00008B/537